Withdrawn
From Stock

OUT FOR THE KILL

Several individuals, occupying a house divided into flats, become connected more than by just living in the same place.

One of the residents, Arthur Crook, receives an unexpected visitor at his flat.

Miss Chisholm, who runs a hat shop, disappears — and this could be the unlikely centre of a criminal operation.

Kay Carter brings herself in to the view of danger when she opens a mystery parcel.

Arthur Crook tries to get Kay out of London to a safe place, but they meet a group of criminals who have other ideas. Everyone is in danger . . .

OUT FOR THE KILL

Anthony Gilbert

·BLACK·
DAGGER
·CRIME·

First published 1960
by
Collins

This edition 2002 by Chivers Press
published by arrangement with
the author's estate

ISBN 0 7540 8612 7

Copyright © 1960 by Anthony Gilbert

British Library Cataloguing in Publication Data available

Printed and bound in Great Britain by
Bookcraft, Midsomer Norton, Somerset

ONE

One evening toward the end of that fabulous English August of 1959, Mr Arthur Crook came back from his office shortly after 7.00 pm to find a stranger waiting outside the front door of his flat at 2 Brandon Street. He and Brandon Street had gone through the war together, but only he, in essence, had survived. No. 2 had lost its delightful air of shabbiness and secrecy that had previously made it such a fitting background for his activities, and he was homesick for the blacked-out windows and for the uncarpeted wooden stairs which he had known for twenty years. During the post-war period everything had gone up, including the rents. An enterprising company had bought the house and turned it into a nest of fashionable modern flats in which Arthur Crook himself was an anachronism. Even the plumbing, that had been so individual and spirited in the old days, had been replaced, the pipes brought inside, with the result that your neighbours couldn't turn a tap or press a button without the whole house becoming aware of the fact.

Crook sighed over the changes, that seemed to tie up with changes in crime, the result of which appeared to be a deplorably slack period for himself. Nowadays the state got the best of everything, including murders. Gangs knifed policemen, and watchmen and bank managers got shot up during daring raids, but how long since one had heard of a Buck Ruxton or a George Joseph Smith? Men seemed to have lost the magnetic individual touch, while the welfare state looked after the spinsters to whom he had once played Galahad in modern dress. The fact was spinsters had never had it so good, they didn't need to fall to the wiles of handsome villains with Peter Cheyney moustaches, and in consequence a lot of the flavour had gone out of life. Look at him, for instance, turning into Brandon Street at this hour, he to whom 123 Bloomsbury Street had been his home between 9.00 am and any time up to midnight, before a grandmotherly government washed your face for you and bought your indigestion pills.

As he jumped out of The Old Superb, the ancient yellow Rolls that had replaced the indomitable red Scourge, his eye was caught by a political poster on the opposite wall.

For National Security, Social Security, Individual Security, Vote . . . It didn't matter which party it was, because they all said the same thing.

Security's all right in the grave, reflected the ungrateful Mr Crook. It's what graves are for.

An empty taxi was waiting outside no. 2 and as he began to ascend the steps a girl flashed past him, gave him a smile that nearly knocked him sideways—it was so like old times when adventure beckoned from every corner—and jumped into the cab.

She ain't going to spend the evening with Mr N. O. Body, thought Mr Crook aggressively. Nor, as it turned out, was he.

He found himself ascending the stairs almost on tiptoe. It seemed an intrusion to make a noise in this refined house. The lady on the ground floor was a stargazer of sorts, worked out individual horoscopes and was never seen without a hat. Probably even wore it in her bath, Crook thought. The girl who had just gone past him lived on the next floor, and the one above was now occupied by a very ladylike person called Chisholm, small and prim as a bird, so neat she looked as if her hair and clothes were painted on her. There was a light in her hall and he knew a sudden impulse to bang on the door and ask if she had any use for his services. He later wondered if he mightn't have done it and so possibly have changed the course of history, her history at least, if he hadn't suddenly got the impression that he was being watched and, lifting his eyes, saw someone leaning over the banisters of the top floor. Instantly his heart pounded; it might only be the man come to read the meter, but at least it was a human contact.

6

He beetled up the last two flights and found a tall thin young man with rakish green eyes under an impudent crest of fair hair, standing guard over a chest that looked for one wild moment as though it might contain a body. The next second he realised it was too small even to conceal a midget. But that thin reckless face put heart into him; it was the sort that didn't give a toss for please and thank you, shared Mr Crook's own view about regimentation, sign-on-the-dotted-line and take-your-place-in-the-queue, and knew that the right place for tranquillity is the churchyard.

Black's black and white's white but what the hell's grey?—that's what it said. A knife in your heart or a gun for your protection, but never anything static or safe.

Out for the kill, thought Mr Crook, his spirits rising mercurially.

'Sorry to have kept you,' he said in a buoyant voice, just as though he'd known all along the fellow would be waiting and was grateful he hadn't got tired, as chaps did so easily these days, and faded away.

'Think nothing of it,' said the stranger. And Crook knew he wasn't wrong, and this was a kindred spirit, because, without another word, he gave Crook the impression it was worth waiting twice as long for the pleasure of meeting him in the end.

'Brought the TV set,' he added.

Crook's spirits fell with such a bump he thought the sound must be heard right through the house.

'Wrong address,' he assured his visitor, fishing out a latchkey. 'Don't want one of those monstrosities here.'

'Have a heart,' pleaded the other. 'Lugged it up about fourteen flights of stairs.'

'Didn't they teach you arithmetic at school?' asked Crook pleasantly. 'You should have a word with your union. No deliveries where there ain't lifts.'

'Lovely thought,' approved the visitor. 'Only I'm old-fashioned. I like to eat; and the number of chaps prepared to exist in holes with no advantages except double windows, central heating, dishwashers, washing machines, spin-driers and a garage, mostly on credit, would surprise you. Can you believe it, some of these places are three storeys high and the tenants don't strike for a lift?'

Mr Crook agreed. 'Leave that damned thing where it is and have one for the road. Been waiting long?'

'Mere twenty minutes or so,' said the young man, heaving up the massive seventeen-inch set as though it were no more than a packet of baby towels and following Crook into the big untidy room that he called home and the conditions of which would have made a woman weep. Papers lay everywhere, with books, files, bottles, the works.

The young man, who was as single-minded as Crook himself, took it all in in one comprehensive, sweeping glance.

'That 'ud be the ideal place for it,' he said, indicating a table under the window.

'I said to leave that outside,' howled Crook.

'Indoor aerial, of course,' went on the visitor soothingly. 'Though you could have those knitting-needle things if you preferred. Still, that 'ud be extra and we don't supply them.'

'You didn't say you were giving the set away,' murmured Crook, opening a scarred cupboard and bringing out a couple of bottles of beer.

'Hirewire Company at your service,' retorted his visitor, snatching a card from his pocket and slamming it on the table. 'Hirewire Company, lowest terms, best service. Local representative—C. Oliver.'

'You C. Oliver?'

'That's right. Got a spare plug anywhere?' He looked around as if he expected one to fall out of the ceiling.

'No,' said Mr Crook gratefully.

'Take the one off the reading lamp.' C. Oliver yanked a knife out of his pocket and got to work.

'I ain't a cat,' offered Mr Crook reasonably. 'I can't see in the dark, not for book work and so on.'

'Won't be troubled with that once you've got our new seventeen-inch Air Master installed. Now, let's see. Aerial.' He picked up a pole and began running around the room like a modern Blondin looking for his tightrope. 'Reception from here, I think.' He dropped the pole into an angle of the wall, plugged the set in and turned a knob.

8

'Probably prefer ITV,' he assured Mr Crook.

'Mind reader?' asked his involuntary host, pouring out the beer.

'We go by districts. Snooty parts of Kensington, Campden Hill, say, they still go for the BBC Culture. International relations. Keep the world safe for democracy. None of these phony quizzes which they couldn't answer anyhow!'

'Drop that knife,' said a steely voice in Crook's ear, and he whizzed around to find himself being threatened by an enormous face staring out of the TV screen.

'Inspector Hawksbee—you'll like this,' said the eager Mr Oliver. 'The man who stands between you and the hoods.'

'Who said I wanted anyone to stand between me and the hoods?' demanded Crook rather peevishly. 'I suppose he's the regular police.'

Mr Oliver's mobile fair brows lifted. 'Are you pulling my leg? You must have heard of Hawksbee. Surely the name rings a bell.'

'Not since the days of Kipling,' promised Mr Crook.

Oliver looked as blank at the mention of Kipling as his companion had at the mention of Inspector Hawksbee. The cameras receded and the enormous face that had dominated the screen assumed less horrific proportions. Hawksbee wearing a raincoat and his hat, although he was clearly in someone else's house, and armed like Galahad, with the tenfold strength of a pure heart, was facing a peculiarly unappetizing-looking young thug, who talked what he called English in the modern fashion, which was apparently to slur practically every consonant.

'In these days of the welfare state can't he get himself a set of teeth?' asked Mr. Crook unsympathetically.

On the screen someone extinguished the lights, the sergeant exclaimed in a fashion that wouldn't have shocked a Victorian duenna, and when the lights came on again the young man had vanished.

The sergeant turned and walked away.

'Where's he going now?' asked Crook.

'He's going back to talk to Sally—Mrs H. to you.'

'Leaving the crime to solve itself?' Crook sounded shocked.

'She's going to solve it for him.'

Crook emptied his glass and refilled it more or less in one movement.

'Why? Is she a lady policewoman?'

'Of course not. She's the man behind the mastermind, sees to it he gets his due allowance of cracklepops or what have you for breakfast and his nice vegetable drink with his lunch. He's going to discuss it with her because she can apply the woman's angle.'

'How does that help?' inquired the obtuse Mr Crook.

'The women like it. You must realise that the greater proportion of regular viewers are women; they don't want to see a woman sergeant bringing home the bacon—jealousy complex and all that, I mean there aren't women sergeants and never can be—but they know women's intuition is worth all the facts on earth, so they like to hear Sally H. tell her husband exactly who did the crime, and then he goes out and drags the fellow in.'

Sure enough Inspector Hawksbee now walked into a modern smart setup that wouldn't have disgraced the lower floors of no. 2 Brandon Street. Sally, who must from her appearance, thought Crook, serve all her meals from tins, came to meet him, removed his hat and made him sit down.

'Doesn't he take off his coat?' Crook asked.

'Those programmes are worked to a time schedule,' explained C. Oliver. 'Thirty minutes including the commercials. If he has to take off his coat Sally has to hang it up and then they have to fetch it and put it on again. So many seconds lost, and if you knew what the advertisers pay per second on this programme you'd feel honoured that he even removes his hat. . . .'

Sally produced a cup of tea, out of her pocket so far as Crook could discover. The great man took it without any thanks. Then he began to talk, but the words were inaudible.

'Sound failed?' asked the intelligent Mr Crook.

'He's telling her what's the position to date,' Oliver told him. 'We know, so we don't want it all over again.'

Sally was nodding and wincing and calculating; then a heavenly sort of smile lit up her face—you almost expected to hear her say, 'I feel sensational'—and the sound came back as she said, 'But Joseph, surely it's perfectly plain. The man you want is . . .'

The picture faded.

'That doesn't seem much of an advertisement for your goods,' complained Mr Crook.

'Commercial,' capped C. Oliver.

'What, right in the middle?'

'Well, obviously. Suppose you got the solution before the commercial. You'd just switch off, wouldn't you?'

Mr Crook supposed he would.

'Whereas now you'll sit through the commercial to find out who done it.'

'Don't we know who done it?—I mean the thug . . .'

'You don't know Hawksbee,' said Oliver in a kind voice. 'He wants the mastermind, not the cogs in the machine.'

'And the chap with the flick-knife was only a cog?'

'That's right.'

On the screen there flashed an immense bottle of some sort of vegetable compound. A frill of faces appeared around it like a kind of human halo. The mouths opened and yelled advice to the viewers:

> Take it cold, take it hot,
> Take a little, take a lot.
> Take it when you're feeling blue.
> Vegade makes a man of you. . . .

Sally made a lightning appearance, clearly toasting the viewers in a glass of what Crook instantly christened The Muck.

The picture faded and now a motherly female with the figure of a hen was seen popping someone's steak pie into someone else's oven. The door of the kitchen opened and a man (hubby, supposed Crook correctly) shoved his head through the opening.

'Dad's got the bird,' he announced.

She slammed the oven door and whizzed around like a tee-totum.

'Dad, you never!'

Crook waited to hear her demand a sit-down sympathetic strike at the works but Dad forestalled her by producing from behind his back a small cage containing a budgerigar. (Delighted laughter, off.)

Dad beamed, showing all his lovely National Health teeth (twenty minutes daily in Klensadent and no one will guess they're not Nature's own).

'Pringle's Budgie Seed,' said the knowledgeable Mr Oliver.

'Pringle's,' chanted an invisible choir, presumably of budgies, 'makes your arteries tingle.'

'Is that good?' asked Mr Crook.

'What's that got to do with it?' demanded Oliver, staring. 'Look out, part two's just coming up.'

Mrs Hawksbee had clearly made her ineffable contribution, for her husband was now on his feet, his hat on his head.

'I knew you wouldn't let me down, old girl,' he said. 'Twenty-three years we've been married, and when I think how nearly I lost you . . .' Forgetful of the criminals who were presumably doing a bit more carving up with flick-knives during the interval, he and Sally indulged in a long embrace. 'You silly old man,' said Sally—even the somewhat violent act of kissing had not disarranged a hair or left a trace of lipstick on her husband's cheek—'you don't really think I was going to let Gloria Golightly get you. Detective-Inspector Hawksbee isn't the only one who always gets his man.'

'Here, I say,' expostulated Crook, really put out, 'that's my signature tune. Can't I sue them or something?'

'Yours? You didn't say . . .'

Crook struck a gesture that, considering his rotundity, his vivid brown suit, and his years—he had been fifty-five for rather longer than is conventional—did him credit.

'Crook always gets his man. Even old Hawksbee must know that.'

The effect on his companion was miraculous. 'You're not that Crook! Well, I'll be . . . What a bit of luck. There was a ladybird on my coat this morning, that always means something good. Arthur Crook in the flesh. Well (he had brought out a pad of green forms during the commercials but now he put it away again) you won't have to pay rental for this. They'll be glad to let you have one free.'

'Who will? Hirewire?'

'No, no, one of the sponsors. There's the Femina Bra Company, f'rinstance. They've been trying to get a suitable ad representative for weeks. You hear these things in the business, you know. The big actresses cost too much, and those they can get don't look right. . . .'

'But you think I should? Advertising bras?' Mr Crook nearly burst.

'They'd play it from the oblique angle, of course. You know— forlorn damsels who've—well—slipped a bit.' He used his expressive hands to outline the perfect female form divine, and then the one whose divinity had got a bit smudged. 'First the damsel in distress treacling after the chap who walks past without a sign. Girl in tears going home to Mum and a good book.'

'Not the TV?' asked Mr Crook.

Mr Oliver paid no attention. 'Then—up you pop.'

'Wearing a bra? Won't they think I'm advertising a circus— always assuming you get it past the censor?'

'No, no. You don't have to say a word. Just your picture—no personal appearances, of course.

> *'Ladies, can you get your man?*
> *Here's a chap who always can.*
> *Take a leaf from out the book*
> *Of famous lawyer, Arthur Crook.*

'They'd have to tidy that up, of course. I'm ad-libbing. Good ad for you,' he went on, 'and don't tell me you can't do with it. There isn't a chap living who can't do with it. Why do you think some of these fellows let themselves be cited in libel actions and what not, if it isn't to get their names in the papers? Even if they pay damages it's cheap at the price.'

A tremendous burst of shooting from the screen caused them both to turn. Detective-Inspector Hawksbee looked like an advertisement for somebody's sporting gun, bodies all around him.

'Where did he find the artillery?' asked Mr Crook interestedly. 'Or did Sally have the gun hidden in her bra?'

'You see?' said C. Oliver. 'You're getting the hang of it right away. I'll leave this here. . . .'

'I don't want it,' protested Mr. Crook. 'And I need that plug for my lamp.'

'It'll grow on you. Presently you'll wonder how you ever did without it. Links the individual to the world. That's our new slogan. Pretty neat, don't you think?'

Mr Crook poured out a third bottle of beer. 'You're not drinking yours,' he said. 'But perhaps you prefer Vegade. Sorry I can't oblige.'

'This a good time to find you as a rule?' asked Oliver, snatching up his glass.

'No,' said Crook. 'If I'm not at my office I'm in the pub.'

'Not any more,' prophesied Oliver, ogling the TV.

'I've told you, you can take that away.'

'Can't do that. Installed under our new three-day free-viewing offer. Besides, another chap collects. I'm only allowed to deliver.'

'You can't make me keep it.' Mr Crook sounded horrified.

'You agreed to let me install it, didn't you?'

'Nothing of the kind.'

'Well, you didn't stop me. Now you've got it for three days. Three days' time you'll hear from us. But you think over what I said. No reason why you shouldn't get your viewing free. Must be pushing off, thanks for the beer. Got a couple more visits before I get home.'

'This hour of night?' He was astounded to realise it was nearly nine o'clock.

'Have to get the husbands to sign the form and they're mostly at work. If they aren't we're not interested in them. Mustn't be late or they've oiled out to the darts game; too early and they're at the table. It's like all great sports, everything's a miracle of split timing.'

He put out his hand. 'If I hadn't let that ladybird go,' he said, 'I'd stuff it and put it in a glass case. Arthur Crook—what do you know? Never be certain I mightn't be needing you myself one of these days.'

'Not you,' said Crook scornfully. 'Before then your monster will have found a way of providing alibis off the cuff.'

'Leave my card,' said Oliver. 'This is my office address. Well, well, what a bit of luck for me the chap in the flat below wouldn't let me in.'

'What's that?'

'Came to give Miss Chisholm a demonstration this evening

but when I got there the boy friend opened the door and said nothing doing. Giving her a bit of demonstration himself, I suppose. " Try the flat upstairs," he told me, so—here I am.'

' Keep it clean,' reproved Mr Crook. ' You haven't met Miss Chisholm. She wouldn't recognise a boy friend without he wore a label around his neck. And then she'd have about as much use for him as I have for that monstrosity.'

' It'll grow on you, practice makes perfect,' promised Oliver. ' The day'll come when you'll be grateful to me for calling.' He slapped a leaflet on the table. ' Any trouble, just consult that,' he said.

Mr Crook didn't believe him—about being grateful, that is.

But it was quite true. Full points for a try, what hopes of a conversion? thought Crook, hearing those feet flash down the stairs. He wished he'd had the adamantine courage of the boy friend who'd refused to countenance the thing in his flat. Lifting his popping brown eyes he met the blank grey face of the invader. He stared at it truculently and it stared idiotically back. On an impulse he leaned over and turned a knob. Nothing happened.

Wrong one, thought Mr Crook, turning another at random. The voice that instantly roared at him nearly sent him through the window; then an immense face faded in, its huge mouth open to yell: ' Are you saved? From gout, arthritis, fibrositis . . .'

Frantically Crook started turning knobs in all directions and was rewarded by another face rotating like a teetotum. Gratefully his eye fell on the booklet the assiduous Mr Oliver had left on the table. He snatched it up and compared the diagram with his own black-magic instrument. Following directions he found at the end of a minute or so that a miraculously clear picture had emerged. At eleven o'clock he was still hypnotised by the thing, and hadn't even been down to the pub. No wonder the country was going down the drain, beer shares falling like hailstones most likely. He picked up the drummer's card and put it on the mantelpiece. Whoever came for the set in three days' time could take that away.

He had no thought then how soon he was going to see C. Oliver again.

TWO

The girl who had caused Crook's heart to lift as he came into Brandon Street that evening was a commercial artist of twenty-three, called Kay Carter. She had been on her way to a cocktail party whence she returned shortly before nine o'clock. Running fleetly up the stairs she was nearly knocked off her feet by a tall, fair young man who came hurtling down from the shadowy floor above. The stranger pulled himself up, gave her a wide grin, said, ' Ought to do something about that bulb,' pulled an imaginary forelock and was off again all in one breath.

Kay leaned over the banisters. ' Where's the fire?'

He looked up, laid a dramatic hand on his heart and flashed out of the door. An instant later she heard the engine of a car throb into life and then the sound of something dashing away.

' Visiting Mr Crook, I suppose,' she decided, since it seemed impossible he should be here for Miss Prism, as she irreverently called her overhead neighbour. Thinking of Miss Prism reminded her of what the stranger had said about a bulb, and, glancing up, she saw that the landing above her was dark. Each floor had an automatic time-push and each push kindled all four electric light bulbs simultaneously. They were so triggered that they were no sooner on than they went out again and it was necessary to press each switch as you passed it. Oh well, she thought, Rhodes would look after that.

Rhodes occupied what had been called the basement. Now it had been prettified, with plants in pots on the outer walls, and rechristened the garden flat. Rhodes, whose tenancy included the job of part-time porter and general dogsbody, was a genial fair-headed grenadier of a man, who emptied the tenants' dust bins, swept the stairs, polished up the knocker on the big front door, and stoked the boilers. He was a tower of strength not only to the tenants of no. 2 but to many of their neighbours, since he was not officially on duty after ten o'clock, and thereafter got his living by 'obliging' anyone who wanted to employ him. He could deal with a faulty fuse, put in a sash cord, knock together a cupboard, wash your windows or your car. There was an immense run on his services, he was so good-natured, so dependable. The tenants of other flats complained that the water ran tepid toward the end of the month because the fuel went short; they said the stairs weren't properly dusted and the paint wasn't washed. No one could say that at no. 2. The water seethed day and night and Rhodes never needed any extra fuel. It was all a matter of management, he said. After the first two months—he had been there fifteen—you knew just what supplies were needed. Similarly he had a standing order for so much soap, polish, flakes, and you could set your calendar by the delivery. The first of the month the coke arrived; the first Monday of the month the delivery boy from Bannerman brought the household necessities. Some chaps tried to diddle the management, a few pence here, a few pence there, but not Rhodes.

'Probably dodging in and out of the income tax regulations like a wireworm through a three-pronged fork,' suggested the unscrupulous Mr Crook, but he had these gentry on his list along with a lot of other kill-joys and was delighted when anyone outwitted them.

Kay went into what was called an American kitchen—a slice of the living-room sealed off by a tasty pastel Venetian blind, and with a few eggs and some milk and cheese and a good deal of skill she quickly knocked together a meal that would have got her a job as a cook in practically any private household where she cared to apply. She washed up, made coffee and, not being plagued with television and finding nothing alluring on the radio, settled down to write to one Bryan Forbes, the young man who had captured her heart and who was most inconveniently at this moment a considerable distance away, the width of the Atlantic Ocean, in short. Her pen flew over the thin pages—she wouldn't use a typewriter for correspondence with *him*—deploring his absence, and with no notion how much more reason she was going to have to deplore it during the days immediately ahead.

17

If it hadn't been for a miraculous opportunity out of the blue she would probably have been Mrs Bryan Forbes by this time, but they both agreed you couldn't turn down a chance like this one. And one of the stipulations for this particular job was that the acceptable candidate should be a bachelor.

'If I pull this off,' Bryan had murmured, his face so close to hers it seemed as large as Inspector Hawksbee's on Mr Crook's TV screen, 'we're made. It's the chance we've both been praying for. Three months, that's all, my darling, and then I shall come over and fetch you.'

'Why doesn't someone offer me an illustrating job in the States?' she murmured wistfully. But it didn't occur to her to try and stop him. He still seemed a miracle to her after more than six months. She had met him quite casually at a trade cocktail party and just stood staring like a child. When he said, in the silly phraseology of the day, 'Where have you been all my life?' she replied dumbly, 'Waiting, I suppose.' She'd meant to marry a blond Anglo-Saxon. Bryan was tall and dark and distinguished, with a kind of inner light burning through everything he did, even the little things. 'You're like a painter,' she taunted him once. 'You always want to perfect just one more detail.'

She found him irresistible, and she didn't know how she was going to do without him for three months, though she'd lived quite happily without even knowing of his existence for twenty-two years. But work fills one's time and absorbs one's energy and she had the good sense not to decry all her other associations because she was in love.

Overweight again, of course, she thought, as she began to shuffle the pages together. When she had put the envelope aside to mail the next day she was aware of a sense of uneasiness for which she couldn't account. People presumably felt like this when geese walked over their graves—why geese? In Kensal Green, say?—or ghosts glimmered in the twilight. She went to the front door and on an impulse she flung it open, holding herself very stiff and rigid but there wasn't a sound. Not—a—sound. And, of course, that was the explanation. The place was quiet, too quiet. One of Crook's complaints was that whereas in the old days he practically didn't know whether his neighbours ever went to the bathroom, now there was no such privacy. Miss Chisholm in a previous incarnation must, thought Kay, have been a precision machine. She rose on the stroke of seven winter and summer, she came back from her job at 6.30. At eleven o'clock she went to bed. Kay could hear the cistern emptying and then filling in the noisy manner of modern cisterns when she had her bath in the morning, and the rush of water at 11.00 p.m. as she prepared to retire.

' I don't really need a watch,' she had told Mr Dove around the corner when she took hers in to be cleaned. 'There's a human time machine on my premises and if anything was five minutes wrong I should know it was my watch and not Miss Prism.' Occasionally this neighbour went abroad, and then an extraordinary air of tranquillity pervaded Kay's flat. She felt she could lie in bed late, play the radio till midnight or entertain friends till the small hours of the morning. Miss Chisholm was a martinet for house regulations. No radio or other musical instrument after 11.00 p.m., said the lease, and though most people loosely read that as midnight, not so Miss C. Play your radio till 11.10 and she would knock on the floor with a stick as heavy as her own tread. If you didn't switch off immediately she would come down in a severe dressing gown and ring the front-door bell.

Kay looked at the watch on her wrist. The time was a quarter to twelve, and absorbed though she had been she could not have failed to hear that sturdy policeman's tramp go past her door and then sound overhead. Miss Chisholm had been in her own flat when Kay went out to her party; if she had returned before nine o'clock she must have given some sign of her occupancy, but there had been nothing, no running tap, no cistern flushing. Ergo—either she had dropped down in a dead faint or she had gone out again and not yet returned.

Well, why not? Kay asked herself reasonably. Only, of course, machines don't suddenly change their patterns. Still, there was nothing she, Kay Carter, could do about it. All the same, she didn't go to bed right away. Where was the sense, when she was sure to be awakened when Miss Chisholm did come in? She sat up playing patience till 12.30. Then reluctantly she packed up the cards and decided to call it a day. But still, she wasn't at ease. Fem. int., Crook would have called it; his shorthand term for feminine intuition. (When this kind of thing happened to him he called it a hunch, but it came to the same thing in the end.)

Perhaps she rushed off to the Continent on a night flight, Kay reminded herself, climbing into bed. And again—Rhodes was sure to know. Rhodes knew everything, was, indeed, Miss Chisholm's only confidant in the flats. She was inclined to speak of him as if he were her particular factotum, popping in and out doing a score of odd jobs that husbands or knowledgeable young women (like Kay Carter, for instance) do for themselves. And you could be sure she wouldn't pay a penny beyond the market price.

Of course, Kay consoled herself, setting her trim dark head on the one little soft pillow she allowed herself, she could be on the town. It was an amusing thought to put one to sleep.

The next morning she woke late. No sound of a bath being run had aroused her, and when 8.30 struck nobody opened the door of Flat 3 and came stomping determinedly out. She ran down a few minutes later to fetch her bottle of milk. The management had provided a small coffin-shaped box beside the front door for each flat, where tradesmen and postmen could leave parcels when the tenants were out; having collected her milk and newspaper Kay impulsively opened the door marked 3. Inside was a morning paper, a half-pint bottle of milk, half a dozen eggs in a box and some cream. A note in Miss Chisholm's neat pointed hand had been left the night before.

That proves she hasn't gone away, Kay reflected. Besides, her car's there.

Miss Chisholm drove a grey-blue Martin Tourer, that she fussed over as a Mayfair lady will fuss over a poodle dog. She would never have gone away and left that parked outside the flat. All the tenants parked in the open these days, but when Miss Chisholm went abroad, which she did in the summer, she either took the car with her or put it in a garage.

Kay had just made her coffee when she heard Rhodes on the stairs and opened her door.

' Morning, Miss Carter,' he said. He had his usual big cardboard container in which he collected the rubbish and put it in a bin in the basement to be collected in due course. ‘Anything I can do?’ Probably the Last Day would find him alert and smiling, she thought, asking just that.

‘Did you see anything of Miss Chisholm this morning?’ she inquired.

‘Well, it’s nine o’clock.’ Rhodes sounded surprised. ‘She’d have gone before now. She put her bin out as usual, though, rather more than usual.’ A number of parcels wrapped in newspaper were already in the container. Kay smiled. It was a joke between her and Rhodes that if Miss Chisholm had only an eggshell to dispose of she’d wrap it in newspaper. ‘Why, did you want her?’

‘I’m worried,’ said Kay. ‘There hasn’t been a peep out of her since I got in about nine o’clock last night.’

‘Having a late morning perhaps,’ suggested Rhodes, though they both knew how uncharacteristic of their prim neighbour this was.

‘She must be ill. Did you ring her bell?’

‘No,’ said Rhodes. ‘Why should I? Now I come to think of it she did say something a day or two back about going abroad.’

‘But she wouldn’t go without saying a word to anyone. Besides, she left an order for the milkman, and her paper’s there. Oh, Rhodes, I was sure you’d know.’

‘You’ll see, she’ll be around presently,’ he consoled her. ‘If she hasn’t gone out, that is.’

‘She can’t have gone out. Her car’s there. Besides, there’s Henry. Did she ask you to look after him while she was away?’

‘She didn’t,’ acknowledged Rhodes, ‘and that’s a fact.’

A bell rang down the quiet stairs.

‘Listen,’ Kay exclaimed. ‘That’s her telephone. Well, she can’t be there or she’d answer it. Unless, of course, she’s died in her sleep. She came home last night as usual; then I went out and since I came back, twelve hours ago, it’s all been as silent as the grave. It’s out of the straight,’ she added, ‘and Miss Chisholm might have been the inventor of the straight and narrow. Still ’—she smiled into Rhodes’ good-natured face (you could see he thought all this was a lot of fuss about nothing)— ‘I don’t know why I should worry about her. She’s not my auntie. By the way, the light on her landing doesn't seem to be functioning.'

Rhodes put out his hand and pressed the switch alongside her door. A light sprang up on each landing.

'Someone having a bit of a lark,' he explained. 'Bulb twisted so it didn't establish contact.'

Somehow that disturbed Kay more than ever. 'What an extra-ordinary thing for a grown-up person to do. I mean, it's not as if there were children up there . . .' She smiled unwillingly as she spoke. The idea of Miss Chisholm with a child was somehow ludicrous; it was hard to believe she'd ever been one herself.

'Kids aren't the only ones to act silly,' Rhodes assured her. 'Gone to see a sick relative p'raps,' he suggested.

'Without her car? You know, it's a funny thing, I've been here a year and I don't even know if she has any relations. In fact, I wouldn't be greatly surprised if someone told me she'd been grown out of a culture in a bottle. I've only once seen the inside of the flat,' she went on. 'It was so tidy I felt as if I was something that had blown in during a gale and didn't really fit.'

'There's a lady can look after herself,' Rhodes assured her, and went whistling downstairs to empty Mrs Sagan's rubbish on the ground floor. She was just the reverse of Miss Chisholm, never wrapped up anything, and usually had odd parcels and bits as well as the kitchen garbage.

Kay went back and poured herself another cup of coffee, still thinking about her neighbour. All she knew of her was that she was a milliner in a small—at all events, a select—way, with a West End workshop. She made hats to order, and on the occasion of Kay's sole visit to the flat had tried to convert her to wearing them.

'So much more elegant than a scarf,' she remonstrated.

'They don't suit my face,' Kay had explained.

'Because you've never found the right one. I make them to suit faces and temperaments. You've no notion, Miss Carter, what a hat can do for you.'

It was a busy morning. The morning's mail brought a com-mission to illustrate a magazine story and an invitation to lunch with the editor of Women's Taste the following day. Working, a painty smock over a full skirt, Kay forgot about Miss Chisholm until a ring at the door in the afternoon made her reluctantly put down her tools. The postman was outside, with a smallish squarish cardboard box addressed in neat printed capitals to Miss Chisholm at 2 Brandon Street, Earl's Court, S.W.5. The word urgent was blackly stamped across one corner. The return label bore a printed inscription: Louise, 2 Hebberden Mews, W.1, and the parcel had been registered. Louise was Miss Chisholm's trade name. 'She seems to be sending hats to herself,' said Kay when the man asked if she knew whether the lady upstairs was away. He had brought the parcel that morning and had no reply. 'Seeing it's marked urgent,' he said, 'I wondered if you'd mind taking it in.'

'I don't mind a bit,' said Kay. 'I'm not sure she isn't away, but probably she'll be back this evening. I'll put a note in her box to say I've got the parcel. Do you want me to sign or anything?'

He gave her a little green slip and a stubby pencil. She signed and the postman said, 'Ta,' and went whistling down the stairs.

Two or three times that afternoon Kay heard Miss Chisholm's telephone ringing and it always rang itself away into silence. On an impulse at about five o'clock she dialled the business telephone number on the parcel she had taken in, but the result was the same. There seemed to be no one there, either.

But she can't have gone for any length of time, she reminded herself suddenly, because of Henry; Henry was Miss Chisholm's blue budgerigar, and was apparently her sole concession to sentiment. Miss Chisholm had had him as a baby bird and had sedulously trained him to speak. 'Come on, you naughty girl,' he used to say. It was a pity, Kay reflected, he hadn't been taught to answer the phone. Remembering Henry, her apprehensions died down.

I'm getting to be a regular fuddy-duddy, she told herself scornfully. Rhodes is right, she went out to see someone, it got late, she decided to spend the night. She'll be back as usual this evening.

At 6.30 that evening she listened confidently for the sound of footsteps, but though she heard Mrs Sagan slam her front door—

23

and how that door remained on its hinges with the treatment it got defeated everyone in the house—no one went up to Flat 3. Kay was going out to dinner and just before she went, at 6.45, she ran up the stairs, carrying the parcel. There was still no light under the door, but that wasn't surprising; you didn't need a light at that hour. She rang and she knocked and then she hesitated about leaving the parcel on the landing. Suppose Miss C. wanted it particularly for this evening? It was a small box but too large to be left in coffin no. 3: still it was registered and might contain something valuable, so she decided to take it back to her own flat. She had scrawled a message—I have a registered parcel for you in Flat 2—and this she pushed through the letterbox.

Then she went out to dinner. It was a duty call to two elderly aunts, half-sisters of the late Dr Carter, who shared a flat in South Kensington. They wanted to know if she'd heard from Bryan and when he was expected back, and didn't Kay think it rather peculiar to accept such a commission when it meant postponing his marriage.

'Not a bit,' said Kay. 'It's his job and a wonderful opportunity. It could change both our lives.' ('And how!' as Crook would have said.)

'Men have changed since we were girls,' simpered Clara and Effie, but since they hadn't been sought even in those distant days it was hard to see on what they were basing their statement.

Kay got away about nine o'clock and the sisters told each other there was something funny about a girl who (a) didn't want to stop and see television, the highlight of their evenings, and (b) could speak so casually about the man to whom she was engaged.

'She doesn't even seem worried that he's gone,' said Clara. 'And yet one hears so much about the enterprise of American women.'

'I'm not sure he isn't the one who should be worrying,' retorted Effie, darkly. 'Leaving her alone in a bachelor flat for three months. She's quite a pretty gel, you know.'

'Mouth's too big,' snapped Clara, whose own mouth was the size of an immature rosebud.

'Those eyes, though, a sort of violet . . .'

'Don't know why she doesn't treat herself to a perm,' said Clara, whose hair looked like the Medusa, lots of little snakes, only grey instead of gold, writhing in every direction.

'It's rather distinguished, that smooth, dark hair—perhaps she has a secret life,' brooded Effie.

Clara sparkled. 'Talking about a secret life, have you switched on? It's time for the serial.'

THREE

As she opened the door of her flat Kay almost fell over the box she had left in its diminutive hall.

Better take it up for the last time, she thought with a sigh of resignation. She discovered, to her surprise, she really wanted to get the thing off her premises, which was absurd. It wasn't large enough to be a nuisance, it couldn't, from the weight alone, contain a bomb, and, being a non-hatter herself, she had no curiosity as to the contents. All the same, she'd like to see it go. But when she pressed the bell of the upper flat the result was the same as ever. No one at home. The emptied dust bin still stood outside the door. That of itself would be proof that Miss Chisholm hadn't returned. Coming down, the box swinging from one finger, she encountered Mr Crook bouncing up, looking as pleased as Punch and not altogether unlike him.

'Been visiting me?' he asked hopefully.

'At this hour?' She smiled and once again he was half knocked off his balance. There had been someone called La Gioconda—he remembered vaguely.

'You don't have to worry about that,' he assured her in eager tones. 'I don't stand by union hours. You'd be welcome any time.'

'I've been up to call on Miss Chisholm,' she explained.

'How brave you are!' said Crook. 'I don't even dare look in her direction lest I be turned into stone.'

'She is rather alarming. She banged on my door once and held out an illustration I'd done for a magazine. "No woman of taste, as according to the text this creature is, would wear that kind of hat with that kind of suit," she told me. "If you wore hats yourself you would have a greater knowledge of *haute couture*."'

'Don't tell me she's eloped with the boy friend,' said the enchanted Mr Crook. Mystery was his meat and drink as well as his bread and butter, and he couldn't think of anything less likely.

'Don't tell me she's got a boy friend.' Kay was so dumb-founded she nearly dropped the hatbox.

'That's what C. Oliver says. I wonder what C. stands for. Charlie, I expect. A proper Charlie.'

'Who's C. Oliver?'

'The human whirlwind. He was here last night.'

'Oh yes. I met him on the stairs. He nearly swept me into eternity, and two vanishing women in one house would be too much.'

'Two vanishing women?'

'Miss Prism disappeared last night—well, to all intents and purposes. If she's there she's not answering bells or telephones or washing her hands or crossing the floor. Even Rhodes didn't know she was going away—if she has gone. Did you hear anything unusual last night—after I'd gone, I mean?'

Crook thought. 'No,' he said, 'I didn't—not from her flat, that is. Mine now . . .' His big mahogany brow creased. 'I'm just beginning to wonder if I didn't hear anything because C. Oliver didn't mean me to. Between him and Inspector Hawksbee you wouldn't have heard the P.M. announcing a new war.'

'You haven't told me what the human whirlwind was doing here last night,' Kay murmured. 'Oh, I'm sorry. I didn't really mean to sound curious. . . .'

'Why not?' asked Crook, genuinely amazed. 'What are we put in the world in our tens of thousands for if it ain't to take some interest in each other's concerns? But it's nice to know someone else has never heard of hawk-eyed Hawksbee. No,

26

Oliver came last night to see Miss Chisholm about a television set.'

'You must have got it wrong,' urged Kay. 'She hates television, she wouldn't have it at any price.'

'Well, so wouldn't I not have it at any price,' said Crook, who, like Humpty Dumpty, believed in making words work for him, rather than becoming their slave, 'but there's a hulking great monster staring me out of countenance in my flat at this very moment, and all thanks to Mr C. O. If you catch sight of him again,' he added warningly, 'you slam the door and put up the chain, or you'll find you've got the invader on your premises, too.'

All this while they were standing outside Kay's flat. 'Why don't we go in?' she suggested. 'You won't mind, will you, if the room looks like the world before the Spirit of Order brooded over it?'

'That's the way I like them,' Crook assured her. 'We'll all be neat and tidy enough in the grave. First time I've been inside any of these flats, bar my own, of course, since the new company started them up.' He sighed nostalgically. 'You never saw them in the old days, of course. Probably still in your pram. There was always something going on then.'

'I wouldn't be too sure there isn't something going on now,' Kay told him. 'Oh, let's get that out of the way.' She opened a cupboard door and tossed the box inside. Crook grinned.

'How come?' he asked, indicating a battered-looking soft black hat hanging on a hook.

'Oh, that was the aunts' idea—I was having dinner with them tonight. Well, half-aunts really, if there are such things. They gave it to me solemnly, when I came here, telling me that when they lived in the country they always kept it on a hook in the hall, so that when the gypsies called, which they did perpetually right through the summer, trying to sell straw mats or asking for water to make tea, they'd get the idea there was a man on the premises.'

'You're making it up,' Crook accused her. 'That sort of thing went out with the 1914 war.'

'Oh, I believe you, but except for the fact that they've invested in a TV they haven't progressed much since then. They're both over seventy.'

27

'Well, what's seventy?' said Crook.

'Some people are seventy years young and some people are seventy years old, and my aunts belong to the second group. Anyway, I promised to keep it hanging on a hook in my flat, and that's what I'm doing. Now, what do you like to drink? There's some gin or there's beer. . . .'

'Beer for me,' said Crook. 'Look, honey, you're getting a thing about our Miss Chisholm. She's free, white and goodness knows she's past twenty-one, she can go away for a night without us telephoning the police. . . .'

'She didn't take her car,' said Kay quietly.

'That open Tourer affair that's blocking the front entrance? So that's who it belongs to. I couldn't park the Superb within three doors, thanks to that.'

'That proves there's something wrong,' Kay insisted. She seemed to have lost all interest in the beer, and Crook thought it was time he took a hand. He opened the bottle skilfully in his own way, which didn't involve the use of a bottle-opener, and looked around for glasses.

'Proves what, sugar? Any tooth mugs handy?'

Kay mechanically opened a cupboard and took out two tumblers engraved with local fauna. 'Sent me by a friend in Nairobi,' she said. 'Will you have the giraffe or the elephant? There was a bison but he got broken.'

Crook said he wasn't fussy and the elephant seemed suitable. He poured out the beer.

'There *is* something wrong,' Kay insisted. 'Miss Chisholm never went so far as the post box except in the car. She thought that if you were meant to walk you'd be given four feet.'

'And how!' agreed Mr Crook. 'Thank God for a girl who keeps her beer in the fridge. But maybe someone called for her. The boy friend, say, and they decided to make a night of it.'

'She's as fussy over the car as she is over everything else,' fretted Kay. 'If she knew she wasn't coming back she'd have put a cover on it. She wouldn't leave it exposed to the insult of common passers-by, not for a whole twenty-four hours. And then there's Henry,' she added.

'Is this the boy friend cropping up again?' hazarded Crook.

28

'Henry's her budgie. Her sole concession to the humanities. If she'd been going away she'd have left a note and a spare key for Rhodes, asking him to feed it. I know she would. She wouldn't leave it to starve.'

'She should have a TV set. Then she'd know you only have to teach your budgie to say Pringle's Budgie Seed, and it can get it for itself.'

'Can you teach it to say that on the phone?' asked the girl dryly.

'Oliver didn't say so, but perhaps they haven't thought of that one yet. Anyway, budgies don't starve in twenty-four hours. Even that lesser order, the human race, don't do that. She could have put in an extra millet spray or bit of cuttle-bone.'

'In that case she should be back tonight, and she hasn't come, Mr Crook, she hasn't come. She'd never leave Henry for two nights.'

'There's still time,' said Crook patiently. 'It's barely ten o'clock.'

'She could have telephoned Rhodes if she'd been kept, but she hasn't, because I asked him; or she could have rung me, if he was out, but she didn't. It simply isn't in keeping for her to have walked out without a word or letter, no papers cancelled, no milk—in fact, goods ordered. Did you say this man, Oliver, was there last night?'

'Called but had the door shut in his face by the boy-friend.'

'Did he see Miss Prism?'

'Said she didn't want to see him or something. Well, maybe it wasn't quite convenient—you know the one about three being a crowd.'

'If she was expecting him . . .'

'Maybe she changed her mind. . . .'

'Or had it changed for her. What time was this?'

'Well, I found him waiting when I got up there, said he'd been there about twenty minutes. Must have called about seven or thereabouts. You didn't hear him?'

She shook her head. 'I'd be washing, changing, running the water. And I wouldn't be expecting anyone. But I did hear Miss Chisholm go storming up at 6.30 as usual.'

'By herself?'

'Well, I didn't hear anyone else. But then, if they walked normally I wouldn't. Besides, her tread would drown an army. I didn't hear anyone go down after I got back from my party.'

'Running more taps, p'raps?'

'No. I was writing a letter.' The quick colour flooded into her face. 'The whirlwind went straight down, though, like coals falling down a chute. I saw him vanish into the hall.'

'And I saw him vanish into his little tuppenny-ha'-penny van and go beetling round the corner. No, if there has been any dirty work at the crossroads it was while you were at your party and I was bein' reduced by the monster.'

'I telephoned the shop,' Kay went on. 'I got the number from the hatbox—at five o'clock, but there was no reply.'

'Shut down for the summer break perhaps. Like dry cleaners. Two weeks in August, and if you spill your soup on your dinner jacket you go out in your pyjamas for the next fortnight. That would explain the hat being sent here. Look, sugar, she don't have to be missing because she don't answer a bell or a telephone. She could have her reasons.'

'One of them being that she isn't there. Mr Crook, she could have had an accident, be in hospital . . .'

'In that case, they'll have got in touch with the next of kin.'

'Provided she has any. Wouldn't they have come round here?'

'Not if she didn't give them the address.'

'She's the sort that would never go out without an address in her bag. Probably carries it tied round her neck, too. Besides, I telephoned and she would have answered if she'd been there. Of course she would. Did you ever know a woman who could resist a telephone bell? Oh, nine times out of ten it's the man coming to read the gas or someone you don't want to talk to or a wrong number, but there's always the million-to-one chance that this may be the call that will revolutionise your existence.'

Crook's heart warmed a bit more; he knew exactly what she meant; he'd got out of bed on innumerable occasions at the bell's shrill summons, and thought if there was such an amenity in the graveyard and it tolled for him he'd push up the lid of his coffin and put out a skeleton hand for the invisible receiver.

'What do you suggest we should do?' he asked. He could see she was like most of her sex, couldn't see a flower in bud without wanting to help God make it blossom before its time, and thought patience was one of the cardinal sins, but he was blowed if he could see what she could do now.

'Shouldn't we let the police know or something?' she suggested vaguely.

'The police,' parroted Mr Crook, 'are a very overworked body of men. They don't like having their eyes wiped any more than anyone else, and the notion that they might be called in because of a lady of mature years has gone off for a night . . .' He put out a huge hand and touched her arm. 'What's your idea, sugar? That she's dropped down in a dead faint?'

'Either she's ill or she isn't there. There was no light on in her flat when I came back and it would be too dark to read without one. Especially with the nylon curtains she has. I don't go for them myself, there's too little air in London as it is. . . .'

Crook shook his big red head wonderingly. He'd never noticed any lack of air in London. Privately he thought the girl was making a lot of fuss about precious little. Being a woman herself, she should know they change their minds more readily than the wind blows, and if Miss Chisholm was having a bit of a scamper over the tiles, it wasn't likely to harm anyone but herself, and it wouldn't have occurred to Crook to worry about what would happen to her, any more than he'd worry about what would happen to a hickory bough when the wind blew. The one he was sorry for was the boy friend. It flashed through his mind to wonder what he was missing on the screen while he chatted here—Wild Westerns, Scotland Yard revelations, pictures of polar bears in igloos. He didn't mean to keep the thing, of course, but when you were given free-viewing for three days you'd be a mug not to take advantage of your opportunity.

'I've thought of something else,' announced Kay.

'I knew it,' said Mr Crook in resigned tones. 'Dames always do.'

'Miss Prism always locks her door when she goes out, even if it's only as far as the butcher to get a chop. She says her insurance company insists on it. Not a very savoury neighbourhood, she says . . .'

Mr Crook bristled at once. 'Let me tell you, I've been living here for more than twenty years and it's never got me down.'

31

Kay looked at him with an amused affection. 'Tell me the neighbourhood that would.'

'P'raps she locks herself in at night, too,' Crook offered. 'Virtue like that must be worth preserving.'

'I don't think it's her virtue so much as her possessions, she has in mind. Now, if the door isn't locked she must be inside.'

Despite all his good resolutions about not counting chickens before they were hatched, Mr Crook's heart began to leap and wriggle like a fish on the end of a line. Oh, too good to be true that there might be a corpse there, he was thinking. Just like old times, the house hadn't lost its magic.

'Let's you and me beetle up and look,' he offered. But in his heart he knew that damned lock would be locked from the outside.

So it was all the more exciting when it wasn't. The lock, for some reason neither quite understood, had been set very low in the door and they both dropped down to squint through the keyhole, and it was perfectly clear the keys were still on the inner side. So . . .

'That's proof,' said Kay simply. 'That something's wrong, I mean.'

'Well, not exactly,' Crook murmured.

'It is to me.' He thought enviously how easily women reduced difficulties, mostly by the Nelson method of not admitting that they exist. Put a posse of women in the Cabinet and dismiss all the males to the bar, and they'd solve most national problems in a highly original but equally competent manner. It occurred to him that probably most other men had realised this already, and that was why they fought so sedulously to exclude women from high office.

Kay, still kneeling, laid her ear against the keyhole.

'Listening for groans?' asked the fascinated Mr Crook. 'A bit late, isn't it? I mean, if she really has been missing since last night . . .'

'I was wondering if Henry was trying to give the alarm.'

'Couldn't she,' murmured Mr Crook weakly, 'have taken Henry with her?'

'Well, the cage is still hanging in the window. I could see that from the street.'

The letterbox, wondered Mr Crook, and they had a genteel struggle as to which of them should be the first to look through. Sadly Mr Crook yielded.

'They must have got all the doors shut—it's only a tiny hall, no more than a few feet of passage. The bedroom and living-room doors open off it and the k. and b. are sort of alcoves with doors opening into the rooms, so we shouldn't see those either way.'

'No body?' asked Mr Crook wistfully, and she shook her head.

'But she could have fainted and be lying in the living-room —or had a heart attack . . .'

'Or been electrocuted in her bath,' added Crook in enthusiastic tones. 'What do budgerigars do when tragedy overtakes the household? Dogs howl and cats miaow. . . . Not that you can blame Henry if he's mute. Probably thankful for a bit of peace; she always gave me the impression of being a managing female. Now, sugar, there's nothing we can do for the moment. . . .' He put out his big hand and touched hers. It was cold as ice. 'Suppose she's just gone off, maybe on the spur of the minute, how grateful is she going to be when she finds the police waiting on her doorstep? If there's been an accident she's bein' looked after anyway—and you're not toyin' with the idea that she's got herself murdered?'

'I don't know why she should be, but then I don't know anything about her. I didn't know she had a boy friend. But I do know one thing—she wouldn't go out and leave her flat unlocked, and the car uncovered and Henry practically widowed, and it can't be locked because the key's on the other side.'

Steps sounded on the stairs below and Rhodes came up. 'Oh!' He seemed surprised at the sight of them on their knees. They must, Crook supposed, make a pretty strange tableau, but no such thought passed through Kay's mind. Like all women, when she was serious a Presbyterian divine had nothing on her.

'I thought as I heard voices, Miss Chisholm might be back,' Rhodes apologised.

'If she ever went out,' said Kay.

Rhodes cast a sharp glance at Crook.

'The young lady has a theory there's trouble brewing,' said Crook. 'Could be she's right, it's a way dames have in the face of all reason and good sense.'

'She came in last night because I heard her,' Kay insisted.

'Now I come to think of it there was a young chap, said he'd come to deliver a television or something. I thought it was a bit queer, knowing her views. I was watering my few pots and things in the front when he bounced out and asked what floor. I told him the third. "Save yourself the trouble," I said, "she'll never let you in."'

'Apparently she didn't,' Crook agreed. 'Chap came up to me. I was stuck with him for an hour and a half.'

'Never take no for an answer,' agreed Rhodes. 'Once you let those chaps inside the place you've had it. My mother let a vacuum chap in once, and before she knew where she was she was signing on for so much down and the rest in monthly instalments till she was eighty or thereabouts. What gave him the idea she'd take a set?' he added, curiously.

'That's what I'm beginning to wonder. Miss Chisholm had a visitor when this chap arrived, so he didn't get in.'

'Did she? I never saw anyone—but of course I don't see everyone that comes and goes and mostly they're for the ground floor. Has some queer birds in *her* nest.'

'There was someone there,' said Crook thoughtfully, 'and this chap came up to my flat and hung about for the better part of half an hour waiting for me. Said the chap in Flat 3 sent him up. Patience seems to be his middle name. He inveigled his way in and he kept me from doing anything useful for the rest of the evening.'

'Did you keep the set, sir?' asked Rhodes. He said it courteously enough, but there was a note of amusement in his deep voice.

'Keep it? I'd have bought the damned thing to get him off my premises.'

'It might be quicker in the long run than filling in one of those forms,' Rhodes agreed.

'I didn't fill in a form,' said Crook in the same reflective voice. 'He said I could have it on approval till tomorrow night.'

'What company?' inquired Rhodes sharply.

34

' A thing calling itself the Hirewire.'

' That's genuine enough,' Kay reassured him. ' My aunts rent through that. Fairly new to the game and extra favourable terms to get the business on its feet. Trust Aunt Clara to get a thing at bedrock prices.'

' God bless Aunt Clara,' suggested Crook. ' That's one point cleared up. All the same, a chap I didn't invite and who didn't call on professional business—not my professional business any- way—calls one evening and that's the one evening someone disappears.'

' You didn't hear anything, Mr Crook?' Even Rhodes' cheerful face was looking troubled.

' An army could have gone by with that monster roaring at me and I wouldn't have heard. I'm just beginning to wonder if that was the way it was meant to be. I wonder if the star-gazer on the ground floor would have noticed anyone come in.'

Like someone who passes effortlessly from orthodoxy to agnosticism scarcely noticing the change, he had moved over from frank, even scolding disbelief to a warm-hearted suspicion.

' No harm asking,' he continued in buoyant tones. ' Here, sugar, you're the one started all this. You come along.'

Like a bird Kay came.

FOUR

Mrs Sagan opened her door wearing the inevitable hat, tonight a pink turban, and a long trailing housecoat. She stared at Crook and the girl as if she didn't quite believe in them.

' Could we trouble you?' suggested Crook, and she seemed to wake up and said at once, ' Why have you come? These are not my office hours.'

' We didn't think this was the registrar's,' Crook assured her, introducing the two of them. (They had inhabited the same house for twelve months but she still seemed doubtful of their identity.) 'It's about Miss Chisholm.'

'Miss Chisholm? Something's happened.' It was a statement rather than a question.

'That's right. Did you expect it?'

'I am particularly sensitive . . . I could see misfortune roll-up for her unless she would listen to me.'

'And she wouldn't?'

'She would not even allow me to draw up her horoscope. Is she dead?'

Full marks for directness, reflected Crook. Aloud he said, 'Well, we don't know, we thought you might help us. Can you remember when you last saw her?'

Mrs Sagan went into a trance. 'Was it this morning?' she wondered.

'If so, you should have a medal, because no one else in the house saw her this morning. How about last night?'

'I remember now—someone called for her. He carried a box. He asked me if there was a lift.'

'Knock on any door,' murmured Crook.

'I—er—happened to be taking a breath of fresh air at my window. I usually take a little refreshment about seven o'clock.'

'You're sure of the time?'

'Not within twenty minutes, say, six-thirty, seven, seven-thirty, what difference does it make?'

'You might be surprised. Happen to see anyone else go up last night? Before the chap with the box?'

Mrs Sagan shook her head. 'I was at my desk. When I am at work I should hardly notice the outbreak of a new war.'

'According to all accounts we're none of us going to have the chance to do that. War travelling faster than sound, and if you hear the bomb at all it'll be in another world. You didn't by any chance notice Miss Chisholm go out last night?'

'Let me think.' Marshalling her mental processes seemed as tricky a job as catching a white mouse that has escaped from its cage. 'Someone came in,' she announced. 'You know this house is a perfect sound box.'

They nodded. They knew.

'You mean, after Miss Chisholm came back?'

36

'Oh yes. A man. I didn't pay much attention. I supposed it would be for one of you. Miss Chisholm has so few visitors.'

'Did you notice him?'

'Look, Mrs Sagan,' Rhodes put in, 'we know a man came to see Miss Chisholm about a television set.'

'Oh, that one!' She gurgled with sudden, unexpectedly pretty laughter. 'Oh yes, a fair young man about as unnoticeable as a bomb. He happened to catch sight of me and asked if there was a lift.'

'That's Oliver C.,' said Crook. 'Was there anyone else? You didn't, for instance, see an ambulance? A doctor's car?'

Suddenly, like a curtain being run down on a play, Mrs Sagan dropped all her absurd affectation and now displayed the robust good sense she had inherited from her Streatham mother.

'What's all this about? What's happened to Miss Chisholm?'

'Don't you see,' cried Kay, 'that's what we're trying to find out?' She explained the situation as far as they knew it. 'Mr Crook isn't as sure as I am, but then he'd never met her, but I'm absolutely certain she'd never have gone out and left the keys on the inside. Why, how would she get in again?'

'She's got two sets,' put in Rhodes. 'If she's expecting anyone she leaves one with me.'

'There's a key on the inside of the door,' Kay insisted. 'She must be there. And yet there hasn't been a peep out of her for nearly twenty-four hours. Besides, there's Henry.' They kept coming back to Henry. 'Her bird, you know. She wouldn't go off and leave him, not without a message or anything. Would she, Rhodes?' she urged.

'Doesn't seem like her,' Rhodes agreed.

'And her car's outside. She'd never have walked. . . .'

'Didn't happen to notice a taxi call last night?' Crook suggested.

'Well, I don't spend the entire evening at the window, like a girl on a switchboard,' Mrs Sagan pointed out. 'I have to have an evening meal like anyone else, and then I wash up. Afterwards I had a telephone call. It came just as I had made myself a cup of tea, I remember.'

That's bought it, reflected Crook. A woman loose on the tele-

37

phone was less reliable than a woman loose in a dress shop with her husband's chequebook.

'First I thought it was a wrong number,' continued Mrs Sagan painstakingly. 'So, of course, I rang off. But it rang again almost immediately, and a most extraordinary person said, "Are you the model? Are you sure you're not the model? Well, is there anyone in the house who is?" I kept saying, "What name do you want?" and he said, "I want the model." So you see, Mr Crook, if a taxi had come I shouldn't have seen it because my telephone's at the back of the flat. So noisy in the front, all the traffic, you wouldn't hear it on your floor.'

'And I went round to the Blue Rabbit as usual after I'd had a bite,' put in Rhodes. 'I didn't see a taxi, either.'

'Then this morning,' brooded Mrs Sagan, 'the postman came about half-past ten, but nothing for me, and at eleven I had Mrs Rollo, while the coal was being delivered. She comes once a week, I think she imagines I'm a fortune-teller, she keeps looking round for the crystal. I must put up a notice. She always wants to know what's going to happen before we meet again. Of course the truth is she's heading straight for an asylum, but you're not supposed to tell them that. She was full of complaints as usual, had nearly fallen over the lid of the coal hole. "Why do you suppose you were given eyes?" I asked her. But of course she's always looking inward.'

'Or upward, for the stars,' contributed Crook blithely, but that was a mistake. Mrs Sagan stiffened, giving the impression that the stars were no affair of any sceptical amateur.

'I had a lunch appointment and Mrs Rollo made me late for that,' she went on. 'I got back about four for another appointment, and—I don't think I noticed anyone else until Miss Chisholm returned at 6.30 as usual. Oh,' she turned to Kay, 'I noticed you go out just before I did at midday. Living on the ground floor,' she added with some dignity, thinking she detected a rapid exchange of glances between Crook and the porter, 'one sees all life pass under one's window.'

'How about the boy friend?' inquired Crook. 'You did say someone came beside the TV chap.'

'Well'—Mrs Sagan sounded vague—'I do have the impression someone came in, a male step—but it needn't have been for her.

38

I simply heard unfamiliar feet in the hall. Or perhaps it was you.' She looked at Rhodes.

'Well, not that time of day. I only come if I'm sent for and last night nobody did. Miss Carter's right, Mr Crook. It doesn't add up.'

'You leave arithmetic to the police,' Crook advised.

'The police!' The words might have been an Open Sesame to the harebrained Mrs Sagan. 'Of course, why didn't we think of them? Perhaps she's been picked up.'

'Picked up?' Three voices rang out in unison.

'Well, what do we know about her? She could have been knocked down by a car and picked up by the police. She could be in a hospital or even a mortuary. Anyway, they're the ones to accept responsibility. It's what they're paid for.'

'Responsibility for what?' asked Crook.

'Well—breaking into her flat. Isn't that what you had in mind?' Her mad brown glance swept them all. 'Obviously we can't sit here and do nothing.'

'I suppose you know a lady can't be officially missing till she's been gone forty-eight hours, and then only if the circumstances are suspicious.'

'Just like a man, trying to dodge the column,' cried Mrs Sagan, catching Kay's eye. 'It's happening all the time, neighbours whisper, but no one wants to look a fool or accept the responsibility. The milk piles up and the newspapers block the letterbox and when at last someone does make a move the odds are they find it's a hearse they need, not an ambulance. I once made a collection of newspaper cuttings on this very subject—I do a little journalism sometimes to help out—and you'd be surprised —one body, I remember, lay in a lift shaft for a week and even the liftman didn't know it was there—well, if we tell the police and they won't take any action, and Miss Chisholm is really dead or dying in her flat, or even been murdered, you do read such dreadful things in the papers, and you don't have to be young and beautiful or even very rich these days, well, it'll be their fault, don't you see?—like being run over on a crossing,' she wound up vaguely.

'What on earth have crossings got to do with Miss Chisholm disappearing?' exclaimed Kay, but Crook touched her hand saying quickly, ' Let it ride, honey. We don't all want to be missing from our flats for the rest of the night.'

' Anyway, I think it's a very good idea,' added Kay sturdily.

Crook telegraphed a message to Rhodes. Trust dames to gang up together, it said, and Rhodes telegraphed back. And how!

Mrs Sagan trotted to the back of the flat and lifted her receiver. Crook and Kay followed, Rhodes waiting in the passage.

' No one's there,' she said, shaking the receiver pettishly.

' Have you pressed the button?' asked Kay.

' Oh, I forgot. I can't get used to these party lines. Every now and again I press the button in the hope that Rhodes—he has the other half, you know (Crook was the only one of the lot who had a line to himself, Kay sharing with the missing Miss Chisholm)—has got a sure tip for the 3.30 and is just putting something on, but he's always arranging to come round and put in a window sash for someone or paint a gate or something. That man must be like you, Mr Crook, work twenty-four hours round the clock.' She was dialling as she spoke. ' I've always wanted to dial 999. Hallo. I want the police. What? Oh, I suppose the local police. No, I don't know the number, but it's urgent. All this red tape,' she added without bothering to lower her voice. ' Oh, is that the police? My name is Sagan, Mrs Florence Sagan, and I live at no. 2 Brandon Street, the ground floor. I want to report a mysterious disappearance. . . . What's that? A cat? I didn't say anything about a cat. I'm allergic to cats, I certainly shouldn't report their disappearance. I should consider it a dispensation of Providence. It's a lady, name of Chisholm, came home last night and hasn't been heard of since. Well, of course something's wrong. It's nearly twenty-four hours. Could you spend twenty-four hours in a flat without even pulling the plug?'

This appeared to shock the station officer into near insensibility for Mrs Sagan got a long, uninterrupted call. Crook admired the economy and skill with which she put her case, rounding and stamping it, till suddenly he thought of his childhood days when butter wasn't sold in the unromantic half-pound slab but was carved out of a barrel-shaped mass, shaped by wooden hands and finally stamped with a cow or a swan.

It was decades, he thought, since he'd seen a swan or a cow in his butter dish.

Mrs Sagan stopped for breath and the policeman had his turn. Now and again she expostulated, 'But, officer . . .' but the police are as good at this game as any civilian. Presently she hung up.

'He says you can't call a lady missing because she's away for the night. Might have stopped over with a friend. Might have gone out in the friend's car and so of course she'd leave her own. No crime to leave a bird alone in a flat for twenty-four hours—"not like a doggie",' she parroted. 'Oh, well, that leaves us a clear field. We've satisfied our official consciences.'

'Meaning?' suggested Crook, his heart warming to her with every syllable.

'Well. Would there be a chance of breaking in through the window? Hasn't she got a balcony and there's a balcony on the adjacent flat? Couldn't Rhodes . . .?'

'I could and all,' said Rhodes, coming in on his cue like any old maestro. 'Lady next door knows me. I did a bit of a job for her a couple of months back.'

'That's splendid. What are we waiting for? You can get over onto Miss Chisholm's little balcony and look through the window. If you don't see any bodies or anything, everything's O.K. Anyway, you could have a word with Henry. I expect he wants a bit of cheering up. You can explain—to Mrs Benson, of course, not Henry—that Miss Chisholm has left her keys behind and has asked you to let her in. I don't quite see her trying to climb the barricade she's erected between the two balconies. You know, I wouldn't be surprised if she lived a secret life.' Her enthusiasm grew with every syllable she uttered. 'It isn't natural to be so anxious for privacy. I suppose you haven't heard any orgies at any time, Mr Crook?'

'I wouldn't notice,' said Crook regretfully. 'I'm not nosy till I'm paid to be.'

'Get along with you. What do you think you're doing now?'

'This young lady consulted me.'

Did I? wondered Kay. Yes, I suppose I did.

'What are we waiting for?' demanded Mrs Sagan. 'Rhodes, you must have kissed the Blarney stone smooth in your time. You'll be able to talk Mrs Benson over, I'm sure.'

'I can try,' Rhodes agreed. 'Mind you,' he added, as they came into the communal hall of the house, 'it's a blooming waste of energy to say nothing of risking my neck. There wasn't a boy in our street when I was a nipper couldn't have opened a lock like that, with a bit of celluloid. Crying shame the locks they put on these flats. I could do it myself if I had a bit of celluloid.'

'If Bill was here,' capped Crook wistfully, 'he wouldn't even want celluloid. Just one glance . . .'

'Conjuring lay?' asked Rhodes smoothly. 'Well, I'll go along and see if Mrs Benson is in.'

'You'd better say she had her bag stolen,' warned Kay. 'No one would believe she'd forgotten her keys.'

They watched him nip up the steps of no. 3.

'The owner isn't going to like this,' observed Mrs Sagan in cheerful tones. 'There's something in the lease about keeping the front door shut in the daytime, but in this overwhelming heat and there being no ventilation in the hall and stairway—I mean, anyone could have come in without ringing a bell. I don't want to sound heartless,' she ran on briskly, 'but a thing like this does seem to—to decorate life a bit, doesn't it? And things aren't very exciting these days, just H-bombs and all that.'

Crook could almost have kissed her.

'And in a way it does seem to go with Miss Chisholm. Did either of you ever see her hats? She's a great one for decoration. I do like a bit of independence myself, all these hats that look as if they came out of the same mud pie . . . Besides, you expect something for your money when you pay her prices, and if you only get a bit of duck's feather that probably your fish-monger would give you for nothing if you made love to him nicely, or a bit of black net sprinkled with gilded butterflies, well, you do feel cheated. Don't you think we should go up and see if Rhodes has got through yet?' She made it perfectly clear that she intended to be one of the party. So they all marched upstairs, and Crook rang the bell.

'No bursting in, mind,' he warned the two women. 'Let's have everything legal and aboveboard.'

'As if you care!' scoffed Mrs Sagan.

Kay, who had instigated the investigation, began to have sudden qualms.

'I do hope she'll understand,' she murmured.

A pencil of light sprang up under the door. It was obvious that Rhodes was inside the flat. An instant later the door opened and there he stood, all the cheek and gaiety gone, like chalk marks from a slate.

'I think you'd better come in, sir,' he said to Mr Crook.

'He can't mean there's really a corpse,' breathed Mrs Sagan.

But that's just what he did mean. Only it wasn't Miss Chisholm's.

FIVE

They stood, the four of them, beside the swinging gilt bird cage, staring at the little bunch of blue feathers that lay on the floor among the sand and the powdered grit. Crook, moving abruptly, jolted the cage, which swung a little, and a tiny gilt bell tinkled on a fairy note. A pink celluloid ladder fell out of position; a blue celluloid replica of the dead bird bobbed on a spring perch. Rhodes opened the door of the cage and picked up the little body. Kay stared in mingled dismay and disbelief.

'Who would do such a thing?' she whispered.

'Someone who knew Miss Chisholm wouldn't be coming back', said Crook slowly. He turned to Rhodes. 'Do you know any regular visitor she had?'

'Well, I'm not around much of an evening, which is when she'd have her visitors. Now and again I stop in but mostly I go to the Blue Rabbit or The Boarhound—that's mostly if there's boxing or something on the telly. They have a set there. Now and again of a morning she'd leave me a key if she wanted some job done inside the flat, but she didn't like doing it, I could see that, would try and nail me for Saturdays when her hat shop wasn't open. I used to think that was a strange thing, wouldn't Saturday be your best day?'

'She makes hats to order, I think,' said Kay in a very small voice. 'She may not even have a display window. And I don't suppose her sort of customers would be much in evidence on a Saturday morning.'

'What was wrong with the woman?' demanded Crook, impatiently. 'Did she run an illicit still, or a counterfeiter's gang? All this fussification about a few personal belongings . . .'

'Perhaps she kept money or jewellery on the premises,' suggested Mrs Sagan. 'If she didn't trust anyone, she probably didn't trust the banks. Does anyone know?'

'I only spoke to her on two or three occasions in all the time I've been here,' said Kay.

'I'm not on duty after ten o'clock,' Rhodes pointed out, 'and though I did quite a lot of odd jobs for her she wasn't what you'd call a forthcoming lady.'

'I only ran into her once or twice,' Crook acknowledged, 'and each time she gave a sort of start as if she thought she'd walked into the zoo by accident. And I don't think she'd have consulted me professionally, no matter what jam she was in. She'd have a very lah-di-dah solicitor with white slips to his weskit and nice thick iron-grey hair. Coming to last night,' he added, 'I was enchained by the Minotaur, Mrs Sagan was being telephoned by a lunatic, you . . .' He looked at Rhodes.

'Frying sausages in my back kitchen,' Rhodes pointed out, and Crook's heart warmed to a chap who could do that with the thermometer past eighty. 'And then round to the Blue Rabbit, like I said.'

'She must have relations,' insisted Mrs Sagan. 'Everyone has those.'

'Not me,' said Crook.

'How unfair! But then men always get the best of everything.'

'She could have put an address on the telephone card,' suggested Rhodes.

They flipped open the little drawer, but there was nothing there.

'No buddy, no brothers and sisters, or maybe she knew the

44

numbers so well she didn't have to put them down. Everyone ought to leave an address or a telephone number, everyone that lives alone, that is '—his glance seemed to settle on Kay— 'makes things so much easier.'

'Who for?' asked Mr Crook woodenly.

'Well, the police if it comes to that.'

'Human nature's so mean,' sighed Crook. 'It don't think about making things easier for the Force. I know it's ungrateful, but I even know chaps who don't like the police.' He looked at them as if he expected them all to drop dead with surprise. 'Well, what can we do now? We haven't a bit of proof.'

'Wait a minute,' said Kay. She opened the bedroom door and looked in. 'Her things are gone from the dressing table,' she said. 'Brush and comb, hand glass and cosmetics, if she used them. Anyway there are none there now.'

Mrs Sagan popped her frizzy head into the bathroom. 'Sponge and flannel, also,' she said.

In the living room everything seemed neat enough. A pair of glasses in a blue leather case lay alongside a book on an occasional table under the window. There were three or four stubs in an ashtray on the main table, where two used glasses stood beside a bottle of sherry on a painted Italian tray.

'The last drink together,' suggested Crook. 'Does she smoke?'

'No,' said Kay and Rhodes simultaneously.

'Then Oliver, C. was right, and she did have a visitor here, someone who stayed long enough to smoke four fags. Someone a bit on edge,' he added acutely, 'they're all stubbed out before they're half smoked.'

'These spectacles,' murmured Kay. 'I don't think they're hers. I never saw her wearing any.'

'Had them for reading,' put in Rhodes. 'Said she couldn't read a line without them. Funny, they made her look quite different.'

'If she's cleared out you'd think she'd take them with her,' ruminated Crook. 'Much more to the point than that muck she puts on her face, that could be picked up anywhere.'

'Perhaps she left in a great hurry, something had happened, and she didn't think about the glasses.' That was Mrs Sagan.

'Or it could be,' said Kay softly, 'that there's something—

45

someone—behind this and whoever that someone is didn't know she wore glasses. Well, I didn't myself.'

'Or, if she was going on an unofficial honeymoon, it might have occurred to her she wouldn't have time to read many good books,' contributed Crook.

'Oh, you can laugh,' Kay cried, 'but you don't think it's all right, do you? You think something's happened, something sinister.'

'Always happy to learn,' murmured Crook. 'Well, we know something's happened, we know she's disappeared. We don't know where and we don't know why, but I'll tell you one thing. Whoever came in either had a key or was known to her, nobody forced that front door; and the place is so neat it 'ud make the proverbial pin look messy. No one's gone storming round hurling open drawers hunting for the missing safe or torn up the floor hoping to discover the miser's hoard.'

'She wouldn't have done that to Henry,' Kay insisted. 'Would she, Rhodes? She thought the world of that bird. If she had to part with him she'd have given him away—or sold him. You can get good prices for a talking bird. Say she was going off with the boy friend and she left Henry to him. Went out so as not to see, he came after, didn't know about the lock.'

'I'd have taken him,' declared Mrs Sagan, much more distressed at the sight of Henry's poor draggled little body than if she'd burst in to find Miss Chisholm with a knife in her heart.

'O.K.,' said Crook at last. 'Let's go. Lady isn't here. No, that at least we can vouch for,' he added quickly, seeing Mrs Sagan was about to raise yet another objection. 'You couldn't hide a good-sized rat in these flats. You looked in the wardrobe, she ain't there, she ain't in the bed or under it, she ain't in the bath. There isn't an ottoman on the premises, she can't have pitched out of the window because she'd have landed in the street slap under our nose, if she was out the back Rhodes would have seen her—no, she just disappeared at a very convenient time when someone knew the rest of the household was engaged.'

'Her place of business might help,' suggested Mrs Sagan.

'There wasn't anyone there when I telephoned this afternoon,' said Kay.

'I was telling Miss Carter, Miss Chisholm did say something about the the place being shut for redecoration,' contributed Rhodes.

They were like people playing a round game, each slamming down a card.

'If it wasn't for Henry the thing 'ud be clear enough. Business shut down, lady goes to Europe to pick up new ideas.'

'There's the milk—and the butter—and—wait a minute . . .' Mrs Sagan made a dash at the kitchen as if it were a rat she meant to take by surprise, and snatched open the door of the refrigerator.

'What does she expect to find there?' inquired Crook.

'There's enough food for days,' Mrs Sagan reported. 'She wouldn't have gone off for any length of time and have left that there. And she hasn't turned off the electric-light switch. Anybody would do that who knew they were going to be away.'

'Like me,' agreed Kay.

'I didn't know the lady,' Crook acknowledged, 'but you'd be surprised how they can act out of focus sometimes. Ask the police if you don't believe me. Say she had a kind of brainstorm and did Henry in . . .'

'I knew a wife once,' Mrs Sagan chimed in, 'very fond of her husband really, been married twenty-two years, when one evening she picked up a coal shovel and dented his head in. A horrid mess. Do you know why? It turned out that every night of those twenty-two years he'd said, "The express for Bedfordshire leaves in five minutes precisely"—every night at half-past ten.'

'Did she polish him off?' asked Crook.

'Oh no. A few days in the hospital and he was as good as new. I don't know where he is now,' she added thoughtfully. 'We didn't meet again. It was after that I took up my astrology. If I'd known about it earlier I might have been warned.'

So might he, reflected Mr Crook, reserving his sympathy for the absent Mr Sagan. 'Let's be pushing now,' he suggested once more. 'Say the lady did suddenly turn up and find us hanging about her premises, we should look like a bunch of peonies.

Now, everyone sure they've not forgotten anything? We can't ask Rhodes to make a second sortie over the balcony.'

They all looked around and then trailed through the door. Rhodes seemed to hesitate a moment before he let it slam behind him. 'If it does come to the police,' he said. 'I suppose they can break their own way in, and if you ask me they could learn much from some of the lads I know.'

With which cynical and unpatriotic comment he accompanied Mrs Sagan downstairs.

SIX

The following morning, having made certain there was nothing in the mail for anyone at no. 2 from the missing woman, Crook took the Superb around to the offices of the Hirewire Company. These proved to be modestly situated in the basement of a building off Marylebone High Street and to be in charge of a man with a massive torso, a pale polished face and not much hair.

He rose as Crook came in, scenting a possible new client. Crook, however, speedily disabused him, slamming down a card and saying, ' Inquiring on behalf of Miss Caroline Chisholm, 2 Brandon Street, Earl's Court. Understand your Mr Oliver—you do have a Mr Oliver here?' he added sharply.

' Yes, yes.' Mr Ayre became expansive. 'One of our most successful operatives. A born demonstrator—and believe me, Mr—er—Mr Crook—no amount of training can compensate for a natural flair.'

' I'll buy it,' agreed Mr Crook generously. 'That chap could sell an umbrella to a hippopotamus. Why, he even left a set with me.'

Mr Ayre began to ruffle through the forms on his desk.

' Oh, I haven't got round to filling in one of those,' Mr Crook assured him. 'I've got the set on the three-day trial plan.' Mr Ayre looked puzzled. 'First you've heard about it? You don't surprise me a bit. But your Mr Oliver's a bit of a psychologist. He knew if it was sign-on-the-dotted-line right away he'd have gone off with a flea in his ear, which mightn't have bothered him, it would be a brave flea that 'ud bite a chap of his gall— but with his set under his arm.'

Mr Ayre recovered himself. 'There are particular circumstances—I told you he was a born salesman.'

' I should imagine there are plenty who signed up just to get him off the premises,' Crook agreed. 'That chap's got Tennyson's "brook" beat. Talk about going on forever. Now, will your record say if this talking wonder had a date with Miss Chisholm on Tuesday night? Seven o'clock or thereabouts. Or doesn't the penny drop till the set's been installed?'

Mr Ayre permitted himself a somewhat lugubrious grin. 'Apparently not always then. Let me see—your name . . .' He opened the lid of a rather amateurish-looking card index.

'Will I be there?' marvelled Crook.

'You should be. Yes. Here's the card. Seventeen-inch Airmaster. L.O.A.'

'Left on approval,' guessed Mr Crook.

'That's right. Have you—er—made up your mind about it?'

'Not altogether. Mind you, your chap's right, it does grow on you. How about asking him to drop in this evening and talk things over?'

Mr Ayre made a note on a bit of memo paper.

'Now check Miss Chisholm,' Crook urged.

But there was no record in the index bearing her name.

'Might have forgotten to put her down?' suggested Crook.

Mr Ayre shook his head. 'Most irregular. Instructions come through me.' He turned to a filing drawer and began to hunt. 'No,' he said, 'I can trace no letter from her—and if she had telephoned, as sometimes they do, I should have taken the call personally.'

'Shot in the dark?' murmured Crook, wondering if this might be a truer phrase than he knew.

'Our representatives would scarcely go round knocking on strange doors,' said Mr Ayre, with a return of his jellyfish dignity.

'Now that indoor aerials are virtually the rule—we ourselves only install outdoor aerials with the greatest reluctance, holding that it should be possible, given a first-class set '—he put out a pudgy hand and stroked one of the cases beside him—' to obtain adequate reception with an indoor aerial—now that these are *so* common,' he went on, grabbing at the loose thread of his sentence, ' there's no knowing whether a set has already been installed on a particular premises.'

' Yes, well, that's what my neighbour, my other neighbour, not Miss Chisholm, was telling me, that the lady had set her rocky phiz against a set, so it did seem a bit odd . . .'

' I will ask Mr Oliver to contact you this evening if his engagements permit,' said Ayre hastily.

' They better had,' said Crook.

' What is the nature of your complaint?' inquired Mr Ayre hastily. Having Crook describe himself on his card as a lawyer had given him a nasty turn. Lawyers and police always spell trouble for someone.

' Well, just that the lady's done a vanishing trick since your chap came calling. Still, fellow like that can probably explain anything.'

He bounded out of the room, up the basement steps and into the yellow Rolls. Mr ' Piggy ' Ayre wiped his brow, then went all through the records again; but he could have saved himself the trouble. There was no mention of Miss Chisholm anywhere.

Hebberden Mews was a narrow opening off a side street in the West End. For the most part it seemed to comprise warehouses; in any case it seemed a queer situation for a milliner, custom or otherwise, but Crook found her there all the same. Louise, custom milliner, said her plate. There was a window heavily veiled in what a woman could have told him was a double American nylon and when he pressed the bell no one answered. Then he saw a small hand-printed notice: CLOSED FOR REDECORATION. LETTERS TO 2 BRANDON STREET, S.W. 5. REOPENING 14TH SEPTEMBER.

Lightning calculation told him this would be a Monday. It all seemed sensible enough and tied up with the box that had been posted to Miss Chisholm's private address. But standing there, listening with the assiduity of a cat that can pick up vibrations through the hair in its ears, he became convinced that, despite the note, there was someone on the premises. He rang twice but nothing happened. He moved away, making a good deal of noise. When he had gone a dozen steps he turned sharply. The nylon curtains fell quickly together. He beetled back and hammered on the door. When this had no effect he stuck a pudgy finger on the bell and kept it there. This was successful. You need nerves of steel to be able to listen to an electric bell pealing without a break and do nothing about it.

Steps came along the passage and the door was grudgingly opened by an anaemic-looking girl with straight dull brown hair and very pale blue eyes almost extinguished by a pair of spectacles with thick lenses and very modish flyaway black frames, which seemed oddly out of keeping with her general appearance.

Wants to be thought interesting, reflected Mr Crook. The black rims matched up with a black pinafore that she wore over her summer dress.

When she saw Crook she gaped; he often had that effect on strangers.

' Is Miss Chisholm in?' he asked brightly.

She shook her head; she reminded Crook of a moon-faced clock in process of running down, each tick seeming a shade slower than its predecessor, so that at any instant it will cease functioning.

'There's a notice,' said the girl, stirring a languid finger. ' Didn't you see?'

' Oh, yes. They taught us to read even at my kind of school. But that don't mean she couldn't be on the premises, only not, so to speak, on public view.'

' You might try the address on the paper,' the girl murmured, but not as though it were any concern of hers or she could be expected to take any interest. Crook wondered why she should bother to put on an act just to impress him; it was obvious her reaction was unfavourable.

' Oh, I've been there,' he said. ' She's moved out.'

' Then I suppose she's gone abroad. She does, you know. She's a milliner.'

' Where was she yesterday?'

The pale eyes widened. 'How should I know? She wasn't here.'

'Then perhaps you're right and she has gone abroad.'

He waited for her to make the next move. She said gently, 'Did you want a hat?'

'Well, no, I don't think she'd accept me for a customer.' He grinned at the appalling brown billycock that had become his trademark over the years. In the billycock in town and checked golfer in the country he must easily have qualified for one of the ten worst-dressed men in England.

'Matter of fact—can I come in for a minute? I've got a message.'

'Who are you?'

'Solicitor,' said Mr Crook expansively. He could have sworn she stiffened a bit at that.

'I only take orders, you know.'

'Hers?'

'Well—naturally. I work here. Only today I'm just clearing up. For the decorators.'

'How about her partner?' inquired Crook.

Her mouth set mulishly. 'I don't know him.'

'But he told you about getting the place ready for the decorators. I mean, if Miss Chisholm had told you, you'd have done it yesterday. It can't take two days.'

Some men who were collecting goods from the Nu-Unit Furniture Depository next door stopped work to watch and grin.

Uneasy colour flooded the girl's cheeks. 'I've told you, Miss Chisholm isn't here.' She tried to shut the door but Crook's enormous foot in its glossy brown Oxford prevented that. 'Very well,' she said angrily, 'come in just for a minute. But I've told you I can't do anything.'

The interior of Louise's was modest enough—he seemed to be dealing in modest premises today, he reflected. There was what Miss Chisholm presumably called her office, a freshly papered and painted room, with a table and a comfortable modern chair, a second chair, for the clients, he supposed, and a little dressing-table effect with a standing mirror and hand glass. There were some papers on the desk secured by a model of a Venetian gondola sign, a brass sea horse, and an ivory telephone.

'This where the customers come?' asked Crook amiably.

'Yes. Miss Chisholm does the modelling herself. She keeps a lot of fashion papers'—she pulled open the desk drawer and Crook saw them—English, French, Italian—'because some of the customers simply don't know what they want. Sometimes they just want a copy of a hat they had last year. . . .'

'Does she let them get away with that?' Crook asked respectfully.

'Well, not as a rule. Of course in the country it's different, you don't want the fashionable line there. But she generally manages to give a hat a slight twist—her clients trust her, you see.'

More fools they, thought Crook, who never trusted women. It wasn't that they were fundamentally dishonest, but their brains or intelligences—call them what you liked—worked differently from those of the more balanced male. He'd never forgotten a client of his who had once poisoned her husband with rat poison; for all his oratory, he couldn't convince her it was murder. 'If he hadn't been a rat it wouldn't have affected him,' was all she said.

'Is she pricey?' he asked, looking about him.

'She charges from three and a half,' said the girl.

'Three and a half,' repeated Crook, trying to sound knowledgeable.

'Guineas, of course.'

'Of course.' No wonder husbands went bankrupt or strangled their wives if they were luckless enough to find themselves saddled with immoral women who spent three and a half guineas on a hat. 'Nice work if you can get it.'

'You still haven't said why you're here,' the girl reminded him, leaning casually against the table with its blotter and card index.

'Oh, but I did. To see Miss Chisholm. When do you expect her back?'

'We're reopening the middle of September—the 14th—you're sure to find her here then.'

Crook was less certain.

'If she should come in or telephone, who shall I say called?'

'I thought you said she'd gone abroad. She wouldn't ring up

53

from there, surely? Not with only the decorators on the premises.'

' I said if she wasn't in her flat I supposed she had. She might be having the decorators there. I take it it wasn't about a hat.'

Crook twirled the billycock speculatively. 'Do you think she could do a bit of renovating on this?'

Suddenly she came to life, leaned forward, almost snatched the hat from him, and said, ' I'll show you. You'll be surprised.'

He followed her through into a big bare workroom, so frugally furnished it would have satisfied the organizer of a nudist colony. There was a long bare table, a couple of sewing machines, two chairs and a long cupboard running the length of the north wall. The girl opened this and he saw the shelves were full of every kind of decoration, imitation fruit and flowers in abundance, rolls of ribbons and velvets, bits of bright material, cards of rainbow-coloured veiling. The girl took up a piece of gold tissue, twisted it around the crown, took a length of vivid-shaded ribbon and secured it, laid a spray of silver leaves over one ear—Crook gasped. It looked horrible, of course. But she had skill and imagination, if macabre in his opinion, and what-ever she was doing here she was no phony. Ladies who wanted their hats inexpensively metamorphosized could do a lot worse than come to her.

' Very artistic,' he murmured, and she laughed and unwound the fabrics, threw them into the cupboard and handed his hat back to him.

' Are you the police?' she inquired, and once again she had surprised him.

' Why? Are they expected?'

' Well, not by me, but then I only work here. I'm wondering what you really want. Yes, I know you said Miss Chisholm . . .'

' If the place is being redecorated what'll happen to the clients who come up on chance?' he countered.

' There aren't usually any at this time of the year. August's a dead month. No one wants to buy summer hats any more and they'll wait till September to see the new models. Miss Chisholm will bring back new ideas. And if you're thinking of travellers,' she added, breathlessly, ' they don't come in August, either.'

'You all alone here? I mean, the rest of the staff . . .'

He saw her carefully manoeuvring to get between him and the door.

'There's only me and Emmy, and she's left to get married—an Irish boy, I must say I don't envy her, all bogs and potatoes and Sean O'Casey. I suppose Miss Chisholm 'ull get someone new when she comes back. I shan't stay after Christmas,' she added, volunteering the first piece of information about herself since his arrival. 'Not enough scope, but you need a year's reference to get in with any of the big houses. One day I might have a shop of my own, only of course it takes capital.'

'I wouldn't have thought it would pay on this scale,' said Crook rashly, and the portcullis dropped at once.

'That's Miss Chisholm's affair, isn't it? I can't tell you any more, I'm very busy. I've got to notify all our customers that we're closed till September 14th. Not that many people come in August, like I said, but there's always the few that think this is a slack time and Miss Chisholm could do a special job sewing on a bunch of pansies or something.'

'Couldn't you do that for them?'

'I told you, I take orders.' Then she sighed. Her pale blue glance seemed to travel up his rotundities like some lethargic fly.

'One of them being not to gab to strangers. You learn your lessons nicely.'

'I don't have anything to tell you.'

'Well, you've told me Miss Chisholm wasn't here yesterday. That's something I wanted to know.'

'Why? Are you blackmailing her?' There was still no emphasis in the lymphatic voice.

He sent her a sharp glance but the pale face was as blank as a sheet of paper.

'What goes on here?' he said curiously. 'First the police, now blackmail. What's behind this hat shop?'

'Just what you can see. Except, of course, there's a wash place out back. That's all I know.'

'Not very much,' Crook agreed.

'I do know one thing. Lawyers write letters, they write as many as they can, because they charge for each one. They don't come calling in person, it wouldn't be economic.'

'You know a lot,' Crook complimented her. The girl flushed.

'Well, if you're not the police and you're not blackmailing her, you must be the husband,' she accused him. 'Only I thought that might be the same thing.'

Crook nearly dropped in a faint at the idea of himself playing Old Dobbin to Miss Chisholm's grey mare.

'It's news to me she had one.'

'You didn't come here for nothing,' she insisted.

'I keep telling you, I want to see Miss Chisholm. Just that. To see her. Not necessarily to speak to her, just to know she's here —or there—still with us.'

Now the colour came flooding into her face. 'You mean, she's —gone?'

'Oh, she's gone all right. Question is, did she go of her own accord? Well, you can't tell me and you've got all those letters to write.' He clapped on the brown bowler. 'Sorry you've been troubled,' he said.

He beetled out and walked a few steps to where he'd left the Superb. The girl glided away as noiselessly as a swan. She stood watching as the car disappeared around the corner, then ran to the telephone and dialled a number.

'Mr Brown? Someone's been here asking questions, like you said he might. Wouldn't leave a name but said he was a lawyer. Drove a yellow car, a Rolls, I think, though I don't know very much about them. An old model. Oh, I'm sorry, no, I didn't think to get the number, but I shouldn't think there were two like it. It was as yellow as—as a daffodil.'

'What did he want?'

'Just wanted to see Miss Chisholm.'

'What did you tell him?'

'That she must have gone abroad. He said he'd tried her flat.'

'That's all?'

'I couldn't tell him anything else, could I? That's all I knew.'

'I want you to go round to Brandon Street this afternoon and get a box that was sent there registered. Bring it round here. The tenant of no. 2 took it in. And bring the key of Hebberden Mews with you. I'll look after those premises.'

'I haven't quite finished notices to customers.'

56

'Well, get those done and then get on. You ought to be finished by lunch, and then go round to her flat. If there's any trouble say the box has a Salisbury postmark and your mother sent it up to be retrimmed. Anyway, get hold of it.'

Mr Crook stepped out of a telephone booth at the mouth of the alley, jingling four pennies in his hand. Now who's she ringing up? he wondered. The mastermind? He can't be giving the affair his full attention or he'd have thought up something better than having the place redecorated. That first room hasn't been done many months and who bothers about a workroom for a couple of girls who are only using it as a sort of passage? The clients don't get that far.

He went back to Bloomsbury Street where Bill had been doing a bit of research.

'Hirewire's all right,' he reported. 'Small but struggling. The chaps work on commission so it's to their interest to get all the clients they can. I give it another eight months,' he added dispassionately. 'That's about the time it's been running to date.'

'Ayre? Any record?'

'Known in the trade as Piggy, mainly, I gather, owing to his appearance. Was manager for another hirewire company that went under, crushed by mass competition.'

'Sounds O.K.,' Crook acknowledged, 'which is more than I'd expect of Louise. That hat shop affair's a cover for something else, Bill. I winkled myself inside because the obvious answer is a nest of convenient little rooms that can be hired by the hour. Wouldn't be the first time by a long chalk that a hat shop's been used as that kind of a front, and with the new vice law coming into effect there's going to be a lot of accommodation wanted. But it wasn't that. The workshop might be fitted up as a dormitory but that's about all.'

'Give her your name?' asked Bill.

'No; she wasn't altogether the amateur, though. She got my hat from me very neatly, hoped I'd have my autograph inside it, I suppose, only I don't have that kind of hat.'

'Don't need it,' said Bill, unfeelingly. 'Can't be two like it in England.'

He was a tall dark man with a handsome ruined face, who looked precisely what he was, the son of a good family who'd taken the wrong turning in youth. The police could have told you a lot about him, and he still had information as to the whereabouts of certain jewels that the police had never traced. If it hadn't been for a bullet wound in the heel five-and-twenty years earlier he'd never have crossed Crook's path, but a jewel thief must be nippy on his pins and a lame man is simply a liability. And jewel thieves seldom work independently.

'What's the Chisholm dame to you?' he added in his unemotional way.

'Just a neighbour, not even a particularly good one. But I don't like being used, Bill, and I get ideas very easy as you know. Well, I left a message with Piggy for the young man to call round tonight. If they're as keen to get orders as he makes out he'll be there; and if there is anything fishy about him, well, he'll still be there, because he'll want to know what it's all about. And, if there's a little crooked dealing going on, my Miss Carter ain't going to be very popular, being the one that started the avalanche. Might give her a bit of advice—you never know. About once in a hundred times they take it, and this might be my lucky day.'

But nobody answered the telephone at Flat 2, and when he rang an hour or two later the result was the same. So he sent a telegram, and then shut off his mental stopcock as far as the Chisholm affair was concerned, and spent the afternoon up to his bristling red eyebrows in something else.

SEVEN

When Kay Carter came back from her lunch appointment she found the telegram shoved into the letterbox. Hang onto the hatbox, it said. She read it, lifted her eyebrows, and, in the inconsequential way of females, decided to use her own discretion should emergencies arise. This particular emergency arose about an hour later. Someone rang her bell and when she opened the door she found a drooping, rather badly dressed girl with straight brown hair and a beret, waiting on the step. She wore glasses with flyaway black rims, which contrasted oddly with her dowdy clothes.

'Have you seen Miss Chisholm?' asked the girl, and Kay said, 'No. I think she's gone away.'

'You don't know where she's gone?'

'I'm afraid not.'

'Oh dear, my mother will be upset. Could I have the box please?'

'Box?'

'Yes. The one with the hat in it.'

Kay shook her head. 'What makes you think . . .?'

'Well, my mother sent it here, it was a hat Miss Chisholm was going to retrim for her, and she wanted it in a hurry. . . .'

'But why here?' Kay looked as blank as a wet weekend. 'I mean, these aren't her workrooms. You aren't allowed to carry on business from here, it's in the lease. I don't count,' she added quickly, seeing the pale eyes move toward the brush in her hand and the paint on her smock. 'Artists are like authors, not important enough to count as tradesmen.'

'I don't know anything about that, but Miss Chisholm said if she sent it here she'd see what she could do. The postmark's Salisbury,' she added.

'But I'm not Miss Chisholm. . . .'

'I know. But the postman could have left it with you, couldn't he?'

'Why should you think that?'

'Because they told me at the post office you'd taken it in,' improvised the girl. 'You have to sign for a registered parcel.'

'Do you work for Miss Chisholm?'

'You do ask a lot of questions. I told you, it's a hat my mother sent up in a hurry—and since Miss Chisholm's away and her workshop's closed there's no sense leaving it.'

'You've come a long way to fetch it,' suggested Kay.

'No. Not really. I work in London. It's my mother who lives in Salisbury, I have a room at Sheepford. Are you going to give me the parcel? If not I—I could call the police.'

'They aren't allowed in without a warrant. Oh, all right, I was only having a bit of a joke.'

'It doesn't seem very funny to me,' said the girl blankly.

'Do you know how I earn my living?' asked Kay in a brisk friendly tone. 'Mainly by illustrating magazine stories, and this is just the sort of beginning Miss Howard would love for *Woman's Taste.* I've sometimes thought I might write the stories as well. . . . All right, the box is here.'

She opened the narrow hall cupboard and the girl saw the neat suitcase, the vacuum cleaner, the hot-water bottle on its hook, the emergency oil stove.

'All ready for the invasion, aren't you?' she suggested suddenly.

'Why, are you planning one?' Kay retrieved the box. 'Will you give me a receipt?'

'Why?'

'Then if someone should come asking awkward questions I can prove I'm not hiding it.'

'Why on earth should you want to hide it, my mother's last year's hat?'

'Do you remember the head in the hat box in *Night Must Fall?* Our dramatic society did it about three years ago. You forget I'm steeped in fictional situations—naturally I have to read the stories or a good part of them before I can start illustrating—this might contain stolen property or . . . Anyway, I had to sign for it, and if Miss Chisholm should turn up—I've never seen you before, remember.'

She had got out a purse diary and was scribbling hastily.

'Just sign that—it's all red tape, but then we're swaddled in it these days. Use my pen.' The girl looked suspiciously at the page she tore out and handed over. 'Received of K. Carter one registered parcel postmarked Salisbury.'

The girl added her name and handed the paper back. The signature read 'A. Smith.'

'What does " A." stand for?' asked Kay idly.

'Aileen. And Smith's really my name if you were thinking of making another joke.'

'Thank you. Now if Miss Chisholm should ask about the parcel I can tell her who called.'

'She won't I don't suppose. Mother will write or some-thing. . . .' The pale blue eyes stared over Kay's shoulder. 'Have you got a telephone?'

'I shouldn't get many commissions if I hadn't.'

'Would you mind if I had a call on it? I'm so late, all this rushing round, and I was meeting a friend. . . .'

'There's a phone booth on the corner opposite the gentle-men's hairdresser,' Kay assured her. 'It's practically always empty this time of day. I used it a lot before I could get a line. I'm waiting for a long distance call myself.' Still smiling, she closed the door. Now why did she want to come in here? she wondered. And, if she had, should I mysteriously have disap-peared like Miss Chisholm?'

Thoughtfully she turned back and shot the little bolt she had had put on her front door that morning.

The girl who called herself Aileen Smith (which was, in fact, her name) took the hatbox to a flat in Francis Street, W.1.

'Have any trouble getting it?' inquired the short compact little man, very dark, with a large nose and a greater capacity than Crook for overlooking a scruple.

'Oh, no, Mr Brown. Well, not really. She did ask for a receipt.'

'What for?'

'Well, for the parcel. It was registered, you see. She said if Miss Chisholm should come back and ask for it, she'd like to have some proof that she had given it up.'

'Did she say anything else?'

'She did say it was funny Miss Chisholm going off like that.'

Her companion, whose original name of Braun had been softened to its anglicised equivalent more than two years before, briefly showed strong, slightly discoloured teeth.

'I hope you told her it was the artistic temperament.'

'Well, no, Mr Brown, I didn't think that was such a good idea. I mean, she's kind of an artist herself. I suppose it is the right parcel.'

'What do you mean, the right parcel? Why shouldn't it be?'

'Well, I don't know really. I mean, I only know what you said. But it does make a person think.'

'That there could be two parcels? Come, girl, what are you trying to say?'

Instead of answering she inquired in her slow soft voice: 'That man who came asking questions—who was he?'

'He told you he was a lawyer, didn't he?'

'Miss Chisholm's lawyer?'

The man's patience began to sag. 'My dear girl, you're talking nonsense. So far as I know, Miss Chisholm's in no need of a lawyer. Of course, if you have more information . . .'

'That's just the trouble, Mr Brown. I don't seem to know anything, and that does make it awkward.'

'Who for?'

'Well, me. When people start asking questions, like this man and then Miss Carter . . .'

'What did she ask you?'

'She was curious about the hat shop.'

'Why should she be?'

Miss Smith was tracing a hesitant pattern on the table with her short stubby fingers in their fabric gloves.

'Well, that's one of the things I don't know. She had met Miss Chisholm. . . .'

'Considering they lived in the same house that's natural enough.'

Up came her head, her eyes startled behind the thick glasses, the hideous beret slipping over the smooth shapeless hair.

'Well, not really. In the house where I live at Sheepford I've been there months and I don't know any of them. None of them have ever come to my room, that's all I have, just the one room, combined room, they call it, and they've never invited me into theirs.'

Frederick Brown leaned over and took up the cardboard box. 'This is the one we were expecting,' he said. 'Post-marked Salisbury, that's genuine enough.'

'That was something else I didn't understand, why I had to pretend the hat belonged to my mother. I mean, I haven't got a mother, that is, she's dead. . . .'

'Then you can't hurt her, can you? And what was there so suspicious about your calling for a parcel for Miss Chisholm who's unexpectedly been called away?'

She dropped her eyes and said softly, her hand still making those silly movements on the table top, 'There really is a hat in that box, isn't there, Mr Brown?'

'Well, of course. What did you expect?' He picked up the parcel and shook it. 'Open it yourself if you're doubtful.'

He watched her fumbling unhandily with the beautifully tied knots. 'Here, cut the string,' he said. He watched her clumsily fold back the brown paper wrapping and lift the lid of the box that it revealed. Carefully she parted the tissue paper; then she began to yelp with laughter.

'Oh, dear, oh, dear. Ha, ha, ha. Oh, I do call that a joke.'

'What is it?' He was at her side in a minute, had snatched up the disreputable old felt ruin, was staring at it, dismayed, furious and, then, apprehensive.

She held it up, a man's black felt hat, the sort of hat her grandmother might have hung in a back passage to deceive beggars. 'Look, here's the hat my mother wants Miss C. to redecorate. My mother's hat! gasped the zombie at his side. 'You never told me she was a gypsy. I don't resemble her much, do I?' She moved so that she could see herself in the glass; she tweaked at the lank brown hair, took off the glasses to say, 'I never heard of a gypsy with pale blue eyes.'

'Be quiet.' The words had the force and effect of a physical blow; she stopped as suddenly as a child who has been struck. 'Is this a trick of yours?' He caught her by the shoulders, seeming taller than she, though he was in fact some inches less.

'How could it be? I mean, the parcel's registered. Oh, you'll tear my dress, Mr Brown.'

'The bitch!' he said softly, letting her go. 'The crafty double-crossing bitch. All the same I don't altogether understand . . .'

Miss Smith stood twitching her dress into a more orderly position. 'That's the way I feel,' she said in the soft voice she had used a few moments before. 'I don't seem to understand anything, since Miss Chisholm went away. I don't understand why she couldn't tell herself, that she was going, I mean. Or let them know at Brandon Street; because she didn't. This lawyer person let that out, I mean that's why he came. You know, it wouldn't surprise me if he expected to find her body there.'

'Oh, stop talking nonsense,' cried the man impatiently.

63

'But what else am I to talk about if I'm not told anything?' protested Aileen. 'I really do think, Mr Brown, it would make things easier all round if you took me into your confidence a little. I mean, for your own sake, really mostly for your own sake.'

The dark eyes hardened and gleamed, like scraps of bitumen.

'Is that supposed to mean anything?'

'Well, suppose the police came to question me?'

'Why on earth should they?'

'I suppose they'd come to you first. And if you know where Miss Chisholm is and can tell them, I dare say everything's all right. Do you know?'

'She had to go abroad in a hurry.'

'Well, that's something else I don't understand. This is the dead season. It's not as if she was a famous milliner and someone might steal her models. And she's always been so—well, pernickety is the only word that occurs to me. If she does things she has a reason for them and she tells you what the reason is, even if it isn't the right reason, if you understand what I mean.'

'No,' said Brown. 'Are you sure you know yourself?'

'She's ever so fussy about what's in the stockroom. She goes round practically counting the pins. And then overnight she's gone. One evening she says, " Good night, don't be late "—you know, she should have had a record made of that, Emmy and me used to laugh like anything—and then she's never seen again. I mean, she'd have telephoned or sent a card or something. Mr Brown, do you know where she is?'

'This is where we came in,' said Brown disgustedly.

'If she's really abroad what's the sense in having orders sent to Brandon Street for that girl to take in?' Aileen Smith persisted.

'Miss Chisholm rang me up on Monday evening and told me there'd been a sudden change of plan; she was going abroad on the night flight. She asked me to let you know about closing the showroom. . . .' Brown spoke with obviously controlled exactitude.

'For redecoration. Yes. I know that's what you told me. But she hasn't had a man in to give an estimate and she's not the sort to give anyone a free hand.'

64

'I'm attending to that,' said Brown curtly.

'What about the orders that'll come in while she's away?'

'I shall go round with the decorator in the morning and collect any mail there may be.'

'Do you want me to turn up or what?'

'I told you this morning, you can take your summer holiday now, get away for a change. Have I got your address? Well, write it down in case I can't lay my hands on it. What was the name of the place you said? Sheepford?'

'Sheepford. It's a suburb of London, ever so quiet, you couldn't believe you were so near the city. It hasn't got a station but there's good buses to Richley, and it's only twenty minutes by electric train. . . .'

'I'll write to you there. Will letters be forwarded?'

'They won't have to be. I shan't be away.'

'Surely you're going to have a holiday?'

'I don't know—I've nowhere special to go.'

'Haven't you any friends or relations? Think, there must be someone. . . .'

'Oh, no. I'm an orphan. I was brought up in an institution. Now I have this room, it's home to me, I don't want anyone else in it. In the institution nothing belonged to you, it was all communal, even your thoughts weren't your own, then I came to London and lived in a hostel, three in a room. It's only this last year I could afford some privacy, it's more wonderful to me than going out every night. . . .'

'Aren't you lonely?' asked Brown curiously.

'Oh, no, not really. And when I've had my supper—you can't cook very much in a combined room so it's a very light meal, and there's a sink on the landing where I can wash up, I go out sometimes, down to the River Gardens—I love the river—or even take the bus to Richley. Only I feel a stranger there, it's quite big compared with Sheepford. I seem to belong there, it's like being part of a pattern. I never seemed to be anyone till I had a place of my own.'

'What are you trying to hide?' asked Brown curiously. 'Some young man who . . .'

'There isn't any young man.' The note of sincerity in her voice was unmistakable. 'Directly someone else comes into your private world they start putting their hands all over it, it isn't yours any more, even little things like saying, "Have you thought of putting the divan against that wall?" or "I think that picture would look better over there," as though it was their bed, their picture. . . . I don't say,' she added more calmly, 'that one day I wouldn't be prepared to share it but not yet. I haven't had it long enough. Mr Brown, what does that black hat mean? It isn't the one you expected to find, is it?'

'Is it the sort of hat you'd expect your mother to wear, supposing you had a mother?'

'No. Who put it in the box, Mr Brown? Not—not Miss Chisholm?'

'Suppose you tell me,' said Brown quite pleasantly.

'I can only guess, the same as you. Do you think it might be Miss Carter?'

'You've forgotten the parcel was registered, haven't you?'

'I suppose you could open one and do it up again.'

Brown came forward and took the brown paper over to the window. Carefully he peeled away some of the surplus wax.

'Perhaps you're brighter than you know,' he suggested. 'Perhaps that's just what happened.'

'So it was Miss Carter . . .'

'I didn't say that.'

'You mean, someone on the way? Who did it really come from?'

'Too bad no one put a note in the box. They didn't, did they?'

'No.' She shook her head. 'I looked carefully through the paper.'

'When did you look carefully through the paper?'

'When I opened the box just now. It's funny, isn't it? I mean, how would Miss Chisholm know who it was from if there wasn't a message inside? Unless she only has the one client at Salisbury.'

'Perhaps you can tell us that.'

The girl's brow wrinkled, the silly blue eyes widened. 'How should I know?'

'Didn't you keep the card index?'

'But this might be one that wasn't in the index.'

His hand, square and large and brutal, came out and caught

66

her arm. 'What does that mean? Were there many that weren't in the index?'

'I don't know that there were any. I didn't write the cards all the time, sometimes Miss Chisholm wrote them, sometimes she tore them up. This client won't be coming to us again, she'd say.'

'And, of course, you weren't interested?'

'Well, not particularly. I mean, it wasn't my business, I just had a job there and I meant to move on after Christmas.'

'Why after Christmas?'

'I might as well get my bonus,' she muttered. 'But there's no promotion there.'

'Tell me something,' said Brown and his voice was still quite calm and cool. 'What made you open the box—before you brought it round here, I mean? Curiosity?'

'But I didn't open it, Mr Brown. I could have laughed fit to bust when I saw what was inside. Perhaps it's a sort of code,' she suggested, hopefully.

'What on earth are you talking about? What sort of code?'

'Well, I couldn't help noticing some rather queer things about the shop. I mean, for one thing, why did Miss Chisholm have so few customers? She couldn't possibly have made a living out of the shop, not when she'd paid Emmy and me our wages, and the rent and everything out of what she made from the hats.'

He jutted his chin at her. 'What are you suggesting?'

'I did wonder if she might have a side line.'

'Such as?' His voice was suddenly smooth.

'I don't know. She was a mysterious sort of person. Some customers she wouldn't let us have anything to do with. We didn't even see the bills, and she always paid in her own cheques. Besides . . .'

'Well?'

'Honestly, Mr Brown, some of the hats, well, I know she was supposed to be very clever, but some of them weren't even very good. I have a—a flair for hats, what's called a feeling for them; I did know.'

'When you're working for people, my dear, you learn to take orders.'

'You mean she had to make the hats the customers wanted.

67

But that isn't true. They came for her to make the sort of hats that she thought was best. But she used to hang them with ornaments sometimes—though she never wore that sort of hat herself.'

'Presumably because they didn't suit her,' said Brown. 'Oh well, if this isn't your idea of a practical joke, it must be some-one else's.'

Aileen whirled around. 'Mr Brown, where is Miss Chisholm?'

'I told you, she's gone abroad.'

'When's she coming back?'

'When she's finished her business, I suppose. Now, you've noti-fied the clients the workshop's closed till the middle of next month. . . .'

'I've written to the names in the card index.'

'Well, isn't that enough?'

'I just told you, I have sometimes wondered if there were some that weren't in the index.'

'If so, that's Miss Chisholm's affair, isn't it?' Brown spoke briskly. 'If you've any sense you won't go round talking like a third-rate actress. . . .'

'Well, I haven't really anyone to talk to, have I? Unless the police . . .'

'What on earth have the police got to do with it?'

'That man who came this morning, saying he was a lawyer . . .'

'Do you think he was the police? What gave you that idea?' Brown still spoke with a studied coolness.

'I don't think he was a lawyer. I did wonder if he might be her husband. . . .'

'Miss Chisholm's husband?'

'Didn't you know she'd been married? Not that she said much . . .'

'But she told you?'

'She sort of let it out. Oh, it was over a long time ago, but—you'll laugh when I tell you this—I did think once perhaps it was you.'

'You're wasted in a hat shop, Miss Smith. You should be writing whodunits.'

'I don't like them, I never read them. . . .'

'My connection with Miss Chisholm, since you're interested, was simply a financial one. Now, that's enough. I hope you're satisfied. You can start your holiday at once, as I told you. Whether you go away or not is your own affair. What wages were you getting?'

The girl hesitated. 'Miss Chisholm had spoken of giving me a rise. . . .'

'That'll have to wait till she comes back. What are you getting at the moment?'

'Eight pounds,' said the girl sulkily, 'unless I did overtime. . . .'

'Since you say there wasn't enough work to make a living for Miss Chisholm there can't have been much of that.'

But a new sly look slipped across his face as he pulled out his wallet.

'Sixteen pounds,' he said briskly, laying the money on the table.

She made no move to pick up the notes.

'That's not enough. There's this week's pay. I'm quite prepared to work till Saturday.'

He laughed abruptly.

'You don't miss a trick, do you? All right.' He paid out another eight pounds. 'Now, did you write down your address? Good. I'll ring you in the morning—I suppose you've got a telephone?'

'Well, I haven't got one of my own, of course. For one thing, I couldn't afford it, and for another, I don't suppose I could get it.'

'Then you'd better telephone me.'

'I didn't say there wasn't one in the house. There's one in the hall. I'll put the number down, shall I?'

'That's right. Will you be in in the morning? What's the best time to get you?'

'Oh, I don't suppose I'll hurry to get up. It'll be a nice change to be able to lie late. Mr Brown, tell me, why are you going to ring tomorrow?'

'In case any business comes in that you could deal with. Or I want to know anything about the morning mail. After all, you're being paid for this week. Don't forget.'

'I don't like it,' said the girl, her lips pale and pressed together. 'I wonder if it would be a good thing for me to go round to 2 Brandon Street and talk to Miss Carter?'

'No,' said Brown briefly. 'What good could that do? Or do you think she's planning to wear the hat, whatever it was?'

'She doesn't wear hats, she told me so.'

'Then she's not the least likely to have unpacked the box. You're making too much of a silly practical joke. . . .'

'Do you think the police would call it that?'

He shook his head impatiently. She was a scatterbrained kitten, whirling in all directions at once.

'Where on earth do they come in?'

'You're worried, aren't you? Why, Mr Brown? Tell me why? Is something wrong? Do you really know where Miss Chisholm is?'

'I've told you, she had to go abroad suddenly. Isn't that enough?'

'Even if it was enough for me, and mind you, I don't say it is, would it be for the police? Suppose one of them should turn up at Sheepford and start asking questions, what should I say?'

'They won't turn up at Sheepford.'

'That's what you say, but suppose they do?'

'Then tell them the truth, of course, as I should in your shoes.'

'Oh, of course,' she mimicked. 'Only they might have asked you before they asked me, and it is important, don't you think, that it should be the same truth? Oh, well, I can't tell them anything I don't know, and perhaps I'm getting too upset about a trifle, only somehow that hat worries me, Mr Brown. I feel it spells trouble, but I've only got to refer them to you, haven't I?' She put on her glasses as she spoke, seeming to quench the person she'd been a moment before. Then she went quietly out.

Shortly after her departure Frederick Brown had another visitor. He was a Jekyll and Hyde character who appeared in one guise at home and in quite another at the Francis Street flat. Everything about him was changed, even his name and bearing were different. This man, you knew, would be able to give all

70

the answers and they wouldn't be the ones in the copybooks.

'Anyone come calling?' he inquired, and Brown said, 'The girl, Smith, has been here. She means trouble, Ben.'

Ben's glance travelled to the astounding old black hat that was lying on the table where Aileen had left it.

'Did she bring that?'

'In the box the postman handed over to Miss—that girl at Brandon Street.'

Ben picked up the hat. 'Not funny?' he suggested, and Brown said, 'Not to me.'

'Does Smith know this is what she brought?'

'She opened it for me, under my eyes. Insisted on opening it . . .'

'So you could see what was inside?'

'I'm not sure. But now she has seen it she'll have to go. She's got the idea that there's something odd going on, doesn't see why she shouldn't cash in. Well, Caroline tried that. The fools! To think they can threaten a man like me. It's amazing that Caroline could double-cross me as long as she did. . . .'

'Does the guv'nor know—about Caroline?'

'I shall simply report that she was no longer reliable and has been paid off. He won't ask any questions, what's one woman more or less to him? It's a pity all the same, she was a clever woman. . . .'

'The really clever ones stand by their allies,' Ben suggested. 'How much do you think Smith has guessed?'

'She's a natural self-dramatiser, talking already about the police. Still, leave her to me. What I need to know is—who's got the hat that should have been in the box?'

'Smith?' guessed Ben.

'I doubt it. I think she'd have played that card right away. Of course, it could be our Salisbury contact, doubling up with Caroline. That's the worst of women, you can never trust them to play straight. They always want something for nothing, just to show their independence. But that girl isn't the fool Caroline seems to have thought. She knows there's some funny business going on, and she'll never have the sense to keep her mouth shut.'

'Caroline can't have told her anything. . . .'

'She got a bit careless. This girl realises there were other clients—she's mouthing ridiculous threats about the police, and now that Crook's muscled in . . .'

'You're not suggesting trying to knock Crook off?' Ben sounded really alarmed. 'Mind you, I don't say the police would shed any tears for him, but if anything should happen to that character you'd find a mob battering down your doors and dragging you out for a lynching.'

'Only if they knew.' Brown sounded quite indifferent. 'This is where you come in.'

'Not likely,' said Ben.

'I must know if he's tumbled, if he's seen the hat. You're not being asked to do anything violent, but—you're the one contact. You could get inside the flat, couldn't you? Could you get in tonight?'

'Shouldn't be too difficult. But do you suggest he's going to sit in a sort of coma watching the TV while I take a run round the premises?'

'I leave that to you,' returned Brown woodenly. 'You're no fool, you must appreciate we're all on pretty thin ice. The girl's more dangerous that I realised—she's been keeping an eye for quite a while from what she said—then that meddling fool goes round to see her—do you know she thought he might be Caroline's husband?'

Ben grinned. 'Did she tell him that?'

'Then,' Brown went on carefully, 'she thought I might be the man. You do see we can't afford to let her . . .'

'Count me out on murder,' said Ben sharply.

'I told you, I'll look after her.'

Ben picked up the black hat and stared at it. 'You're sure she won't spill the beans before you've time to shut her mouth?'

It was clear he felt no more pity for her than a farmer who proposes to induce myxomatosis to rid his land of a pest.

'I've told her I'll ring her in the morning. She'll wait. She thinks she's got us—got me—like this.' He opened his big hand and shut it firmly as though he were crushing something. 'By the way, this place, Sheepford, where she's living—you get around—do you know where it is?'

'On the river, about fifteen miles out. Commuters' town

72

mostly, got some famous almshouses put up by a God-fearing widow in '94 and never been improved since. What's she doing there?'

'Lodging.'

'With a family? You want to be careful. Suppose she talks to them tonight?'

'She won't; she doesn't know any of them. She just has a room and keeps herself to herself. No boy friend, no family. A sleepy-looking type, the sort that generally comes to a sticky end.'

They made an appointment for the following day and Ben went out. He had his job to do and he knew that even his position wasn't too healthy. Brown would use him and pay him as long as it suited his book. On the whole he thought his was the tougher job of the two. Knocking off a girl wasn't so difficult, but Crook spelled trouble in five letters. He was the sort of chap who, confronted by a brick wall, either climbed over it or, if it proved too high, battered his way through. And probably would batter out the brains of anyone who got in his way.

EIGHT

That was just before six o'clock. About five minutes later Crook telephoned to Kay from the booth by the gents' hairdresser.

'Just coming up,' he warned her, 'so let down the drawbridge. Any developments?'

'Someone came for the hatbox!'

'Who?'

'A girl called Aileen Smith. I got a receipt.'

'You mean, you gave her the box? Didn't you get my wire?'

'Yes. But I thought I'd better use my own judgment. It was registered.' Crook's groan was audible over the wire. Women using their own judgment were about as safe as hand grenades with the pins withdrawn. 'The post office told her it had been taken in,' she added quickly.

'Not the only one,' riposted Mr Crook. 'O.K. Watch where you see my white plume shine—meanin' watch the window for the Superb and wait for me to give the countersign. I'll whistle " My Bonnie " through your letterbox. Y'know, I have a feeling you may be getting other visitors before the night's out.'

Less than five minutes later he knocked twice and blew some peculiar notes through the letterbox. It didn't sound at all like ' My Bonnie ', but then nothing Crook did was quite in accord with other people, and he might have a particular tune. She drew the little bolt and let him in.

'So you got rid of the box,' said Mr. Crook, looking at her thoughtfully.

'I told you I'd use my own judgment.'

'So you did, sugar.'

She took his hat that he yielded very reluctantly, and hung it on a hook inside the cupboard. There was another hat hanging there already. Crook shook his big red head.

'I feel like I was living at the bottom of the garden all among the fairies,' he confessed, clenching his big jaw with a sound like a hare stamping. 'How come your ratty old felt hat has changed into a natty little white number? With half Covent Garden hanging on the side of it?'

'Well, I had to give her something, and exchange is no robbery. I mean if you shake an empty box you can tell it's empty, and I didn't suppose she'd open it on the spot.'

'A registered parcel,' whispered Crook.

'I was very careful. Luckily there was no special seal. Someone had poured on the wax and just stamped it down with the end of a pencil or something. . . .'

'And what one woman has done another can do.'

'And I dare say her fictitious mamma will look just as handsome in the old black felt as in this.' She nodded toward the hat she had taken from the hook and that now lay on the table. 'I had one frantic moment,' she said, 'when she wanted to use the telephone. I hadn't thought of her coming in and the hat was lying on the chair. Of course, if she didn't know what was inside the box she might have thought it was mine, but when X finds out about the swap . . .'

'When you get into *Who's Who*, sugar,' said Crook very, very gently, 'you can put "shoving my head in the lion's mouth" under Recreations.'

Kay looked hurt. 'Wasn't it a good idea?'

'If you're tired of life I can't think of a better one. Don't you see, you've tipped your hand well and proper now. That hat obviously meant a lot to X or he wouldn't have sent the girl round for it. When he finds your black monstrosity that's going to make him put his thinking cap on, and what he thinks ain't going to be very pleasant—for anyone. I suppose it was the same girl?'

'Straight brown hair, black-rimmed glasses, blue eyes that look as if they've been sent to the laundry too often, a beret . . .'

'That's my beauty. Any letter or anything enclosed?'

She shook her head. 'I looked most carefully.'

'Well, that makes sense. Then if it did go astray there'd be no tracing it. Salisbury's a largish place. My hunch tells me there's something wrong about all this.'

'There's certainly something wrong about the hat,' agreed Kay vigorously. 'I've drawn this kind for the fashion papers, they're all the rage this year or were at the beginning of the season.' It was hand-sewn in a thick white silk material and meant to be pulled down over the head. 'Everything depends on line in a hat like this, it's what they call tailored, and this is a very good example of its kind. You can get them in most of the better London shops, they run from six to eight guineas, but whatever happens they're never, never trimmed, and certainly not with a monstrous affair like that.' She flipped the cherries with an indignant finger.

'Well, but Miss C. goes in for decoration in a big way. Flowers, fruit—I'm not sure I didn't even see a pineapple—that cupboard of hers was a regular still life. It's what the head shrinkers call compensation,' he added vaguely. 'You know, a small plain body like Miss Prism has to gay up her hats. . . .'

'Not if she's a milliner worth her salt,' Kay insisted. 'Anyway, who would buy it? Oh, you might use a thing like that on a dark heavy felt intended for country wear in a drear-nighted

December—because the country can do with a bit of brightening in winter. . . .'

'And how!' said Crook feelingly. To his way of thinking it could do with a lot of brightening all the year round.

'But—you know, I feel like Alice, this gets curiouser and curiouser. These cherries are only sewn on by a few threads. If Mrs Smith wanted the hat changed she only had to get a pair of scissors and snip the threads. . . .'

'Ah, but she wanted a nice bunch of pansies or something in their place,' Crook reminded her. He took up the hat and pinched one of the cherries thoughtfully. 'Don't pass the word round,' he said, 'but I begin to think I'm slipping. One of these days folks 'ull begin to cotton onto the fact that my retirement pension ain't as far off as I like to pretend it is.' He whipped a knife out of his pocket and carefully cut the stitches. 'What are these trimmings generally made of?'

'Oh, almost anything. Material stuffed with a light filling, painted wood, plastic—glass even.'

Crook was working delicately around the mouth of one of the imitation cherries where it joined the stem.

'Get me a sheet of paper, sugar,' he besought her. He released the little wired stem and very gently shook the receptacle over the piece of paper she supplied. A little white powder poured out.

'You have to hand it to them, it's neat,' he observed generously. 'Five cherries, and I wouldn't be surprised if there was something in the twig affair as well. You could walk through the Customs in that, it could blow away on the boat, someone could rescue it, the stuff could change hands in transit. Oh, very neat indeed.'

'What is it?' asked the girl.

'I'm not sure. I'll get my friend, Macrae, to test it, but I'll tell you one thing, it ain't sugar and it ain't salt. It could be " snow " I suppose or it could be hyoscine. The police are up to their ears in trouble trying to track down these dope smugglers. They're as artful as alley cats. When I was a young man between the wars the stuff was sent over in packets of playing cards, just a little—" snow " for the most part, cocaine to you—a few grains between the face and the back; I remember a big brandy swindle,

too '—he was working cautiously on another cherry as he spoke
—' a young woman kept crossing the channel carrying her leetle
babby—no bother about allowances and not much about passports in those days—and she could have gone on till all-get-out if
one of the Customs officers hadn't been a family man himself
and thought it odd the baby never seemed to grow any bigger.
So they investigated—those were the blessed days when children
were muffled in long robes and shawls—and there it was, a
lovely wax infant, just too good to be true. It all comes of lack
of forethought—which is another word for conceit '—he
emptied the second cherry on to the sheet of paper, it was the
same as the first, which was what he'd anticipated—' if they'd
replaced the infant every two or three months they'd have been
safer than most houses these days. Last thing I heard they were
passing the stuff in plastic lobsters fed into a particular lobster
pot.'

He straightened himself. ' I wouldn't like to guess how much
that little bunch of cherries is worth. We'll take the rest of
them along to the police, don't want any funny business about
me trying to pull the official leg. And I'll tell you something
else,' he added, running on like the famous clockwork man that,
once wound, couldn't stop till he ran himself off the end of the
pier, ' that workshop or whatever she calls it was full of stuff
like this. Whether the strawberries and what not were full or
empty I couldn't say, but it shouldn't be hard to find out. Someone's going along in the morning to collect the whole lot, if they
do call it redecoration. Nice if we could spike their guns,
wouldn't it?' He sighed, and another sheet of paper blew off
the table.

' Suppose this is a blind?' Kay was frowning.

' I told you, I'm going to take this along to Macrae; maybe
he'll be closed but I have the key to the side door. Don't let
anyone in while I'm away.'

' Why should you think anyone would come?'

' Figure it out for yourself. When X opens the box and finds
your old hat there he'll realise you've tumbled. On second
thoughts,' he added, ' you'd better come along with me.'

' No,' said the girl stubbornly. ' I don't think so.'

' I'm doing the thinking, honey. We've already got one woman

77

vanished, possibly in for the Cemetery Stakes. I don't want my sole witness doing likewise. You're in danger. Don't you understand that?'

'Of course.'

'This chap may be watching the flat, he must have realised by now that I'm on to his little game, or let's say, interested in Miss C. or the late Miss C., and once he knows you're on your own he could move in. That ratty little bolt you've had put on wouldn't keep him out.'

'I've thought of all that.'

'Then . . .'

'You're not the only citizen of the Empire,' flamed the girl. 'I'm in on this, too, and there's more than my safety to be considered. You say drugs are being passed and I don't quarrel with that conclusion. Well, I'm a doctor's daughter, I know what drugs can do, particularly to young people. When I was seventeen there was a boy in our village I'd known since we were kids together. Oh, we had all sorts of ideas—boy-and-girl nonsense you can say, but I knew his family—he came up to London and—I never understood before what could be meant by being inhabited by an evil spirit. He's twenty-four now, but he's done for. . . . Don't you see, if someone came, even if I didn't open the door, and of course I wouldn't—I could see him from the window—give a description, the number of the car perhaps —I swore then when I saw what had happened to Teddy that if ever I got a chance to help—it's no good, Mr Crook, I'm not coming.'

'O.K.,' said Crook, who knew when he was licked. 'But stay where you are till I give you the word. I shan't be longer than I can help and the police 'ull be glad of a word from you and I'd like to have you in shape to answer their questions. Which reminds me,' he added, as he reached the door, 'I'm expecting a visitor. The human whirlwind, if Mr Ayre gives him my message and he can tear himself away from mesmerising some other poor boob long enough to look in. If you hear him, sugar, chat to him through the grille, keep him amused. Not that you'll need to do much talking, Niagara Falls is a trickle in the hills compared with that fellow.'

'Do you expect him to be able to help?' murmured Kay,

thinking it was a case of the pot calling the kettle black. Mr Crook in his day could make Niagara look a bit silly.

'Well, according to him he saw the boy friend on Tuesday night, how well I don't know, likewise I don't know how much he'll feel like spilling.'

'And you think the boy friend's the one who sent for the hat?'

'You're coming on,' said Crook approvingly. And he was gone.

As he came bouncing and buzzing down the stairs like some enormous ginger-coloured bee he saw Rhodes going into his own back gate.

'Hi,' he called. 'Going to be around for the next hour or so?'

'Boxing on the telly,' said Rhodes, with a grin. 'I'm off to The Boarhound at 8.30.'

'Should be back by then,' said Crook. 'If not, give it a miss for once. Might get a chance to do a bit of boxing on your own.'

'Come again, guv'nor,' Rhodes said politely. But he could see the devil-may-care lawyer had got something on his mind.

'Might be a visitor come along while I'm away,' he said.

'Coming for you?'

'Well, I'm not sure. It's not likely to be for Mrs Sagan, because there's no light in her flat so she must be out. . . .'

'Goes to the witches' circle or something on Wednesday,' Rhodes confirmed.

'And I'm out and Miss C.'s out—temporarily if not for the count—only Miss Carter's there, and she could do with a St George in case the dragon shows up before I get back.'

'You really do think there's dirty work at the crossroads, don't you?' murmured Rhodes.

'Don't you?'

'I wouldn't give it another thought if it wasn't for the bird. I admit I don't like that much. Well, I dare say I could fox up something. You taking your car?'

'You bet I'm taking my car,' said Crook.

'Pity, I could have been washing it down for you. Oh, well, I dare say I can put the electric light out of action and put it right again. Want me to do anything special?'

'Someone could ask for Miss Chisholm.'

'That's easy, she's away.'

'Or for Miss Carter.'

Rhodes said, looking puzzled, 'You think she might be in some danger?'

'I darn well know she might, but she's like all these janes—knows her way's best, and nothing to show she ain't right. It's a maddening attribute of the sex to be right when by every law of probability they should be wrong. I've told her not to let anyone in. . . .'

'O.K.,' said Rhodes resignedly.

'If young Lochinvar should turn up, fair chap—oh, but I forgot, you've seen him, brought the TV set . . .'

'Coming to collect it?'

'Don't think his union will let him. Still, he's coming, so if I ain't back tell him to possess his soul in patience, give him a nice glass of Vegade . . . I've left similar word with Miss Carter.'

He bounced out; a moment later he bounced back again.

'Happen to notice anyone drive away Miss Chisholm's Martin?' he demanded.

'What's that?' Rhodes came rushing down the stairs. 'Well! It was there when I went out this morning.'

'I left the Superb at the garage on the corner,' agreed Crook. 'Otherwise I'd have noticed she wasn't in my way. Wonder if little Cinderella could have anything to do with it.'

'Cinderella?'

'Young lady from Hebberden Mews. She came calling on Miss Carter. Didn't look like a lady driver . . .'

'How can you tell?' exclaimed Rhodes incredulously. 'Half of them look like nothing on earth.'

'Could be. Still, she's tied up with Miss Chisholm and, if I win my guess, with the boy friend, too.'

'You know her?'

'Called in for a minute or two this morning. She don't like answering questions. D'you know'—indignation momentarily got the better of him—'she had the gall to suggest I might be the missing milliner's old man.'

'Go on,' said Rhodes. 'That one never said I will.'

'Our Miss Smith seems to think she did. Maybe Mr Chisholm had ideas about settling down with another dame and she wouldn't untie the knot. . . .'

'People have by-passed that one,' suggested Rhodes.

'Maybe the second choice has the bacon.' He rubbed his finger and thumb together with vulgar suggestiveness. 'It pays to marry them then. Well, say Miss C. wouldn't untie the knot, it could be X decided to do a bit of untying himself. It wouldn't be the first time.'

'Wonder if the chap on beat duty noticed anything?'

But he hadn't, of course. He asked Crook if he wanted to report a stolen car.

'Well, not precisely, but there'd be no harm your chaps keeping their eyes peeled for a grey-blue Martin Tourer model—number?' He looked at Rhodes.

'ABC 129,' said Rhodes. 'Mind you, she could have sneaked back and taken it off herself.'

'In that case why not sneak up the stairs to no. 3?'

Rhodes heaved a deep sigh. 'Wouldn't you guess it 'ud be the one day Mrs Sagan's not at the window.'

'Oh, well, you know the one about spilt milk.'

'Do you wish to make a charge?' inquired the policeman.

'I'll probably be calling at your station later in the evening,' Crook told him. 'I'll try pulling a string or two then. Inspector Perrin on duty today, d'you know?'

The policeman's face took on a more respectful air. It didn't do in his experience to be too short with chaps who knew inspectors by their names.

'Yes, sir.'

'Might have a little sweetener for him, never can tell. Don't forget about young Lochinvar,' he added to Rhodes. He went around to the garage and collected the Superb and drove away. His friend, Macrae, was one of those obliging pharmacists who stay open till 6.30 and business didn't seem very brisk, so he could attend to Crook's bit of trouble right away. As Crook had suspected, the stuff was hyoscine, about as deadly to its addicts as a nest of puff adders.

'Where did you find the stuff?' asked Macrae.

'"Cherry ripe, ripe, ripe, I cry, Full and fair ones,—come

81

and buy!" And at a price that 'ud knock you backwards, Mac. Well, I'm off. You might even have the police round here, but that's nothing to be alarmed about. What's more to the point is I shall have them cluttering up my place, and that won't suit some of my clients a bit, and like all good lawyers, I only exist to please my clients.'

Then around he went to the model new station where he inquired for Inspector Perrin.

'He's expecting you,' said the officer on duty with a wry grin. 'Got something handsome for him?'

'A nice headache,' beamed Crook.

'Not murder by any chance.' Like every other manor in London they knew the aphorism: 'Where there's Crook there's crime.'

'I won't make any promises, but—he can hope.'

Perrin was a small dark sturdy man with a manner that wouldn't have disgraced a machine gun.

'A report from 2 Brandon Street last night?' said Perrin. 'From you?'

'Tenant of the ground floor, a Mrs Sagan. Universal anxiety felt because our neighbour, Miss Caroline Chisholm (once, possibly, Mrs Something Else but we don't know who) hadn't surfaced for twenty-four hours.'

'I don't believe even you, Crook, had the gall to get one of my chaps round because a lady friend had turned up missing, probably of her own free will, for a night.'

'He wouldn't come. And we're not so sure about the free will.' He outlined the case briefly—Henry (deceased), the car— now missing—the unlocked door, the goods left by the dairy, the box sent through the mail and subsequently called for.

'Your chap kindly said we could contact him again if the mystery deepened. Well, it has. Still no news of the lady, car vanished suddenly, and above all—this.' And he produced the twist of hyoscine and the rest of the cherry spray, still unexamined.

'It did occur to me,' he said with deceptive meekness, 'it might pay you to make a surprise raid on 2 Hebberden Mews. The young lady told me the decorators 'ull be in tomorrow, and I'd say locusts might be a better name for 'em. That cupboard's got quite a lot of stuff in it that my Miss Carter tells me no self-respecting woman would dangle from a lid. . . .'

'So we look in tonight. I get you.' It was characteristic that Perrin didn't seek to prove Crook's story. Crook might be a pain in the official neck and a thorn in the official side, but when he put a lead in your hand as often as not it led eventually to the Central Criminal Court.

'Who's with the girl?' asked Perrin. 'The one who changed the hats, I mean.'

'I've left a chap on guard, if the claims of the telly don't prove too strong. Tell you what, you give me a ride down to Hebberden Mews and let one of your men take the Superb back to Brandon Street. Then if these fellows should have any funny ideas they might hold off. If they see a cop—beg pardon, a constable—parking the car it might give 'em to think, and if they just see the car, well, they'll be as sure as God made little apples I'm inside. Oh, and you might put out an alert for the Martin Tourer model, ABC 129. These chaps mean business.' It was odd how much the incident of the little bird troubled him. Because there hadn't been any need for that small brutal act. Someone would have remembered the bird and got it out and it wasn't as if it could talk, barring its one idiotic phrase. No, whoever had wrung its neck had done so for the pleasure it gave him. It made him feel a bit sick, and though it's difficult for a man whose face looks as though it has been hewn rather carelessly out of a chunk of mahogany to change colour, he managed it; the effect was greenish and ghastly.

'I'll put a chap on to watch the place,' said Perrin, watching him narrowly. It wasn't like Crook to get the wind up over things.

'Put a chap on to watch the girl,' suggested Crook. 'You know what they're like at that age, all presumptive Grace Darlings or Miss Marples. And one woman's vanished already. . . .'

'You can't absolutely rule out the possibility that that was voluntary,' Perrin reminded him.

'And pigs might fly,' agreed Crook, 'and I dare say before I inherit my six feet of earth and the conquering worm some clever chap will have taught them to do it, but till then I go on the evidence of my five senses, and it don't make sense to me that a lady that can't read a letter without her glasses should leave them on the table. Still, that's your funeral, and it won't be your fault if it ain't hers, too.'

The authorities, persistently harried by the taxpayers not to waste hard-earned money, had economised on the lighting in Hebberden Mews. There was a lamp at the entry but the rest of the passage was a yawn of blackness. The police car turned in cautiously. There was a dark bulk near the end of the passage with only a rear lamp showing, which proved to be a small furniture van. As the official car drove up a man adjusted a padlock on the door of the furniture depository Crook had noticed men filling up that morning and came around the side of the van. He was a small dark man who stopped and stared when he saw the police.

On impulse Crook poked his head out of the car window and said, 'Seen anyone around here, mate?' indicating Louise.

'You're too late,' said the driver. He cupped his hands around a match and dipped his head to light a cigarette. 'Shut down till further notice.'

'We're aware of that,' said Perrin briefly.

'Chap hasn't been gone above twenty minutes,' the man went on.

The inspector stiffened. 'What chap?'

'Search me. Driving a Martin Tourer. A nice job.' He spoke in the regretful voice of a man who's lucky if he can run to a second-hand Ford.

'What colour?'

'What, the man or the car?'

'The car.'

'Well, I couldn't see much—you chaps must love crime, the way they don't light the streets—lightish, blue or grey.'

'Didn't notice the number, of course? Well, why should you? Did you notice the driver?'

The other was vague. 'Fairish. I wouldn't know that if he hadn't asked for a flashlight. Come for a hat for his wife, p'raps,' he added with a grin. 'Had a key.'

'Didn't occur to you to wonder what he wanted here this hours of the night?' the inspector suggested.

The little dark man jammed his hat defiantly over his eyes. 'Why ever? I keep my nose clean and I don't poke it into other people's affairs. He might have asked me what I was doing here. Getting a bit of furniture out of the warehouse for some old lady—you know how they are. Move into a furnished flat and park their stuff and then find they can't manage without a special chair or whatnot.'

The inspector nodded. 'Could be we shall want your evidence,' he said. 'Give the constable your name.'

'My guv'nor doesn't like getting tangled up with the police,' said the fellow sturdily. 'Anyway, what's cooking?'

'You'll hear,' said the inspector. 'And you tell your guv'nor that if his record's clean he's got no reason to be afraid of the police.'

Crook gave an audible gasp. Ananias, he thought, had been struck dead for less than that.

'Oh, well, he won't like me losing time and I can't identify the chap, but since you're so pressing it's Ted Hayward, working for the Nu-Unit. All the same—fact is, I was doing a little in my spare time. Chance to turn an extra quid or so . . . You understand?'

'That's no concern of mine,' said the inspector, woodenly. 'Give me your home address, if you like.'

'Fourteen Unicorn Street, Potters Bar. Don't forget to take the number of the van,' he added sarcastically.

'That was a bit of bad luck for him,' murmured the inspector, with a grin. 'Of course, he was doing a little job on the side and he doesn't want his boss to know about it. Oh, well, we may not need him. But that could give us a line on the missing car.'

They rang the bell at Louise as a matter of form, and, as they anticipated, there was no one there. But seeing that all the cherries had yielded their deadly poison, they hadn't much hesitation about breaking into the place, and the policeman got to work on the lock.

While he worked Crook said uneasily, 'Ever had a flea, Inspector? You know, you can feel the little beggar bite, but

85

when you look he ain't there. Come to that, he ain't anywhere, and you wouldn't believe in his existence if it wasn't that he'd left his mark.'

'What are you driving at?' demanded the inspector.

'There's something wrong. I can feel it'—he clapped his hand theatrically to his arm as if to trap a non-existent flea—'but I don't know yet what it is.'

'We know a chap came here in a car resembling the one we're interested in,' said the inspector patiently. 'Pity the driver didn't get the number, but naturally he couldn't know that was important.'

Crook fidgeted about till the chap got the door open. He had a feeling Fate was waiting in the wings to hand them no end of a wallop; and, like most of his hunches, this one was correct.

The door was unfastened at last and they all surged in, and came to a dead stop. Barring the curtains at the window, and the reason why they'd been left would have been obvious to a half-wit, the interior was as bare as a schoolboy's chin. No desk, no chair, no little dressing table. The built-in cupboard in the room beyond resembled the one belonging to Mother Hubbard on a historic occasion. Only a little scrap of greenery was left, fallen on the floor as the villains made their haul.

'Your girl gave them the red light,' observed the inspector. 'When they found the hats had been substituted they realised the game was up.'

'And if she hadn't substituted them you'd be right back where you were this morning, sitting on your backsides wondering how the hell the stuff was being passed,' Crook returned smartly. But he wasn't looking for his flea any longer. He had located it.

'I don't think,' he suggested silkily, 'that desk and chair were taken away in a Martin Tourer, not if it was all the colours of the rainbow. I think it might have been instructive if we could have seen the inside of that plain van. *That's* what's worrying me. Y'see, when I was here before, there was a van unloading furniture and it had the name painted on the side, and since it was a depository why be so careful to hide your identity? Matter of fact, I don't know why he wanted to tell such an elaborate story. He could have produced an order, said Louise was being redecorated and they wanted the stuff cleared out, but, of course, they knew I'd rumbled 'em and they probably didn't expect the police to be quite so smart getting on their tail. If the chap on the beat had asked questions, well, it all looked plain sailing. They couldn't guess a boatload of cops was going to turn up just to find out what was going on at Louise.'

The telephone hadn't been disconnected and Perrin got onto his boys to order them to go into their normal routine, fingerprints and what not. There was always the chance they'd turn up a duplicate print.

'Funny he should mention the car,' suggested the constable who was to return the Superb to Brandon Street.

'Not a bit of it,' contradicted Crook. 'Suppose we'd asked to see what he was carting away? No, that was a red herring all right, and a bit of luck for the forces of law and order really, because if he wasn't in the game how come he knew a blue-grey Martin Tourer was involved at all?'

NINE

Rhodes was leaning against the front door, smoking a cigarette when Crook came back, having told the police car to drop him off a short distance away.

'Don't want to advertise to the world I'm in cahoots with the bluebottles,' he explained.

'Your chap came all right, Mr Crook,' Rhodes said. 'I told him to go up and wait. There's one's got the gift of gab. I wouldn't trust him within a mile of the spoons.'

'Anyone else?' asked Crook.

'Not since I got here. No news about Miss Chisholm, I suppose?'

'Only that she or someone else is anxious to blot out her record. The whole outfit's skipped from Hebberden Mews since morning—most likely I put them on the trail,' he added, gloomily. 'No bodies there, if that's what you're thinking. If she's still with us the odds are they won't take any violent steps against her, too dangerous with all those boy scouts on the track. . . .'

'You don't think she might have slid back and got the car? No, I asked you that before—but it didn't move of its own accord.'

'It didn't have to. Seen Miss Carter?' he added.

'Knocked on her door after showing your visitor upstairs. No one's been calling there, either, not since you left, that is. She said a girl came this afternoon to collect a parcel. . . .'

'That's right. Addressed to Miss Chisholm. Well, that's O.K. The girl came from the shop—Louise—I saw her myself this morning. Though how much interest Miss Chisholm's still able to take in hats is what's called a moot point. How long's young Lochinvar been here?'

'Young—oh . . . Quite a while.'

'I'd better beetle up and make sure he isn't trying to bust his own way in,' Crook suggested. 'He don't give me the impression that patience is his strong suit.'

Skipping jauntily up the stairs he was arrested by the sound of voices from behind the door of Kay's flat. There was a footstep and the door flashed open. Kay stood there with C. Oliver at her elbow.

'I've been entertaining your visitor,' said Kay demurely.

Crook bent his big mouth into a smile. 'Has he sold you a set yet?' he asked.

Oliver shook a regretful head. 'Young lady doesn't want one.'

'You're not telling me you'd let a little thing like that stand in your way?' Crook sounded flummoxed.

'Ladies generally know their own minds. That's one of the things you learn in my job. Mind you, I don't say we ever take no for an answer, our motto is " If at first you don't succeed . . ." '

'Best put the bolt up next time you hear him,' Crook warned the girl. 'We don't want two of those things in the house.'

'Piggy said you were asking for me,' Oliver went on.

'So I was. Something I thought you might be able to tell me. What does C. stand for, by the way?'

Oliver made an odd face. 'You'll never guess. Charterhouse.'

'No one could be called Charterhouse,' Crook protested.

'You'd be surprised. I know a chap who came back from the Middle East and found his son had been christened El Alamein. You'd think padres would know better, all the education they get. No, my Mum and Dad met at Charterhouse, so she thought it 'ud be a nice idea to call sonny boy after the most beautiful place in the world.' He sighed. 'She should have consulted a fortune teller. She and my Dad parted before I was five, and after that she couldn't stand the sound of the name, so she gave me a dear little pet name.' He grimaced. 'Mr Ayre told me you wanted a word,' he went on in the same voice.

'Coming up?' said Crook. Charterhouse Oliver took the hint and walked up to the top floor out of earshot.

'What made you open the door?' Crook asked stonily of the girl.

'Well, you wanted to see him, and he might have got tired and gone away. He did say something about it becoming an occupational disease with him, studying the outside of your front door. Did you find out anything?'

'They've flown,' said Crook. 'I don't like it, I don't like it one bit. What are you doing tonight?'

She told him she was going to dinner with a friend of Bryan's —a dear old thing, she said. It turned out he was thirty-four.

'See he brings you back,' said Crook crossly.

He felt he had had enough of female contrariness for one day; if the sex wanted to commit mass suicide who was he to stop them?

'Going to keep the set?' inquired Oliver in buoyant tones as Crook appeared. 'What did I tell you? You could have signed the form at the office, but, of course, it does me a bit of good if I get your name. Piggy's thrilled. . . .'

Crook wasn't paying any attention; he was like a man who hates cats and knows someone's hidden a cat in his room. Or he was like a dog whose ball or bone has been secreted and has realised their hiding place; he stands by it or under it, head lifted, hair quivering. Every hair of Crook's thick red thatch emulated the dog. He knew, without having to go around looking for fingerprints, that while he was away someone had been in the flat. He saw Oliver watching him and came out of his daze.

'Haven't made up my mind yet,' he improvised. 'Miss Chisholm now . . .'

'Don't tell me she wants a set, after all.'

'If she does I don't know and I don't suppose anyone else could tell you, either. Fact is, she vanished the night you called. . . .'

'I didn't take her away in my pocket,' protested Oliver.

'It's a funny thing,' said Crook slowly. 'Your Mr Ayre had never heard of her, not till I introduced the name.'

'Nothing strange about that,' Oliver assured him. 'I hadn't mentioned her.'

'You said something about an appointment. . . .'

'Not exactly. I said I called to demonstrate the set. I didn't say she knew I was coming.'

'Meaning she didn't know?'

'Meaning just that. Fact is, you have to do a bit of bulldozing in my job.'

'You mean you just go round banging on doors haphazard? Oh, come, I can draw a pretty long bow myself. . . .'

'No, not that way, of course. But—fact is, we've got a client, a Mrs Dodds, living in Fulham. I had a great job persuading her she really needed a set. She filled in one of our inquiry forms— we distribute them into letterboxes locally, and of course they're advertised in the various radio journals—so twenty-four hours later round I went. When she saw me she went into the usual routine. "Oh, I don't really want one. I was inquiring for a friend." Naturally, we're used to that, and we don't let it stand in our path.'

'Could be true,' suggested Mr Crook.

'I dare say.' Oliver's manner said he cared less about the truth than jesting Pilate. 'Anyway, I brought the set and gave a demonstration, and she said she'd think it over. A month later I called again to see if she'd changed her mind. It so happened there was a good programme on—it was the morning, but she was there all right—pictures of the Queen and the Duke—that got her. You have to weigh up on psychology on this job. I could see she was the sort that's nuts on the royal family. . . . Well, anyway, she said, "I never believed, Mr Oliver, you'd persuade me to rent a set. I believe you could even wear down my friend, Miss Chisholm." I said, naturally, "Give me the chance, where does she live?" and she hesitated a minute and then gave a sort of grin and said, "Well, she has a flat at 2 Brandon Street, in Earl's Court, but she isn't there during the day. She runs a business, fashion, you know." I asked what sort of fashion and she said, "She's a milliner. Makes very good hats, if your wife . . ." I said it was the first time I'd heard of ghosts wanting hats and we had a bit of a laugh over that. Then I looked through the programmes and saw there was one called Atop the Tresses.'

'You're making it up,' accused Crook.

'You don't know this layout—yet,' Oliver assured him. 'Well, that's why I got there at 6.50. Programme came on seven o'clock. Don't ask me why, you'd think people 'ud have something better to do at that time of the evening than look at hats, but there it is. I thought, three minutes to get in, two minutes to get the set fixed, five minutes for the patter and getting the aerial so the picture wouldn't look as if we were in a coal cellar, and then she could see the hats, and well—it seemed a sporting chance.'

'And she didn't know you were coming?'

Oliver shook his head. 'If you ring 'em up they say, "No, I shan't be at home." So round I went but I never saw her.'

'But she was there?'

'Well, since I didn't see her . . .'

'You said you heard her. . . .'

'I heard someone.'

'Female?'

'Well, I thought so. Have to be careful when I'm talking to the law,' he added explanatorily.

'Happen to remember if the landing light was working when you came up?'

'I wouldn't know. Wouldn't need it that hour.'

'How about the lady's flat?'

'No light there, either, except what came through the transom.'

'All doors shut?'

'That's right.'

'How well did you see this chap who opened the door?'

'He was wearing a hat.'

'What? In a lady's house?' Crook sounded shocked.

'No gentleman,' Oliver agreed. 'Only it did seem to me no dalliance could hardly have started.'

'Tall, short, dark, fair—oh, come, chap with your gifts must be able to tell me something.'

'Say, about five feet six inches, dark, might almost have been Latin type. No accent, though. Didn't waste his time, either. Just called out, "You expecting a TV?" and the voice said, "No. Must be the wrong flat." So B.F. said, "Try the one above," and shut the door.'

'Didn't notice anything special about him? Didn't have a mermaid tattooed on his wrist or anything like that?'

'Might have been covered with them, but I didn't get the chance to see.'

'Think you'd know him again?'

'What? To swear to in a police court? Not likely. After all, it wasn't him I was interested in. He wasn't going to rent a set. No wonder Piggy looked a bit weird,' he added candidly. 'He's like most honest men, the less he has to do with the police the better. He said you asked a lot of questions.'

'Nothing to what they'll do when they get round to you.'

'If it's not being inquisitive, have they turned up a body?'

'Not Miss Chisholm's.'

'Well, sooner them than me. Corpsing was never in my line. How about it?' he added, in businesslike tones, indicating the set.

You had to admit he knew his onions. When he departed fifteen minutes later he had Crook's signature to a form that posed more questions about your private life than you'd have expected anyone but a government department to think up. He also had Crook's cheque in his pocket.

'Just before you go,' urged Crook, 'what's this Mrs Dodds' address? Going to make us all look a nice lot of fools if it turns out the missing Prism went round to see her and strangle her accidental-like for sending you along.'

When Crook went down later he found Rhodes still hanging around.

'Come off sentry go?' the porter suggested in hopeful tones.

'Oh, I don't think anyone else will come tonight,' Crook agreed. 'But it wouldn't surprise me if we were to see a dark stranger hanging around within the next few days.'

'What do I do?' murmured Rhodes. 'Give him the flying tackle? Or do you want to deal with him yourself?'

'I fancy Miss Carter's the one he'll be interested in. It's a matter now for lead and the ocean.'

'Lead and the . . .?'

'Wait and see,' Crook explained. 'It was a standard joke at my school—but that 'ud be long before your time. By the way, how long does it take to respray a car?'

'What, at a garage?'

'If you wanted it done in a hurry, and not too much spot-light?'

'Do it yourself? Spraying doesn't take long, it's the drying. There was a book I read once where they used a special quick-drying paint. . . . You're thinking of Miss Chisholm's car, of course.'

Crook nodded. 'Mind you, the sensible thing would be to shove it in a private garage and lose the key.'

'If you had a private garage.'

'That's the point.'

'You couldn't spray it in the open without someone coming to watch like a horse looking over a fence,' Rhodes objected, 'and it's not the kind of job you can do in your own house. And if X knows you're interested in the car he's not going to chance turning it over to the experts, even if the licence plates are changed. It might look a bit fishy wanting a perfectly good Martin—because it was in mint condition, if Miss Chisholm had seen a spot of dust on it she'd have wept a tear of grief that would have washed the dust away—I mean, why have it resprayed?'

'Well, the police can do that little job,' Crook decided. 'Shame to take all their fun away from them. Oh, by the way,' he half turned on the steps, 'you're sure no one came past you tonight except young Lochinvar?'

'Only if he was the invisible man,' said Rhodes.

'And one more thing—the night Miss Chisholm disappeared —you didn't see anyone go up to her flat?'

'This TV chap.'

'But that's all?'

'That's all I saw, but someone could have gone up earlier before I got back. I told you Mrs Sagan did say she thought she heard somebody. . . .'

Only, as both Rhodes and Crook knew, that kind of story cuts no ice with amateurs, let alone the police.

'Well,' said Crook, 'I've got to be going. Date with a dame,' which was as near the truth as he ever bothered to come.

At about the same time Brown was preparing to leave his flat. He had reached the door when the telephone rang.

'Hallo!' he asked.

A voice that might have come from anywhere and indeed sounded as though it came from the depths of the grave said, 'Nothing to report,' and the line went dead again.

TEN

Mrs Dodds was a large woman with small black eyes set rather close together and a shelving bosom.

'Caroline Chisholm here?' she exclaimed in response to Crook's question. 'Of course not. Have you tried her flat?'

'She lit out from there a couple of days ago. Disappeared from her workshop, too. Or maybe she's moving into more commodious premises, only no one seems to know where they are.'

'You mean, she's left Hebberden Mews?'

'Well, everything portable's vanished, and she seems to have vanished, too.'

'She's probably gone abroad.'

'Leaving her flat unlocked, her bird unfed . . . I thought, seeing you're a friend of hers . . .'

'Who told you about me?'

Crook grinned slightly. 'The chap who sold you a television set.'

The little black eyes opened; they sparkled; an amazing quality of vitality shone in the big dough-coloured face.

'You don't mean he persuaded Caroline . . .'

'I don't doubt he could have, but he didn't get the chance, didn't get in. Came up to me instead.'

'Landed you?' suggested Mrs Dodds.

'He'd be there now if I hadn't agreed to give the thing a trial. Well, so far as anyone knows, anyone I've been able to contact, that is, that's the last evening Miss C. surfaced. And even then . . .' He frowned.

'You'd better come in, hadn't you?' suggested Mrs Dodds. 'Then you can tell me all about it.'

It was obvious Miss Chisholm wasn't there. She couldn't have lived twenty-four minutes, let alone twenty-four hours, in a place so delightfully haphazard.

'How about the workshop? Haven't they got any news?'

'Oh, that's shut down, too, and if our Miss Smith knows anything she ain't talking.'

'Smith?'

'The Cinderella at the shop.'

'You mean, Caroline's done a flit?'

'Know any reason why she should?'

'If the place went bankrupt . . .'

'Why, wasn't she a success?'

'I didn't know a lot about it, but she only kept a couple of girls and that's no way to run a hat shop; and Hebberden Mews —I always wondered what it covered up, only it wasn't any concern of mine, was it?'

'She did make hats,' Crook offered.

'I know. But—oh, well, I suppose she could afford a hobby, if she liked. Only the funny thing is—you'll die when you hear this—I was in Kensington High Street once—that's about my price—and I saw her, buying a whole lot of shapes. Well, these high-class milliners are supposed to mould the thing on the customer's head, or so I've always understood. . . .'

'Remember the shop?' asked Crook.

'A place called Benson's, quite well known for hats for

what's called the middle-class purse. Not that most people bother with shapes these days.'

'What precisely are shapes?' inquired Mr Crook.

'Just buckram—shapes—moulds . . .'

'Hats before they've got any clothes on? Yes, I see.'

'If you're clever you can do very well with them. Say you've got a suit of a particular material and you want a hat to match, same colour, same stuff . . .'

'I'm with you,' said Crook resignedly. 'Well, thanks a million. Known her long, Miss Chisholm, I mean?'

'We met in the war, both of us working in the censorship. She'd travelled quite a bit on the Continent, talked French and German. We were up North, which suited me well enough because Arthur—my husband—was doing essential work there, and if I hadn't got myself a job they could have put me into a factory—no family, you see. . . . I've been widowed for six years,' she added. 'Caroline was married in those days. . . .'

'So there really was a husband?'

'So she said. She met him abroad after the war. Escorts, duennas, I don't know what they were called, were wanted to ferry B.A.O.R. wives and female personnel from England to Germany and vice versa, and she volunteered for the job.'

'So she used her maiden name for professional purposes only?'

'Well, I gathered it didn't work out. It doesn't surprise me,' added Mrs Dodds in a burst of confidence, 'I should think she'd drive the average man up the wall. It was—pathological—is that what I mean?'

'If you don't know, how should I?' inquired the fascinated Mr Crook.

'I mean, if you went to see her and put your gloves on her table she'd whisk them off before they scratched the surface.'

'What are your gloves made of? Chain mail?'

'Oh, it wasn't just gloves, a book, a newspaper, anything; she'd have been the kind that follows her husband round with a brush and pan in case he drops a bit of cigarette ash on the carpet. I did wonder,' she added reflectively, 'if it wasn't what used to be called a marriage of convenience. I mean, he was a foreigner, that I do know.'

'Get his name?' asked Crook like lightning.

Mrs Dodds frowned in a tremendous effort of concentration. 'I did know it once, it was the sort of name that could easily be anglicised. Now what was it? It was German,' she added. 'Braun? Or was it Schmidt? Or Fischer? I always thought of her as Caroline Chisholm.'

'Never saw him?'

'I don't know if he ever came over to England. I met her one day in Oxford Street, and she told me she was married. I wouldn't be surprised if he was in the black market—I mean, how was it Caro got hold of goods in scarce supply like nylons when the rest of us were queueing up for a single pair and then probably being put off with silk that laddered within the week? Oh, yes, she had them, she offered me some, thirty shillings a pair.'

'What did you say?'

'I didn't buy them if that's what you mean. She said she'd been sent some from America but they were the wrong size. The next I heard of her was she was working for a milliner, and I said, " Well, that should pay her because you know—at least, I don't suppose you do—but it's one of the hardest things in the world to get a hat that seems a part of your personality." She said one day quite soon she was going to set up on her own and she'd send me a card. And later on she did.'

'When would all this be?'

Mrs Dodds, who seemed a first cousin to Mrs Sagan, considered. 'It was about '51 when I heard she was married. Then from '52 to '55 I really never saw anyone, because Arthur had his stroke and I nursed him. We'd had such a struggle keeping a roof over our heads during our married life I wasn't going to have him die in a state hospital. Then it would be the following year, I think—I remember telling her I was a widow—that I met her, and I think it would be '57 that I got a card from her telling me she'd set up in Hebberden Mews. Well, I didn't go round there right away because I'd just discovered a wonderful little woman off the Kensington High Street, who had a sort of second sight where hats were concerned. But she went to keep house for a widowed brother in Devon last year, and then I went to Caroline.'

'At Hebberden Mews?'

'Yes. Have you seen the premises?'

Crook nodded.

'What was your reaction?'

'A bit on the modest side, I thought,' suggested Crook.

'You know, I felt the same. I know that space in that part of London is worth its weight in gold, but I did think something slightly more showy would have paid off. Mind you, it's amazing what squalid offices some of these big businesses have, but then it's like that Yorkshire saying—I'm not rude, I'm rich. If you're known to be in the money you can settle in Houndsditch if you want to. She told me her marriage had broken up and she'd gone back to being Miss Chisholm. I didn't ask any questions, I thought really she was lucky not to be in the churchyard. Arthur was the sweeetest-tempered of men, but if I'd badgered him about his newspaper and mud on his shoes and all the rest of it he might well have picked up a hammer and put a stop to everything.'

'You're sure she never said anything else about her husband?'

'She showed me a snapshot of herself and some other people and she pointed to something like a little black dwarf in the corner and said, 'That's my husband.'''

'The small dark man,' murmured Crook.

'That's right. She seemed to be doing quite well,' insisted Mrs Dodds. 'I mean, her clothes never came off the hook, and she wore Italian shoes. You can always tell. Not that I wear them myself, suffering as I do from fallen arches . . .'

'But she made good hats?' suggested Crook, feeling like a hairpin that's got into the vacuum cleaner and goes around and around and around. 'A bit strong on parsley round the dish, wasn't she?'

'Parsley?'

'Decoration—trimming—whatever it's called. If she'd used real stuff for her creations, she'd have been a boon to Covent Garden.'

'She didn't persuade me to have a lot of trimming,' declared Mrs Dodds.

'So you stuck to the penny plain?' said Crook cordially.

'Getting a hat is like getting a husband,' said Mrs Dodds

seriously. 'It doesn't matter how decorative or smart they are if they don't suit you. My husband, during his latter years anyway, looked like a football with a bowler on top, but he suited me. Oh, I dare say she could have run me up no end of a creation, now I come to think of it she had got a hat practically finished covered with great waving roses . . . Whoever's going to wear that will be riddled with greenfly, I warned her—but—look, I'll show you . . .' She vanished into an inner room, and Crook mopped his forehead. He felt he'd been trying to do a four-minute mile and something had gone wrong with his watch. Mrs Dodds returned with a large dome-shaped purple erection in which she could have made a good-sized blancmange; she jammed it down over her thick masses of black hair—she wore it *en pompadour* and it was obvious that no hairdresser was making his fortune off her—and said, 'Well, now, you do see what I mean. A hat should be an extension of the face.'

Crook nodded weakly. He couldn't have put it better himself; the blank expanse of plain dark felt seemed to have grown on the broad sallow forehead.

'Oh, you're not going, are you? I was just going to make a pot of tea.'

But Crook said he was a busy chap himself and he could see she was the same, and all the washing-up . . .

'Oh, I always have time for the unexpected,' said Mrs Dodds easily. 'Housework can be done at any time.'

Crook said faintly he supposed so, but it did occur to him there were rather more articles of feminine apparel lying around than you'd normally expect at this time of night—and he could see the kitchen stacked with unwashed crockery. He thought she probably went on the good old practice of using everything and then having a grand clean-up.

'What's really brought you round?' asked Mrs Dodds. 'Has something happened to Caroline?'

'Did you expect it to?'

'I told you, I rely on the unexpected. You didn't say who you are.'

Crook produced a card. 'A lawyer? How fascinating. If I hadn't been a wife that's what I should have liked. You know, get all the facts and then arrange them to suit your client. I always loved jigsaw puzzles.' He saw one was laid out on a table near the window. 'I've been weeks doing that,' Mrs Dodds went on. 'I think some of the pieces must be missing. Oh, must you go? Well, I've done a lot for you, haven't I? I mean, you didn't even know she had a husband till I put you in the picture, so now it's your turn to do something for me.'

'Such as?'

'Keep *me* in the picture,' said Mrs Dodds cosily. 'I mean, if it turns out that he murdered her—is that what you suspect?'

'Who said anything about murder?' demanded Crook.

'Oh, I know the police never put anything down in black and white. . . .'

'The police? Have you had them here?'

'Now, you mustn't think I can't add two and two. And of course I'm not taken in by this.' She indicated the card he had laid on the table. 'Lawyers don't come bursting in on perfect strangers, asking questions as you did. Of course I know you were supposed to tell me who you were before you started, but I dare say you thought I wouldn't tell you if I knew.'

'And wouldn't you?' wondered Crook aloud.

'Well, I'd be careful—naturally. Talking to the police must be rather like coming up before the Archangel Gabriel. But I promise you one thing, I'm not hiding anything. Do tell me one thing. Do you think conceivably Caroline has been murdered?'

'Since you ask me,' said Crook, 'and not being the police despite all appearances, I rather think I do.'

ELEVEN

Aileen Smith, that poor silly sheep, returned to her dormitory village in a mood of defiant triumph. Although she had no suspicion of the actual truth she had the wit to realise that the hat shop was a cover for something presumably crooked and that her boss, who didn't seem at all troubled about the disappearance of Caroline Chisholm, was worried as all get out by the exchange of hats.

He's mad, that I know, she reflected, and that gave her power. If he thought she was really going to be satisfied with three miserable weeks' wages he must be crazy. I'll have a flat of my own, she thought blissfully. Perhaps I'll open a business. I'll do the employing. She dreamed the lunatic visions of her kind, pictures in one of the women's weeklies, shiny photographs by a big name of the girl who began life in an orphanage and now ran a cosmetics business or—not hats, she was sick of hats, and anyway that 'ud only be copy-catting Miss Chisholm.

She switched off to think about Miss Chisholm, where she really was. Hiding from the police? But why? Really gone abroad without a word? Or concealed somewhere . . . One thing, she was convinced that Brown knew, and was shaking in his shoes in case she should come to share his secret. Recalling that bitter implacable face, her faith in her own ability wilted suddenly. Others must have pitted themselves against him and where were all of them now? If Caroline Chisholm had been the last . . .

It might be smarter, perhaps, to go to the police right away with her story. She'd get the publicity all right—or would she? Would the police take the credit? But she might get an interview on television. The girl who helped to unravel a mystery. That was what she wanted, a place in the sun, she who all her life had occupied a north-room hovel while other people spread themselves on sun-drenched verandas.

She went home and cooked her unpleasing meal—she was no cook and anyway what could you do in one room? The food rapidly disposed of, she stood at the window, staring out. This was the hour of the day when bitterness possessed her, when the world put off its working clothes and donned its glad rags. She opened the narrow wardrobe; there was one dress there she had bought but never worn, a green and gold brocade, very slender and plain, a cocktail dress, the saleswoman had said, looking at her dubiously as though wondering when on earth such a Plain Jane would wear such a garment.

She hadn't known herself, but because the dream must persist

she had bought it and some spindle-heeled light tan shoes with
tiny buckles on them. If ever she did go on TV, got picked for a
quiz, say, or one of those special programmes like ' What's My
Line?' that's what she would wear. She took it down and held it
against herself. Then she laughed abruptly. What opportunities
would there be to wear such a garment in Sheepford?

She found she could not rest. ' I go out sometimes,' she had
said, ' down to the River Gardens. . . .' She hung up the cocktail
dress and tied a scarf around the lank hair. Down by the river
the young couples gathered on the benches for a bit of pleasure
after the old folk and the young mothers had gone home. The
gardens fronted the river and the folk from the Old People's
Home and the almshouses came and sat here in the sunlight
and chatted or just sat and did nothing, remembering the past,
she supposed. A dreadful prospect. The only more dreadful thing
would be to have no past to remember. She reminded herself
valiantly that in a few days her own situation would be very
different, she would have money and a sense of power. ' I could go
abroad like other people—a coach tour—Italy, say,'—there was
magic in the very name—she picked up her handbag and went
out. The sky, that had been so bright and hot earlier in the day
had darkened now, the air seemed thicker; it would be pleasant
to get down to the river and feel a cool breeze blowing off the
water.

She came quietly out of the house, wondering a little as she
passed the closed doors about the lives of the people who slept
and ate there. They weren't all combined rooms, some of them
were real flats, like the one she had visited this afternoon to pick
up the parcel. In the street she found the air was oppressive;
thunder lurking there, and a promise of heavy unrefreshing rain.
She walked into the High Street where life moved fastest. Not
that anything went very fast here. If you wanted excitement
you took the local bus into Richley that had three cinemas,
two espresso bars and quite a number of restaurants that stayed
open until eleven o'clock.

A young man coming out of the Bear and Baiter seemed to
give her a long discriminatory stare, and she put up her head
and pulled at her shortie gloves and felt excitement begin to
burn up in her veins. Fortunately she didn't hear him turn to

the friend who had only stopped to pay their shot and say, 'There's one won't make the price of a night's lodging.' They walked in the other direction and forgot about her at once. Some of the shops here left their lights on all night and she lingered in front of the dress and cosmetic shops, looked at some exotic hairdos and wondered if a permanent would help her.

A couple—they couldn't have been more than seventeen or eighteen—drifted up and the girl, who was small and dark and round and cosy, pointed to one outsize photograph and said, 'There, Les, see what I mean. I bet I'd look smashing with a hairdo like that.'

'You talk a lot of kerfuffle,' said the boy, thrusting her back into the little porch. Aileen saw him press his lips silently, soft as a butterfly, on the young brown cheek. His mouth moved over her face, up to her ear, his arm about her waist tightened.

'Les! You be careful.' There was a whisper of laughter in the smothered voice.

'What of it? There's no one here.'

No one. With her standing by. She might be invisible, a ghost, a Miss Nobody, and, of course, that's just what she was. But not after tomorrow, she thought, furiously, not after tomorrow. Tomorrow would make her a person with some power; the minute Frederick Brown phoned she'd make him realise he wasn't dealing with a softie. Turning away from that couple, now tenderly engrossed, she shot across the road. That, any Bobby can tell you, is how accidents happen. A car, that had been hugging the shadows, suddenly sprang into life and bounded forward; she heard it, only half-realising what it meant. Then for an instant came the paralysing thought, 'It's going to hit me,' and she dodged wildly; someone screamed, the car swerved, then a brake was applied and she heard the squeal of rubber tyres. Fearful immediately that someone was going to attack her verbally for that crazy dash across the road—hadn't she read somewhere of a pedestrian being charged five thousand pounds damages against a third party in a car because of his own carelessness that precipitated an appalling road crash?— she made for the small slope that ran down to the River Gardens. The car driver righted the car and found himself being stared at by a young couple, innocent and startled as fawns.

'That was near,' breathed the girl, the one who'd screamed.

'What made her do it?' asked the driver, tugging his dark hat over his eyes. 'You frighten her or something? You frightened me, come to that,' he added sourly. 'What's the idea? Hiding in corners and yelling blue murder? Trying to put death on the roads or something?'

'Me and my friend happened to be looking in that shop window,' retorted Les, up in arms at once. 'Do you mind? As for putting death on the roads, we don't have to trouble our heads when there's chaps like you going round doing forty-five on a narrow road like this.'

The driver settled himself in his seat. 'Who was she, anyway? Friend of yours?'

'Well, of course not,' said Lou, surprised. 'We didn't really notice her till she suddenly dashed over the road.'

'Lucky for me you were here really,' acknowledged the driver in a grudging voice. 'If there had been an accident you'd be witnesses she bolted like a hare. Not my fault if she had been mown down. Mind you, they ought to put more lights on this road. I didn't even see you as I came along.'

'That wouldn't trouble us,' said Les, and the man grinned and drove away.

'Lucky nothing did happen,' remarked Lou. 'Don't want our names dragged into a police case. I told my dad I was meeting Yvette Saunders tonight.'

'You should stand up to him more,' Les told her tenderly, his cheek against her hair. 'After all, it's not him I'm proposing to marry.'

They forgot about poor Aileen Smith, the driver, the near accident; only when the news was in the papers next day Lou said to herself, 'I wonder if that could be her.' Only, since she couldn't tell the authorities anything, she decided to keep quiet.

Startled by what she believed, correctly, to have been her proximity to death, Aileen went down to the River Gardens and stood looking across to the water. It was funny she hadn't even seen the car, but of course her thoughts had been absorbing. Too bad if something should happen to her just when life was promising to blossom. She opened the upper gate of the gardens and walked slowly in. As a rule there were three or four couples on the benches, and sometimes there was a tramp who used to sneak in for a kip until Mullins, the gardens keeper, locked the gates at 10.30. He always occupied the same bench, the one at the far end quite close to Mullins' cottage, that went with the job; here he'd stretch out in all weathers under a spreading tree, and sleep as easily and unconcernedly as an animal.

It was growing dark now, and darker than usual because of the overcast sky. The other benches were all empty and, indeed, as she walked down toward the water the first drops of rain began to fall. She would have gone back but she feared the car driver might be waiting to accuse her, might even have called a policeman, and, like most people who have never experienced security, she had little faith in the police. They went with the tide, with the settled people, not with the lone cats that walked by themselves.

At the foot of the gardens close by the river there was a large wooden shelter overlooking the water and she hurried toward it. She hadn't thought to bring an umbrella or plastic raincoat. The storm had blown up almost as suddenly as the invisible car had started. Still, one knew these summer storms. Violent while they lasted, they were usually of short duration, and once more, speeding down the gravel path to the shelter, she congratulated herself on the way in which she had kept her life uncluttered by domestic bonds. No one would look up when she came in to say sourly, 'What ages you've been. I thought you were never coming. It's been such a long evening.' And her sense of independence was still too recent for her to guess at a day when she might long to hear that voice, however nasally whining, to be reassured that she had some place, no matter how insignificant, in the pattern.

The shelter was empty, and she sat down and pulled out a packet of cigarettes. She never smoked at work and she wouldn't smoke in her room after, say, eight o'clock because the smell hung about and seemed to taint everything. But she felt quite sophisticated sitting here smoking and staring at the water. The tide was low tonight and in the expanse of mud the water revealed she saw some swans poking and stamping. Astonishing, she reflected, they looked so lovely on the water, as though they were made of alabaster or porcelain, fairy birds, but when you saw them on land on those short black legs and broad black feet, they lost half their grace and charm. Common sense should have told her that such heavy birds needed reinforcing but she didn't think like that.

She looked along the line of the river path and saw that the tramp was there tonight, a conglomerate bundle covered with his immense ragged cloak. She had met him once or twice, though he never spoke or appeared to see her; she wondered why they did it when there was work for all, and the National Insurance had to provide you with shelter and medical care. I suppose he doesn't want to work, is sick of being told to go there and wait here and do this and sign that and come back on Friday and clock in and remember union rules. . . . She felt more sympathy with him tonight than she had ever done before; and it was nice to think there was one other human creature near at hand; she was going to be free herself soon of all that regimentation, she thought. And so, in fact, she was, though not precisely in the way she imagined.

It was cold sitting in the shelter, but the persistent rain kept her where she was. Her shoes weren't made for this kind of weather and it couldn't last. She lit a second cigarette which made her cough a bit. It seemed as though ghosts were crowding around, ghosts of other solitary women who had sat there and smoked defiantly and told themselves how fortunate they were not to have to go dashing back to some invalid parent or querulous husband. And the others who, like her, had dreamed great dreams, and had dissolved into anonymous dust with none of them come to fruition.

It was quite a relief when she heard steps coming down the path. They came quietly, yet there was a deliberation about them that held the attention. She thought, If it's a couple, well, I was here first, and I'm not going to be driven out into the rain to please them. If it's a man and he gets too free I can yell for that old tramp. Not for Mullins, who might have been the original troglodyte for all anyone ever saw of him till 10.30 when he emerged like a hedgehog from a bed of leaves and came waddling around to lock the gates and make sure no one, like that old tramp, for instance, was still in the gardens. The steps came closer and she knew a throb of excited anticipation but a little apprehension, too, so she held her lighted cigarette in her right hand, the glowing tip extended, because the kind of books she had read and films she had seen had taught her that this can be a useful if very temporary weapon.

So for another second she waited for Murder to come in.

As Rhodes had explained to Crook, there was boxing on the television that night, and when the bouts were over the other channel was showing a sports item, so it would have taken a new war to rouse Mullins. He lived alone in the little cottage and daily thanked the God in whom he sketchily believed that his daughter May was in Canada with the soldier who'd been crazy enough to wed her, and no marauding widow had ever managed to dent him. He didn't notice the strength and intensity of the rain until it had stopped. Only when the smiling face split the screen in a final grimace of goodwill and 'see you again next week' did he slowly stretch and go to the window and look out over his domain.

Must have been quite a shower, he ruminated, taking in the dripping leaves and the general damp dark appearance of the flower beds. He looked at his watch. Ten-twenty. Might as well lock up, no one'll be coming here any more tonight.

He stopped by the tramp's bench and shook him. 'Time to go, old-timer,' he said, his language having been coloured and/or debased by too much viewing.

Stephen Grist, who wouldn't have looked out of place in a statuary room at the Victoria and Albert, woke at once, quick and alert as an animal. He was a magnificent specimen, with a shaggy crop of greyish hair falling to his shoulders, and years of sleeping rough, eating when he could and drinking what he pleased, had done nothing to impair his physique.

'Go on,' he said, 'what harm do I do kipping here? You can let me out in the morning before any of the customers turn up.'

But Mullins shook his head. 'Much as my place is worf.'

'Well, how much is it worth?' The old tramp grinned contemptuously, showing teeth that would have been the despair of any dentist anxious to make his fortune.

'House goes with the job,' said Mullins, amazed that so simple a reply hadn't occurred to the old ruin.

'Who wants to live in a box?' asked the tramp. Next to his weather-beaten carven face Mullins looked small and crumpled and colourless, as though, exposed to even a little of the fresh air to which he was practically a stranger, it would dissolve like the faces of mummies unearthed after centuries from their honourable graves.

'I'll expect to find you gone when I've finished me rounds,' said Mullins, looking with distaste up the length of the gardens to the shelter at the top. 'Not likely to be anyone there, but I best look. Someone else might have thought of kipping down— or someone left a kid there. It's a wonder to me they haven't thought of it before. Doorsteps and church porches are about played out by now, I should have thought.'

'It's a funny kid if it's not howling at this hour, unless its mum's been left along of it,' said Stephen Grist, knotting a piece of rope more securely around his middle and preparing to move.

Mullins, who walked in a crablike fashion—he'd been a waiter as a young man home from the 1914 war and had hovered on the fringe of the black market between '43 and '50, till a thoughtless government started removing controls and put him out of business—tottered along in the direction of the shelter. Old Stephen Grist had just reached the lower gate, the one by Mullins' cottage, when a raw shriek stopped him dead.

''Ere, you, old-timer,' he heard. 'Come 'ere.'

Baby attacked him, p'raps, mused the tramp, grinning as he strode back up the path.

Mullins had glanced inside the shelter and found to his surprise a young woman sitting crouched in a corner; she made no sign when he came up and he thought for an instant she must be asleep. 'Here, miss,' he said, but she didn't stir and he decided she had either fainted or had had too much to drink. 'Can't spend the night there, miss,' he insisted. But she still said nothing, and he reflected it must be a faint, so he pulled his light out of his pocket and flashed it at her.

It was then that he let out the shriek that had arrested Stephen Grist and brought him hastening back up the path. A lifetime of living with nature, as you might put it, had hardened the old man's nervous system.

'Scream all you please, you won't wake *her*,' he said. He looked down at the dreadful cyanosed face, the swollen tongue, the starting eyes, with no particular horror. 'It's nasty, that's what it is,' he announced. 'Done deliberate, see.'

'Most times you strangle someone you do it deliberate,' quavered old man Mullins.

'I mean, he must have come along here just to do for her,' the old tramp explained. 'If it had been one of passion's rages, there'd be marks on the throat, and— turn your light a bit— there's none. Chap caught the two ends of her scarf—see— pulled 'em tight. Must have got her to look the other way—that a boat on the water? Who's coming up your side?—something like that, and then—flick. Easy really.'

'You seem to know a lot about it,' said Mullins, his voice still quivering like a sheet of tissue paper in a wind.

'Met a chap once waiting to be topped,' he explained.

'You been inside?' Not that that was surprising, come to think of it.

'No visible means of support,' said the tramp. 'Not prepared to wash steps and weed a path. Once you start that lay you're done. Story gets around. Chap has his pride. This'll be for the police,' he went on with no change of tone.

'Here, you can't go yet,' exclaimed Mullins. 'You're my alibi. You can tell them I never come out of my house all evening.'

'Me?' said the tramp in tones of genuine surprise. 'You could have been dancing on the lawn in your birthday suit and I wouldn't know. I only come in here to kip because they put these nice wide seats in for the old folks, see, and the kids can't bust them up, the way they do the seats along the river. Besides, lots of those don't have backs and backs are a great comfort. But, of course, you wouldn't know.'

'Anyway, you stay 'ere and I'll ring them. And if anyone else should come in . . .'

He hesitated, then ducked his little frightened shabby head and scuttled for his own home. The tramp waited till the door had swung behind him, then he quickly left the gardens by the upper gate. The police, he knew, would come by way of the High Street, and he was a noticeable figure, so he turned right, along the lane running beside the water, pressing in among the shrubs, identifying himself with them as the wild things do, the partridge that sinks so that you may pass within a foot and not know she is there, the stick insect, the wild beast adapting colour, shade and the movement of the undergrowth to its own ends.

'Lock the gates,' said the station officer, 'and don't let that chap go until we come. And don't touch a thing. Not a thing. Understand?'

Mullins gibbered. He'd seen dead bodies during the first war, of course, and accidents now and again, but nothing like this, a girl wandering into his gardens, no beauty even before someone had done that to her, and getting herself murdered. . . . It was the first time he'd let himself use the word.

He locked the near gate and trudged up to fasten the upper one; it was then he discovered Stephen had gone. He stood there, swearing weakly, though he didn't in his heart blame the chap who was lucky enough to be able to duck from under. Not surprising really, he wasn't one for filling in forms and answering questions—'Where's your National Health Card? Where were you last employed? What are you living on? Where did you sleep last night?'—but it did leave him, Mullins, to the full blast of authority's displeasure. Because quite unfairly they seemed to think it was his fault.

'I told you to keep him here till we came,' insisted the pot-faced sergeant.

'By the time you got round to saying that he must have gone,' Mullins told him sullenly. 'A man can't be in two places at once, not even the police, at least not that I've heard.'

'Can't he see this lays him open to suspicion?' the sergeant demanded.

'Crummy, you're not going to try and pin this on the old man?' Mullins sounded shocked. 'If he was that sort, which he isn't, he wouldn't have come back to his bench for another snooze. That's all he came to the gardens for, a place to sleep.'

'What's his work?' asked the sergeant.

'He doesn't work. That's why he's a tramp. Well, it's a free country, isn't it, and if that's the way he likes it . . .'

He had sometimes been heard to hold forth on the lack of citizenship betrayed by men who wouldn't conform, let the other fellow pay the taxes, but there is a kind of unspoken trade unionism operating against the police—very unfair, no doubt, but there it is. He answered the sergeant's question as well as he could, but it was obvious he was not giving much satisfaction. 'No,' he said, 'I don't know who she was. If I'm going to take a note of every chick that comes into the gardens after dark I'll never have time to make myself a cup of tea. I don't say she was never here before, I just say I don't recall her, and somehow she doesn't seem to me the type the boys go for, even before this happened.'

He had been stuck in front of the telly all the evening, ever since he washed up after his welsh rarebit.

'No, I didn't notice anyone,' he repeated violently. 'I was in my house, I'm not a court of morals, all I have to do is see the regulations are kept and no indecency takes place.'

'Has anything been touched?' demanded the sergeant.

'Well, not by me.'

'How about this tramp—what's his name, do you know?'

'I call him old-timer. Grist's the name, I think, but I don't know anything about him. He never makes any trouble that I know of, just lies down on a bench and has a bit of a sleep. Well, these gardens are meant for the old people, aren't they?'

They found him an unhelpful witness, in fact he could tell them nothing. There was no clue to the girl's identity in her handbag, an envelope-shaped plastic affair that could be bought for under a pound in almost any big store. (Aileen had a theory that it was unwise to carry any note of your name or address in your bag. Suppose someone attacked you and got hold of your address he might hang about waiting for you. If you asked her who, she'd have said vaguely, 'Teen-agers or hoodlums,' though in fact she had never been disturbed by either.) Handkerchief, plain, unmarked, a cheap powder compact, lipstick ditto, a plastic purse with a little change in it, no wallet, no envelope, nothing.

'That chap, Grist, he might have removed something,' the sergeant reflected aloud.

'What, for the bit of cash she might be carrying, a girl like

III

that?' Mullins sounded scornful. 'I tell you, if the old-timer wanted money that bad he'd work for it. He's not like you or me, he's an educated man.'

'Someone 'ull report it if she doesn't get back,' said the sergeant. 'If she comes from Sheepford, that is.'

'No one 'ud come over from Richley on a night like this,' retorted Mullins. 'There's not much to do at Sheepford. No engagement ring,' he added, 'and no one's touched her watch.'

It wasn't much of a night for the routine boys to do their stuff, and photographing for fingerprints was a thankless job when you realised how many people had probably used the shelter during the past twenty-four hours, but once the doctor had seen the body, declared the deceased had died from strangulation in the manner pointed out by Grist, probably during the past two hours, they got out their cameras and did what they could. An ambulance came and took the body away to the mortuary at Richley—Sheepford was too small to boast such an institution—and the usual report was made to the coroner. There was no record at the police station of anyone reporting a girl missing, but it wasn't yet midnight. As a matter of fact, no one in the house where she lodged even knew that Aileen had been out that evening. She could have gone away for a week without attracting much attention. One thing seemed obvious, that she was a respectable girl and that robbery and/or sexual interference was not the motive for the crime. That was as far as the police got that night.

TWELVE

Poor Aileen Smith who had longed for notice during her life received publicity enough after she was dead. It was the next morning before she was identified. Then the paragraph in the local paper to the effect that a woman had been found strangled in the shelter in the gardens brought a number of visitors to the mortuary, one of whom soon supplied her address.

'Lives at Acacia House,' she said. 'I've seen her going in and out.' No, she didn't know her, nobody knew her. Had a job, said the tenants of the ground-floor flat, went to London every day, no friends that they knew of, but often went out of an evening. Since they genuinely couldn't conceive of any girl going out just to walk along the river bank and watch the swans or sit on a bench and read, they supposed she went out to meet some man. She had never, so far as anyone knew, brought anyone back to the room. Most of those who heard about her sized up the case as one more silly girl fishing in waters that were too deep for her. Sheepford was law-abiding enough, goodness knows, nothing there for an ardent young reporter to get his teeth into, but river banks were notorious and if a girl wandered about alone after dark, well, she was asking for whatever came to her.

The old people, to whom the gardens were a daily boon, told each other, in offended tones, that if she had to get herself murdered she might have had more tact than to meet death on what they regarded as their domain. No consideration, they agreed; the whole of the river bank, bushes and ditches and bits of waste ground galore, but no, she had to come into their gardens and—well, say what you like, murder isn't nice. One or two of the old dears even announced their intention of staying away from the gardens for the future. Never know who you may meet—though they were always gone like cuckoos in August before the darkness fell.

Another, more spirited, said, 'Might chance my luck down there. Many a good tune played on an old fiddle.' Not being angels but ordinary selfish human beings, they thought of her death from their personal standpoint. There was some speculation as to whether the dead girl was pregnant, which might provide a motive for the crime, but the medical evidence demolished that. Innocent as the day she was born, so why kill the poor creature? She wasn't a person of any consequence. Might be blackmailing someone, they said. And what sort of job did she have? She never talked about it, and she never got letters and that's a funny thing. People have relatives or friends or responsibilities; and no one rang her up, either. So far as any human creature could be a shadow, Aileen Smith had achieved that inglorious end.

And then Mr Crook came galumphing into the picture. It was Kay who put him on the scent. When she opened her *Morning Record* and saw that a girl had been found murdered in Sheepford, memory said, 'Sheepford? Where have I just heard that name?' and remembered Aileen Smith. After that she hadn't any doubt at all, even before she read about the thick-lensed spectacles found on the floor beneath the seat. She rang up Mr Crook, and he said, 'Well, you have to hand it to the chap, he doesn't waste any time. Been onto the cops yet?'

'No. I thought I'd tell you first. I could be wrong.'

'The sun could rise in the West, but you'd have to turn all Nature's rules upside down to achieve it,' was Crook's vigorous reply. 'No, this 'ull be our Miss Smith all right. I'll have a word with Perrin.'

'They won't want me to identify her, will they? I only saw her that once.'

'In any case you won't go down there on your loneyo,' Crook promised her. 'Y'see, this has become a hanging matter now. Multiple murder. They could have poisoned Caroline C. or chucked her out of a window or run her down by a car or chopped her head off, but none of those are capital crimes, not unless she's a lady policeman in disguise, which somehow I don't think she is. No, don't tell me we don't know where she is. Just take my word for it that when she does surface she won't need anyone's attention but the undertaker's. Same way they could have choked poor Aileen Smith and got away with about ten years, but the two together spell the rope.' It never occurred to him that the two deaths weren't connected. 'Stay where you are, sugar, till I ring you back. By the way, where's your young man?'

'I never said . . .' Kay sounded staggered.

'I know you didn't, but don't try and pull the wool over my eyes. Of course you've got a chap even if you don't wear a ring.'

'He's in America, doing very important work. It was a special job.'

'You write him an airmail and tell him there's a still more special job waiting for him in London, and if that don't bring him back you give him the air.'

'You're serious over this, aren't you?' said Kay.

'Oh, have a lick of common sense,' begged Crook. 'One woman's missing, presumed killed; we've got a second corpse. You've been monkeying about with their property—how much more evidence do you want that you're the next on the list?'

'They can't be sure of that—that I changed the hats, I mean.'

'You don't know you're born,' Crook told her kindly. 'That type doesn't take any chances, give the other fellow the benefit of the doubt. And, to be frank with you, it won't do you any good when it's known you're in cahoots with me. It's an odd thing, the police don't like me and the criminals don't like me, either, like that chap denied by heaven and hell. Now, remember, sugar, if anyone comes asking questions you play it dumb. Do you know where this chap of yours is?—the States is a large place.'

'He's with the Mortimore people in New York, it's a terribly important assignment. . . .'

'Too important to come back and keep a loverly eye on you? Or don't you rate that high?'

She looked as if she'd like to clout him.

'Now look, in his place I wouldn't thank an old buffer like me for taking on his girl. You write him, better still send him a cable, and till he comes back for you, you stay nice and safe behind your own door.'

Because he didn't trust janes as far as he could see them the cunning old so-and-so sent a cable to Bryan Forbes on his own account. 'Come back pronto if you want your girl outside of a coffin, Murder Inc. on the trail,' he said, and signed it Crook. Even if his name didn't ring a bell, and modestly he agreed there was no special reason why it should, the fellow could at least spring a few dollars to ring up his lady love, and then, hey presto! He'd be a match for Murder Inc., whoever they might be, and Nature, intoned Mr Crook piously, never meant me to be a nursemaid. The fact that the old firm might come gunning for him didn't cross his mind; he'd accepted that possibility as an occupational risk years and years ago.

In Sheepford Les said to Lou, 'See about this girl in the shelter? Sounds like the one nearly run under that car last night. Anyway, she was wearing fancy peepers.'

'Seems like her,' said Lou.

'Well, when you see someone nearly killed—Lou, I got an idea.'

'Hold onto it,' said Lou politely.

'You remember that car suddenly came whizzing through —from nowhere? Well, where did it come from?'

'The top of the High Street, I suppose,' said Lou, obtusely.

'I didn't see it—not unless it was ambushed around the corner in Park Lane, and where's the sense of anyone hanging around there?'

'Nice bit of dark,' suggested Lou, dimpling.

'But the chap was alone. There wasn't any bird with him.'

'P'raps he was waiting for a pickup.'

'Funny way to do it, try to run a girl down. Anyway, she didn't look that sort. Lou, I told you I had an idea. Say he meant to do for her, tried out a hit-and-run attempt . . .'

'You're mad, darling,' said Lou. 'Chaps don't try and commit murder with witnesses on the side.'

'What witnesses?'

'Well, you and me—or don't we count?'

'He didn't see us—we were standing under the porch of that shop. He said as much. No, he thought he had the scene to himself and it not being much of an evening and there not being a lot to do in Sheepford at the best of times, he hoped to get away with it. There wasn't anyone else about because if there had been they'd have showed up. I'd have said that girl would never have been nearer death than she was that minute.'

'You did, Les,' Lou reminded him.

'So he meant to get her.'

'We don't know that,' Lou insisted.

'Well, someone did—get her, I mean. There weren't many people around. Pity I didn't notice the number of the car. It was a Martin Tourer, I could see that.'

'She wasn't killed by a car,' Lou insisted.

'Thanks to you behaving like a screech owl. But if that was his idea, no reason he'd ditch it because the first attempt didn't come off. Look at it this way, Lou. Who goes alone into those gardens at night?'

'Girls like that Aileen Smith.'

'We don't know that she did go alone. She might have gone to meet someone—no, though, because in that case she wouldn't have been hanging around the shop window. Besides, it was a bit late for a meeting. Probably didn't want to get wet and saw the shelter and made a beeline for it.'

'And he had second sight and knew she was coming.'

'He didn't have to be there first. Good lord, Lou, don't you ever look at the telly? He could have drawn up farther down and watched where she went. I mean, if you want to kill some-one, you don't give up and go home to a nice cup of cocoa just 'cause you don't win out the first time. Concentration, that's the word.'

'You mean '—Lou's charming little pussy-cat face was pale—' he saw her go in and went after her? Why didn't she scream?'

'I suppose she might have. No one was likely to hear. Unless there was someone in the shelter, there wasn't likely to be any-one in the gardens. And if there had been I don't suppose X would have taken the chance. Besides, if there'd been anyone there they'd have noticed. There was a piece in the local rag about the place being deserted except for a tramp asleep—well, we know that one. Nothing short of the trump of doom would wake him.'

'You don't think he . . .?'

'Murder isn't a bit of occupational therapy,' said Les with less truth than he knew, since that's just what it is to people like Murder Inc.

In any case the police had already exonerated Stephen Grist. The rain that had been falling heavily had turned the gravel paths into excellent print recorders, and there was only one mark of Grist's feet, going to the shed with Mullins' alongside, and none of his returned to the bench where he had been sleep-ing.

'You're not thinking of going to the police, Les?' asked Lou and now she really did look alarmed.

'If there's a murderer going round Sheepford—why, it could be you next.'

'See me hiding away in a shelter waiting to be killed?'

'No, but you could be crossing a road. I'm in earnest about this. That chap knows there were two of us because we came out of the porch when he pulled up; I don't say he'd recognise us again, the lighting in Sheepford isn't much, not even in the High Street as he remarked, but if he thinks there's a chance of us putting two and two together . . .'

'Dad won't like the idea of me being dragged into the courts,' said Lou uneasily.

'Better than coming down to identify you in the mortuary, I suppose. Lou, don't you see you could be in danger? Nobody knows who this fellow is. Nobody saw what happened but us. There could be another accident, a real one this time—one that comes off I mean. . . .'

Lou's father was junior partner at an architect's firm, he didn't approve of his daughter going out with Les, whose old man kept a filling station and garage on the Huntersby Road. One day Les would step into his shoes, and very warm and comfortable they'd be. But Lou's father, who was a Tory to the backbone and believed in Bring Back Capital Punishment and Keep Britain White looked higher for her. 'There isn't going to be any high or low by the time my children grow up,' Lou protested. 'Maybe,' said Mr Rayne, 'only I don't want your children to have a garage hand for their father.'

Les' father believed in no such nonsense. As soon as he had heard his son's story he grabbed his hat, told the assistant to hold the fort, and took Les along to the station.

'I'm not going to have my son grilled for trying to help the law,' he said. 'But I'm not going to be grilled myself for keeping your mouth shut when it ought to be open.'

Kay had already identified the dead girl and told the police the little she knew about her by the time Les and his father arrived.

By the time they reached the station with their story of the runaway driver in Sheepford High Street, matters had advanced a step farther. Les said he hadn't really seen the man properly, because he was wearing a hat pulled over his face (anyway it was the darkest part of the High Street, which was the reason, of course, why he and Lou had chosen it, as the police realised, though neither side referred to this) and must have been an ace driver to pull up the way he did. He was driving a Martin Tourer. Les hadn't noticed the number, and he didn't pay any attention to the chap's further movements. He'd gone on down the hill. Yes, he agreed, that was in the direction of the river. He and Lou had gone along to an espresso later and they hadn't given him any further thought.

The police saw Lou as a matter of routine, but she couldn't help them, either. She had been standing behind Les and had been thinking more about the girl than the driver of the car.

The police didn't like it. Here was a short dark man—Les said he seemed certainly no more than average height from the little he'd seen—turning up once again, and wherever he went trouble went with him. First appearance—Miss Chisholm's flat—and Miss Chisholm vanished. Second appearance—in the mews outside the workshop, and the contents of Louise were stealthily removed. And now at the wheel of a car, and a girl who might prove tiresome to a short dark man was found strangled near by.

The supposition that the car seen at Sheepford was the one that had been removed earlier in the day from Brandon Street was too strong to be denied. Rhodes, interviewed, said he was certain it had been there when he went out to do a job near by at about 10.30 in the morning. Crook had left the Superb at a garage around the corner for a minor overhaul, so he hadn't noticed the car was missing when he returned. It followed, there-fore, that someone had removed it between 10.30 a.m. and say, 5.30 p.m. It was possible that Smith herself had been given the keys and had driven it away, but it seemed to Crook—and to the police—at least as probable that the short dark man had calmly picked his time and removed it. By this time, no doubt, the plates had been changed, it might even have been resprayed. In that case it could be locked in a private garage, abandoned at some place a considerable distance from Sheepford or Brandon Street, or ditched somewhere. The sensible thing would be to keep it in a private garage. It was going to be difficult for the police to examine every lockup in the country. Of course they could circularise the garages in case it had been brought in, and ditto the second-hand dealers.

But as it happened they didn't have to put themselves out, because the very next day the missing car came to light.

THIRTEEN

It was discovered at a remote place on the East Coast called Benton Cove, by a zombie type named Trayson, whose redoubtable old mother had a stall in the local fish market. The zombie went out very early in the morning, whenever the tide was right, to dredge for a certain kind of shellfish that his mother sold. The tides on this part of the coast were treacherous and unpredictable, the current running very strong and the rocks rising from patches of sinking sand that occasioned the local authorities to put up danger boards all along the cliff. About a year previously there had been a local tragedy in which two young men, visiting the neighbourhood, had been caught and killed by the pitiless sands. The zombie, as shapeless as if he had been made out of a ball of string, had an animal wit lacking in those silly strangers who came over in charabancs or private cars to look at the famous sands. No one was quite sure of his age, which might be anything from twenty to forty; the old mother looked as if she had been carved out of granite and discovered in a cave, perhaps a generation earlier. The zombie had only been known to voice one wish all through his life—he wanted to own a car. Girls, animals, the drink, none of these registered, but his simple mind, as unfurnished as an empty room, ran on a dream in which he miraculously acquired a car.

When he came pushing around the bend in the cliffs, for he knew precisely where the best crayfish were to be found, he was brought up short by the sight of a car wrecked on the great rocks that were said to have been split by the Ice Age and were known as the Black Icicles. He knew nothing of any missing car—in fact there had been nothing about it as yet in

the press—but if there had been it would have made no difference to him, since reading and writing to him implied work
without pay. He recognised that it was a Martin—you couldn't
fault him on this one subject—and his slow blood boiled to see
something that represented all the wealth of the world to him
treated with such savagery. He didn't think that a wrecked
car in such circumstances presumably involved a dead body.
He only thought someone drove that over the cliff—murdered
it.

He stood considering, his slow mind brooding on the problem.
Full tide last night had been between seven and eight o'clock.
The car must have come over the cliffs some time in the late
evening or very early morning. Hanging his pailful of crayfish
on a hook of rock and carefully securing his net, he climbed as
agile as a monkey over the intervening rocks. Scrambling like a
mountain sheep he pulled himself over to where the car precariously hung. He crouched down, touching the chassis reverently with his enormous hands. He almost looked as though he
expected to pick it up and carry it ashore on his own shoulders.
Then his eye moving downward, for he was never wholly
unaware of the work he had been sent out to do, he saw something that glinted in the steely morning light. Something silver,
feminine, useless. But because he was accustomed to picking up
every sort of salvage—in addition to getting his crayfish he
helped in a salvage yard for a small wage and a share of anything that wasn't wanted that he could transform into something else only he could desire—he climbed carefully down
and took it in his hand. Then he almost dropped it. For his
treasure was a flat-backed plain silver hand glass, and when he
turned it over he saw it was cracked all across the surface.

A cracked glass was worse than useless, it brought bad luck,
even to handle it might prove a misfortune. But because it was
the most delicate thing he had ever touched he could not lay it
aside. There was a single letter, all flourishes and folly, set in a
medallion on the back; he tried to trace it with his big finger.
He had gone to the village school and learned his letters but it
was hard for him even to spell out the name of a road or a
house, and memory served him better than his dim wits. C, he
thought. Or that other letter that was so confusedly like it—

G. If the glass hadn't been smashed, someone with a name begin-ning with either letter might have given him a few shillings for it. This wasn't the usual trash they got in the salvage yard. It was bright, couldn't have been there long. And anyway he knew it hadn't been there the day before. He might have missed the glass, he could never have missed the car.

The sea racing in with a kind of savage buoyancy recalled him to everyday life. Scrambling back over the rock, the glass pressed against his side, he regained his pail. There were fewer crayfish in it than his usual but he'd show Mum the glass, she might like to have it or at least know where to get the best price. In any case it would be useless to go on looking for cray-fish. When the tide came in at this roaring pace it put a stop to all fishing or dredging. He found his pail and net and made his way up the shelving shingly beach. Here he waited until he heard the sound of wheels and a truck full of air servicemen flashed around the corner. He stopped it by standing in the middle of the road. He was instantly recognised.

'Loopy Sam,' said the sergeant. 'Tired of life at last.'

When they could make out what he was trying to tell them, two of the men went with him to the cliffs. The car was clearly visible, though on that deserted coast it might have been days before it was discovered.

'Any signs of a body?' they asked, but Loopy shook a vague head. He had hidden the silver hand glass under his coat and hoped no one would notice he had got it.

'Don't envy the chaps who're going to raise that,' said the sergeant. 'Got itself wedged between a pair of boulders that must have been there since the Ice Age. What you got under your coat, Loopy?'

The zombie shook his head and backed angrily. As the ser-geant came closer he uttered a growl.

'O.K.,' said the sergeant. 'But don't say we didn't warn you.'

What puzzled him was what a car was doing on the cliff edge after dark. There was a perfectly good motoring road about a quarter of a mile inland, and even if the driver had lost his way the surface of the cliff would surely warn him of danger. The truck went on to alert the police, the sergeant remaining with Loopy Sam. He stood staring over the sea, barren and steel-grey in the unwinking morning light. He longed suddenly for something to break the monotony, a school of porpoises, even the fin of a shark would be something, so long as you were safe on shore. Then the police came up—they were Benton chaps, not the local Sergeant Hibbs, a slow jolly chap who always rendered 'Father O'Flynn' at the local concert—asking questions and frightening the zany out of his wits.

'He's all right,' said the sergeant sturdily. 'Lives with his mum in the sort of hovel you wouldn't bed your dog in, meet him prawning in the mornings when the tide's right. He saw the car and stopped the truck.'

'Just how we're going to get that up is nobody's business,' said the police sergeant. 'People who're going to have accidents should have a bit more consideration. Any sign of bodies?' he added.

The R.A.F. sergeant shook his head. 'Open car, probably chucked out, and whether it was male or female probably won't be known till the sea gives up its dead.' He hesitated, then added, 'That chap picked up something, don't know what it is, might be helpful.'

When they saw Loopy's mirror they said that proved one thing, the driver had been a woman.

'Queer sort of woman,' said the sergeant, 'carrying a great mirror like that about with her. Someone should tell her you put your things into a bag.' But, of course, the impetus of the fall could have crashed open the locks and scattered the contents—only, in that case, where was all the rest of the debris?

'Tide won't float that off,' said one of the policemen in assured tones.

How did he find the mirror? the sergeant wondered.

'Isn't there a lookout being kept for a Martin Tourer this colour?' one of the police officers recalled. 'Belonging to a lady from London.'

When they checked up they found the numbers didn't tally, but they reported it just the same. The authorities salvaged it in due course at some risk to official life and limb and it was taken back to Benton on a truck. No one in the neighbourhood was reported missing, and an expert declared that the licence plates had recently been changed. Then the silver hand glass with C on it was found to tally with a silver-backed clothes brush found on the dressing table of the missing woman's flat, and that was really the first bit of the puzzle they managed to get into place. Next, Rhodes was asked to examine the car; he had washed it pretty regularly during the eighteen months of Miss Chisholm's tenancy and he had no hesitation in recognising it. 'See that burn on the cover on the back seat?' he pointed out. 'Some passenger did that, I remember her pointing it out to me. I said she could surely claim it under the insurance and I wouldn't be surprised to know she did, but she didn't replace the cover.' The odd thing was that there was no luggage found; the boot was empty except for some newspapers and a rug. If Miss Chisholm had intended to clear out she had done so with the minimum of paraphernalia. The car being an open one, any luggage could have been pitched out and lost in the sands—only that didn't explain the hand mirror. It was Crook who suggested that perhaps the car had been empty when it pitched over the cliffs.

FOURTEEN

The case of the missing milliner was proving a tough mouthful for Inspector Perrin. He knew that the car found at Benton Cove had belonged to Miss Chisholm, but he had no evidence how it had got to Benton. It seemed probable that it was the same car that had been used in the murder attempt on Aileen Smith. The licence plates on it when found were traced to an ancient Morris recently disposed of for scrap. The police followed up this clue but it led them nowhere. Inquiries made in the Benton neighbourhood brought little more satisfaction. The cove was a solitary spot where, but for the incidence of the zombie prowling for crayfish, a car could go over the cliff and remain unnoticed for days. The currents were notoriously dangerous and small boats seldom rounded that corner of the coast; similarly no bathing was permitted there and even the hotheads who like risking their miserable lives in order to get a thrill were repelled by the notion of those shivering sands.

The cove stood two miles from the town of Benton, a flourishing market centre, with lines going to London and to the North. A train left for the metropolis at about midnight, and this was usually more than half full; a stranger travelling by it would attract no attention unless he put himself out to do so. Regulars on that line had noticed nothing unusual. Any fit person could ditch the car, walk the two miles into Benton and return to London before morning. There was a milk train just after four and on this he might be noticed if he were unusually well dressed, say, or in any way remarkable.

'But he don't have to be unusually well dressed,' Crook demurred. 'He don't even have to be a little clean-shaved chap with dark hair. There's wigs and those disfiguring scars you get at kids' puzzle shops, there's hair dyes, there's fake moustaches. No one's explained to me the biggest puzzle of all, and that is why a lady packs a large silver-backed hand mirror in her car all on its lonesome.'

There was still remarkably little information about the woman who had run a crook hat shop under the trade name of Louise. Inquiries at Somerset House had elicited no information regarding a marriage that could conceivably have been hers, but even that proved little. It merely showed that Caroline Chisholm had not married in her own name and her own country, but did nothing to disprove the theory that she had married abroad, possibly under a false name. The fact that no one knew the name of the man, her alleged husband, increased the difficulties of the authorities. They had worked around to Mrs Dodds, but her memory was more haywire than ever. Now, in addition to Schmidt, Fischer and Braun, she had suggested Meyer and Stein.

'The fact is, the woman's more than half round the bend,' Perrin confided wrathfully to his subordinates. 'Or else she's got the idiot notion that it's no end of a game trying to pull the official leg.'

The missing woman appeared to have no friends and no acquaintances sufficiently interested to come forward. There were clients, of course, but the few who had surfaced had been unable to give the police any assistance.

With the exception of the Dodds woman, Caroline Chisholm might have been born the day she moved into Brandon Street. Even her birth certificate was in some doubt. A number of women of that name had been born more or less in the appropriate year, but not all these could be traced. Crook wasn't surprised at the situation. He knew that women disappear every year without there being any hue and cry for them; and every so often the police find themselves with a body no one can or will identify. Family ties are broken by death or indifference, people move around, change their country, even their continent.

'What's cooking?' Crook would ask with maddening brightness when he encountered Perrin on his home ground. 'Who blotted the lady out?' Because officially she wasn't dead, not without a corpse or at least enough circumstantial evidence to presume death.

'Surprises me you can't tell us,' growled Perrin.

A short while later it was to surprise Crook also.

That morning's mail included a cable from Bryan Forbes, a stiff prickly affair, like a paper hedgehog, that announced, 'Am communicating with my fiancée direct. Forbes.'

'*Anglice*, keep off the grass,' Crook told himself. He banged on Kay's door as he went downstairs.

'Your young Romeo,' he said.

'What about him?' Her eyes were very bright and direct. 'Not heard?'

'Certainly I've heard. He wants me to go and stay with his mother at Pursey.'

'Country?' guessed Mr Crook intelligently. 'Ah, that's tough. Still, it won't be for long. Only till Romeo comes back.'

'A matter of seven weeks,' Kay agreed.

'Here, hold it. It don't take seven weeks to come back from the States. These jet machines . . .'

'He's not coming back from the States, not till the job's finished,' Kay said gently, with that gentleness that precedes a storm. 'What he's doing is very, very important. He says so. Look.' She held out a cable form and he read : 'Regret impossible change plans immediately. Suggest your going Mother till trouble blows over. Bryan.'

'He's going to be a nice careful husband,' Crook assured her. 'Thrifty and not chucking his money about.' It had occurred to him at once that a really devoted chap would have shouted, 'To hell with the expense,' and bought one more word—Love—it was staggering the difference a little thing like that made to a girl who was presumably over the moon for the absent swain.

'Who's Mother?' asked Crook.

'Mother is Lady Julia Forbes. She'll be as pleased to see me as if I was a serpent wriggling through her letterbox.'

'Snake charmer?' suggested Mr Crook brightly.

'You're so witty,' taunted Kay. 'Mother thought Bryan should marry into the peerage or at least someone with a fortune in cotton or—or something.'

'Something,' agreed Mr. Crook. 'There's no fortunes in cotton any more, not in the Old Country. Well, here's your chance to convert the old battle-axe. Yes, of course you can. I never knew a dame yet couldn't do a thing if she gave her mind to it.'

'It doesn't matter,' said Kay in so airy a voice that he realised she was sick with disappointment at her lover's reaction. 'Because I'm not going.'

'Oh, come now,' expostulated Crook. 'I can see you might be a bit put out but it's playin' it a bit dirty to go and commit suicide just because your Romeo can't tear himself away from Big Business at the drop of a hat.'

'Who said anything about suicide? To hear you talk anyone would think we were living in the age of Sherlock Holmes when serpents really did come through letterboxes.'

'I don't know about letterboxes,' Crook agreed, 'but the serpents are still there, if nowadays they're more likely to wear bowler hats and carry dispatch boxes. No, you go along to— where does the old lady live?'

'At The Manor House, Pursey; and she's not an old lady. She's fifty-three. And it's not really a manor house. It's the lodge, rechristened. The big house went long ago.'

'Snugger,' insisted Mr Crook optimistically. 'You be guided by your Uncle Arthur, sugar. Ring the lady up . . .'

'She won't have a telephone. She says if people want to see her the least they can do is write a letter. She calls telephones commercial.'

'Well, does she deign to open telegrams? Send her a wire, then, and take your cable along with you. Not that she won't be expecting you, dear Bryan will have sent her a duplicate, you mark my words. Probably counting the hours till you arrive. What's Pursey like?'

'A little island surrounded by seas of desolation. At least one change, if you get the express, and two if you miss it.'

'All the better. Less chance for X to come prowling. Now you let her know you're on your way and pack your grip. Travel second class, if possible in a Ladies Only. We don't want any of this British stiff-upper-lip-and-travelling-solo and who's-afraid-of-the-Big-Bad-Wolf spirit. The more people in your carriage the better, and if there are kids that 'ud be best of all. Kids don't have nice feelings like their demented elders, if anyone tries to commit a murder when they're around they'll howl —most likely with appreciation—but at least they won't sit quiet and refined behind their newspapers and carefully not see the chap wipe the blood off his flick-knife. Now take that black look off your face and remember I've forgotten more about skulduggery than you'll ever know.'

He got her promise, reluctant, unconvinced, but he got it. 'Of course what's burning her up is that young Romeo didn't drop everything and come over,' he told himself. 'He's not going to be much of a husband for her if he's going to put business before pleasure.'

It wasn't that he had anything against business, but you must hold the balance true. For himself his work needed everything he'd got; he never missed romance in his own life because if he'd met it face to face he wouldn't have recognised it, and anyway the minute it saw him coming it went down a side street, which, in his view, was very accommodating of it. No one wants to be rude if it can be avoided.

He had a bit of trouble getting the Superb away from the pavement, because they were delivering coke at no. 2, which showed it was the first of the month. Rhodes was standing by, counting the sacks.

'Can't be too careful,' he told Crook. 'When I was at a block of flats Hampstead way, before I came along here, I got landed once with seventeen sacks instead of twenty. And, of course, it was all my fault.'

The delivery man grinned. 'Wonder to me you don't weigh the sacks,' he said. 'You town chaps . . .'

'What's wrong with us town chaps?' asked Mr Crook quickly.

'Well, I'm a countryman myself, only the government took away my job. "We'll find you something else," they said. Unproductive, they called it. Just how productive is it paying M.P.s a thousand pounds and expenses, but no one ever thinks of shutting down the House.'

'Lots of people do,' Mr Crook assured him. 'Only not M.P.s.'

The man grinned and continued on his leisurely way.

'Here, how much longer are you going to be?' Crook wanted to know. 'I've got to get to work.'

'Shan't be much longer.' The coalie shot another sack of coke down the chute.

'Sixteen,' said Rhodes.

'Miss Carter's going for a little trip to the country,' said Crook affably. 'Going to get better acquainted with her prospective ma-in-law.'

'I'd sooner stay here and take my chance,' said Rhodes simply. 'I had one of those once—didn't last long, my girl just floated off with some Yank and I put up the bolt and didn't draw it again for a fortnight. I always thought it was the old lady's fault. If you marry a woman you don't marry her whole family. . . .'

'That's just where you're wrong,' said Crook.

They talked for a minute or two, then Rhodes signed for the coal, crossed the disappointed man's hand with silver, and said 'O.K., Mr Crook, I'll remember what you said,' and Crook hopped into the Superb and dashed away.

In her flat Kay packed a small case, because, whatever Mr Crook might think, she wasn't going to spend seven weeks with that old sourpuss, Lady Julia Forbes; telephoned an agent from whom she got commissions giving her change of address, very temporary, she said; put paint and paper and pencils on top of the case and snapped it down, wrote out a note for the milkman, wrote out her address for Rhodes to forward letters and reminded herself to ask him to stop the papers. One thing, Lady J. would dislike the invasion as much as she herself disliked being the invader. Then she went to the window and looked out, feeling rather like someone who's been unexpectedly condemned to a long term of penal servitude.

'Interfering old nanny goat,' she muttered. Crook would have been shocked to hear her. He'd been called a lot of things in his time, but never that before.

Of course, as Crook had realised, she wasn't sharpening her dagger to stick into him but into that laggard in love, Bryan Forbes. She told herself resolutely she was unreasonable to expect him to drop everything like a hot potato and come beetling back across the Atlantic just to be at her side. Yet she'd imagined he'd come whirling on the heels of a cable with a special licence in his pocket, drag her around to the nearest registry office, and whizz her back to New York. That was the kind of romance girls wanted these days, not immense showy weddings with bridesmaids all quarelling because the colour chosen for their dresses was sure to be unbecoming to one at least. She wondered what Lady Julia Forbes would say when she turned up. Presumably Bryan had cabled her, too, but just in case he hadn't she sent a telegram: 'Arriving 2.40. Kay.'

It was odd how Crook's apprehension had affected her, she really did begin to have bloody thoughts. In the old detective stories you hailed a taxi and the driver was a thug. She had just locked her case when the bell rang. She hesitated in the hall, then called out, 'Who is it?'

'It's me, Miss Carter. Rhodes.'

'Oh.' She opened the door. 'I'm getting as jittery as a barn-door fowl,' she acknowledged.

'Not surprising,' said Rhodes, who looked as serious as Crook had done. 'Are you ready?'

'Ready?'

'Well, Mr Crook said you were going to the country.'

'And you've been nominated nursemaid, I suppose.'

For the first time since he had known her she seemed thoroughly out of temper.

Rhodes—wouldn't you have guessed it?—supported Crook. Men always gang up against females.

'He's right, Miss Carter. You give yourself a bit of a holiday till this trouble blows over.'

'And how long's that going to be?'

'Well, with Mr Crook and that inspector on my tail I'd melt away like a shadow,' Rhodes admitted. 'Packed yet?'

She nodded. 'I've missed the 9.15 express but I may as well go on the slow train with the two changes. It doesn't get there till after two but the only other quick train doesn't go till 2.30. I shan't need a taxi for this one bag, I'll go on the Underground.'

'No need to do that,' said Rhodes. 'I've got a car at the door.'

Kay's eyes smouldered. 'Is that another of Mr Crook's brilliant ideas?'

'You can't blame him for thinking of his reputation. It's all he's got.'

'His reputation?'

'Well, your safety as well, but the two go together. Already the police are saying that if he hadn't jumped in head first, gone around and seen that girl, she might still be alive.'

'How very unfair!' Now she was Crook's supporter again.

'Yes, well . . .' He stooped and collected the bags, and they went down the stairs. Some bits of coke still littered the pavement.

'Remember the war?' said Rhodes. 'Well, no, of course you wouldn't. But I remember seeing some old girl nip out of a house after coal had been delivered down the road, and collect a few bits that had been left in the gutter. Do you know they nicked her? Oh, yes, coal was our lifeblood or something and she was a vampire for taking it.'

'But that was crazy.' She got into a little blue car that had a Hospital Car Service label on the front window. 'What's that in aid of?' she demanded.

'Mr Crook's idea. No one's going to try and ram an H.C.S. car.'

'He thinks of everything, doesn't he? Rhodes, doesn't it ever occur to him that X may be gunning for him?'

'If you were in the war, Miss Carter, you'd know that no chap at the front ever really saw himself being killed—other men, yes, but not him. Oh, I don't say a few poets and so forth, but not the average man. I know, I was there myself.'

They drove off.

He wouldn't let her sit beside him. 'You're supposed to be sick,' he pointed out, so she let him have his way.

They hadn't been long on the road when she was sitting erect, staring out of the window.

'This isn't the way to Charing Cross,' she said. Then she laughed angrily. 'No, don't tell me, Mr Crook's had another bright idea. You're to take me to Pursey and deliver me in person.'

'I've never known him in a state like this about anyone,' Rhodes confessed. 'The car was his idea. When he found you couldn't get the express—you know how they say things go in threes? Well, we've had two mysteries—Miss Chisholm and Miss Smith . . .'

'And he's afraid it's going to be a case of Three Corpses Lay Out on the Shining Sands . . . I only wonder he didn't insist on driving me down himself.'

'Well!' Rhodes sounded faintly shocked. 'He has got other clients.'

'Lady Julia will think I've had a mental collapse, probably think you're a warder or something.'

'If she knows her onions she'll be glad to see you in one piece.'

'Lady Julia doesn't like onions, she thinks they're vulgar. You suppose it occurred to Mr Crook that X might be on our tail?'

'Well, why should he be?' argued Rhodes. 'Did you tell anyone where you were going—bar Mr Crook?'

'No. Mrs Sagan was out, I thought I might send her a picture postcard, she's enjoying this like mad.'

'Well, if you haven't told her or anyone else—you can't think this Lady Julia is mixed up in it?'

Lady Julia, who resembled one of Ivy Compton-Burnett's terrifying matrons, looked sinister enough to be mixed up in anything, Kay reflected. 'I really think if anything did go wrong, she'd consider it an answer to prayer and probably offer to pay for the defence of my murderer.' Even if she had liked the woman she wouldn't have been happy about clearing out like this. She remembered a woman she had met in a newspaper office who told her that during the war she'd spent one Christmas out of London, and that was the year Hitler chose to try to repeat the Great Fire of London. 'I came back first thing the next morning,' she said. 'I felt like an arch traitor. I hadn't slept away a single night since the bombs started, and when I went this had to happen.' Kay felt much the same.

'Running away never solves anything,' she exclaimed aloud.

' " He who fights and runs away, May live to fight another day," ' Rhodes reminded her.

Presently she recalled something else. 'Lady J. may arrange for the train to be met,' she remarked. 'It's not like London, you don't get any transport unless you fix up beforehand. It's even in the cards, though highly improbable, that she might come herself.'

Rhodes said nothing.

' In one minute,' said Kay, dangerously, ' you'll be telling me that Mr Crook thought of that, too.'

' As a matter of fact, he did,' agreed Rhodes in an apologetic voice. 'He telephoned her to say you'd be coming the whole way by road, and not to bother about a car.'

There was not a great deal of traffic, and when they threatened to get into bottlenecks the hospital label gave them priority. Kay leaned back in the darkened car, her hands clenched on her knee, not speaking, hardly seeing the countryside flash past in the brilliant midday sunlight.

' You O.K.?' asked Rhodes presently.

' I'm not so good at cars,' Kay confessed. ' Do you suppose there's any place where we could get a cup of tea? Or did Mr Crook give you a packet of sandwiches for my lunch?' she added.

' Well, even Mr Crook can't think of everything.' Rhodes sounded reproachful. ' I've got to get some more petrol soon. There's often a café by a petrol station—nothing very high class, I'm afraid, but the sandwiches and things you get at these places have to be good, or the drivers who use them would wreck everything.'

About a quarter of an hour later they drew up in front of a

filling station, the Lion Garage with the lion on his hind legs spitting fire and waving a tail as curly as a pig's.

'Any hopes of a cup?' asked Rhodes, and the boy operating the pumps pointed to a little café just beyond.

'I'll get us both a cup and see what they've got in the way of sandwiches,' Rhodes offered.

'I don't want anything to eat,' said Kay. 'Well, only a biscuit. See if they have any cigarettes,' she added.

'Don't want to go in for that,' said the boy at once, indicating an automatic cigarette machine.

'All right.'

Kay got out of the car, stretching luxuriously like a cat in the golden sunlight. She put a florin into the machine and received her packet of Players. She offered one to the boy, who grinned, indicating the No Smoking notices that hung around the garage.

'Still, there's always inside, isn't there?' he added, taking one and sticking it behind his ear. 'Thanks very much.'

Kay got back into the car and lit up; she was feeling sick and the thought of tea, hot and strong and sweet, as it always was from these cafés, refreshed her.

Rhodes came back carrying two cups.

'They gave me a couple of aspirins,' he said. 'Some people can't take them, I know.'

'They don't do a thing for me,' said Kay. She drank the tea thirstily. 'That's what I wanted.' She offered Rhodes one of the cigarettes, but he said he'd wait till they were on the road.

Rhodes took the cups and returned them, then went down the path marked Gents. The boy said, 'You feeling better, miss? Got far to go?'

'Pursey. Is it far?'

'Thirty miles to Whitestone,' said the boy, as Rhodes came back and produced a wallet to settle for the petrol. 'Pursey's about sixteen miles on, I suppose. Market day in Whitestone, you'll find it crowded. Detour by The Shepherdess,' he added, giving Rhodes his change. 'Doesn't add much to the journey, though.'

'Have you been telephoning to Mr Crook?' Kay murmured.

134

'Mr Crook,' she added to Roy Bartlett, 'is my guardian angel, self-appointed.'

He smiled a little uncertainly; she did look queer, leaning back in the car, with her bag open, playing around with a pen as if she didn't know what she was doing.

'Sure you feel up to going on?' asked Rhodes, solicitously. 'We needn't hurry, we've made quite good time.'

'I ought to have come by train,' said Kay. 'This car was a mistake.' A line she had once read floated around her mind and she murmured it aloud. 'God pity me for I am near to death.'

The boy looked at the label on the front of the car. 'Is there a hospital at Pursey or is the lady going home?'

'I'm going to stay with my prospective mother-in-law, her name's Lady Julia Forbes.' Kay's voice sounded strange even to herself.

The boy went back and said uneasily to his father, 'They shouldn't have let her leave the hospital so soon, she did look bad.'

'Bed wanted, I expect,' said Bartlett Senior, who was filling in his football pools and didn't want to be bothered.

Rhodes drove off carefully, but when they were ten miles out of Whitestone the car began to cough in an ominous fashion.

'Does it have to do that?' whispered Kay.

'It shouldn't.' He managed to slide into a convenient parking spot and got down to trace the damage.

'It's the petrol pump,' Rhodes discovered a minute or two later. 'Pity I didn't use my own car but Mr Crook said no. Not much traffic on this road,' he added gloomily. 'If we could get back to that garage we might get a tow. I could do with that cigarette now,' he added.

'Of course.' Kay opened her bag, looked inside, peered at the floor, then moved along the seat.

'You didn't pick them up?' she suggested.

'Me? No. I never saw them.'

'Well, I certainly had them, I gave one to the boy. They were on my lap.'

Rhodes helped her to look. 'Well, they're not there now. They must have slid off into the road as you shut the door.

Never mind. I've got a couple.' He offered her one, but she shook her head.

' I think not, thank you.'

The sun was now at full heat, she was feeling drowsy; the sky was a stainless blue, the fields burned golden brown by that peerless summer; even the birds were silent.

' Just think of living in the country,' said Rhodes. ' You'd feel you were in the middle of life everlasting, with nothing changing forever and ever.'

After about twenty minutes' vigil they heard the sound of a car coming up behind them. Rhodes ran into the highway and signalled. It was a long white car, driven by a single man, and carrying no passengers.

For an instant it looked as though the driver wasn't going to stop. But reluctantly he braked.

Rhodes went forward to explain.

' I haven't got a tow rope,' said the man, shooting a glance at Kay. ' I might give you a lift into Whitestone, there's a garage there, they could send a chap back, I dare say. How about the young lady?'

' I could wait here,' said Kay at once. ' I'd rather.' But Rhodes shook his head.

' You shouldn't, not the way you are. I feel responsible.'

' Nothing's going to happen to me,' she insisted.

' Mr Crook 'ud have my blood if it did,' said Rhodes simply. ' Besides, you can get a drop of brandy at Whitestone. That café was teetotal.'

He picked up her case. Reluctantly she moved out of the little Austin, looking distastefully at the ostentatious Ranger. Cars like that, she thought, should be reserved exclusively for weddings. She opened her bag and produced a powder compact. As she had feared, she looked like a lineal descendant of the Witch of Endor.

' Even Mr Crook couldn't blame Lady Julia if she sent me round to the back door, looking like this,' she muttered. She dabbed powder on her pale sweating face, painted on a new mouth; on the whole it wasn't an improvement.

She turned despairingly toward Rhodes who was standing by the white car. She took two steps forward, then flung her hand over her mouth. She shook her head, eyes wide and dismayed, and disappeared into the bushes and long grass behind the stationary blue Austin.

'What's the matter with her?' inquired the driver of the Ranger. 'Not going to be sick all over this car, I hope. It's hired.'

'She'll be all right in a minute. Sun turned her up a bit. Not to worry,' he added soothingly, as Kay reappeared. She felt shaky and her step wavered as she crossed the path, but Rhodes was at her side, taking her arm, taking her into the car.

'Now we'll go a bit slow,' he promised. 'You'll feel better soon.'

She lay back, drowsiness now definitely beginning to overwhelm her. The world outside went by in a blur; presently through it she saw someone approaching them on a bright yellow motor-cycle. She struggled to sit erect.

'Tell him about the car,' she muttered. But Rhodes didn't move, and the Ranger held on its way. She wondered if she had really spoken out loud, but then the white car turned a corner and she caught a fuzzy glimpse of the driver's face in the little mirror above his head. It was hard and merciless, mouth set in a vice, skin swarthy.

After the little blue car had gone on its way the boy at the Lion Garage drifted inside and lighted the gift cigarette. It was a quiet time of day, not much to do. Presently the trucks would be coming along and they often wanted a fill-up, there wasn't another garage for miles, not till you got to Whitestone. This was when the café did good business, too. Truck drivers were always thirsty chaps and the sane ones stuck to tea while they were on the road. Roy finished his cigarette, switched on the radio, but there was nothing to hold a chap there, and presently he drifted out again to look up the long white empty road. And then he saw, lying just where the car had stood, a packet of Players cigarettes, practically full.

'Must have dropped 'em as the car pulled away,' he thought, going forward to pick them up. He took them inside the office to offer one to his old man. But when he had pulled out the flap he stood staring, because there was something there you don't usually find inside cigarette cartons, not even in these days of fierce competition, with everyone trying to give you a coupon or a price reduction. It was a pound note. He took it out slowly.

'What you got there?' asked his father.

'It was put inside on purpose,' said the young man. He turned the packet over. 'There's something written on it. "Ring BLO 1726. Mr Crook. Say Blue Austin RLA 1946. *Urgent*."' The last word was heavily underscored. 'That was the name she said. "My guardian angel," she called him.'

'Someone having a joke with you,' said Mr Bartlett heavily.

'Expensive kind of joke. No harm ringing up.'

'You leave that phone alone,' said his father. 'Don't want to make a fool of yourself.'

But the boy had been reared on TV, and it all made perfectly good sense to him.

'Abducted, p'raps,' he said, diving for the telephone. 'Well, the girl left a quid, and even a London call won't cost anything like that. Taking money under false pretences if we don't ring,' he added virtuously.

At approximately the time that Kay was dropping her secret message at the garage Lady Julia Forbes was staring at two telegrams, both of which had arrived that morning. One of them said:

'ARRIVING 2.40. KAY.'

And the other:

'PLANS CHANGED. WRITING. KAY CARTER.'

She wondered why the girl should suddenly become formal in the second wire. Something had happened and she did wish people would take her into their confidence. Still, she was relieved the girl wasn't coming down; and really, what manners, writing out of the blue to announce your arrival without even asking if it was convenient. Even in 1959 with youth claiming the earth as never before, it struck her as pretty cool. But the modern young woman was like that. Lady Julia couldn't approve of the young—with the exception of her son, of course.

She hadn't liked the engagement when she heard about it, and she was convinced that, if the marriage could be postponed for a reasonable period, Bryan would appreciate the folly of marrying a girl with no people and no money. She had pulled sufficient strings to make a cat's cradle to get him offered the American job, and even then she had been afraid the girl might try and stop him. But she had had the sense to agree to that. Fancied herself as the wife of a tycoon, no doubt, decided Lady Julia, who for all her exalted heritage had a mind as common as a kippered herring.

Bryan had written most enthusiastically about his progress, he knew his mother loved to hear even the non-essentials. But in one letter he had said he was getting rather odd letters from Kay, who was getting involved in some sort of mystery apparently—it all sounded deplorably vulgar. Three months' separation would give him a chance of measuring the girl up against other, more suitable brides. The telegrams caught her short because Bryan, who had the parsimony so often detected in rich and successful men, hadn't gone to the expense of a third cable, telling himself that Kay could easily wire and there was really no sense chucking money away.

FIFTEEN

When Mr Crook reached Bloomsbury Street that morning he found a pile of correspondence that might have daunted an M.P., but it didn't bother him. Let 'em all come, was his motto. Yet for some reason his heart today wasn't wholly on the job. He had once told Inspector Perrin that he felt like a man after an elusive flea; he supposed he had caught and scotched his, but here it was biting him again, and he couldn't track it down. The trouble had started that morning, that much he did know. Then—he was worrying over Kay. But she was going down to Pursey. He realised that she hated the idea, but he never doubted that she'd go. What he did wonder was whether by this time next year she'd be Mrs Bryan Forbes. Still, that wasn't his pigeon and wouldn't account for this feeling of discomfort, that he'd missed something, something that should have given him a clue. He'd been held up by the coalie for a few precious minutes, and he was a man whose time was worth its weight in gold, but he had too much sense to let that prey on his mind. Time could always be overtaken by a man who could put in an extra spurt just when it's most needed. The chap hadn't scratched the paint of the Superb, he'd noticed that. And anyway coke isn't like coal, it's light and clean and . . .

He sprang to his feet. 'Staring me in the face all this time,' he explained. 'I should start wearing glasses.' He picked up the telephone, started to dial Inspector Perrin and then stopped. Because when you're going to bring a serious charge it's as well to have reinforcements. So he called Mrs Sagan instead.

'That friend of yours who nearly fell down the coal hole last week,' he began.

'Oh, don't bother about her,' said Mrs Sagan. 'She's what's called accident prone. If it hadn't been the coal hole it would have been a banana skin or something. That woman could fall down a flight of steps in a flat.'

He appreciated the picturesqueness of her imagination, a quality in her sex which was seldom deficient, but he wasn't really much interested if she fell into a hole in the churchyard. She wasn't one of *his* clients.

'Remember the date?' he said.

'Wednesday of last week. She comes every Wednesday like clockwork; I'm expecting her now. Though how she thinks her horoscope can have altered since last week . . . She's like a lot of people, she thinks I'm a superior kind of fortuneteller. Sometimes I think I'll hang a notice on my door: No crystal balls, no cards.'

'I should,' said Crook absently. 'Thanks a million, Mrs S. Not going out today, are you?'

'I told you, I'm expecting Mrs Rollo.'

'And she's bringing her sitting breeches along with her? I get you. Be seeing you.'

He rang off.

'Shades of Crippen,' he said. getting on to the police station and asking for Inspector Perrin. He wasn't there, so Crook left a message to ring him back. And he had hardly hung up from that call when his bell pealed again and it was a young man from a place he'd never heard of, telling him that murder number three was well under way.

'Now, listen,' said Crook, as electric as a firecracker. 'What was he like, the chap driving the car? Come on, dark, fair, tall, short . . .?'

'Fair, clean-shaven, thirty-three or thirty-four. 'Bout five feet nine inches, weight I should say eleven stone. . . .' He might have been a police officer making a report and the police 'ud be lucky to get him at that.

'Be seeing you,' Crook said and slammed the receiver down. He called to Bill, 'They've got the girl.' Here's the number of the car, dark-blue Austin. If anything happens to her I'll be guilty of accessory before the crime. Get after the police. I'm going after the girl—and much good may I do her. One thing, she knows she's in a trap, so she'll be on her guard. Wonder how she discovered the fellow.'

He snatched up the telephone and rang the Hirewire office. 'C. Oliver there? Well, that's my first bit of luck today,' said Crook. 'Now cancel everything, let all your prospective clients have a treat and one more day's liberty. You're needed. Battle, murder and sudden death and it could be yours—any of the three.'

'I'm on,' said Mr Oliver obligingly.

'Be with you in five minutes,' promised Crook.

He was at the wheel of the Superb like a flash of fat ginger lightning; he crashed a red light and treated a policeman's screech with the Nelson touch. He went around a corner that said NO ENTRY and tore through a street market. scattering fruit in every direction. He mounted a pavement and nearly killed a black cat. 'Praise the pigs that one got away,' he thought superstitiously. 'No luck if I'd added that scalp to all the rest.'

The young man was standing outside the Hirewire office; he must have been an acrobat at some time, Crook supposed, because he'd wrenched the door open and was inside at such a rate the car barely seemed to reduce speed.

'Any time you've got any breath you might put me in the

picture,' he murmured. They tore over Hammersmith Bridge and up Roehampton Lane, following the road that the blue Austin had taken.

'I'm a reasonable man,' said Mr Crook, and C. Oliver stared. But he saw that his companion was in deadly earnest. 'I'm all for things goin' accordin' to nature, and that goes for human nature, too, and when they don't that's the time to look for squalls. Know how Miss Carter realised we were one tenant short at no. 2?'

'You tell me,' offered Oliver.

'Because there was no sound of taps and what not in the flat above. It's when things are out of the ordinary . . . Miss Chisholm had a routine, and she always followed it. Rhodes likewise. So when you find the routine being bent like an old hairpin, you can guess there's dirty work somewhere. Operative word— dirty.' He emitted a sort of chuckle that ended as a grunt. He hoped his companion didn't realise quite how frightened he was.

They swept around another corner, dodged between two trucks, sort of leap-frogged over a bicycle ridden by a boy who wasn't using his hands and were halted at a crossing by an old lady, who stood on the first of the white lines and smiled in Crook's direction. Realising that even he couldn't sweep up an old dame on his bonnet and carry her all the way to Pursey, Crook stamped on the foot brake. The old lady's eyebrows rose; furiously Crook waved. The old lady looked surprised but waved in return.

'Come on,' Crook yelled. So she started, then changed her mind and dodged back, dropped a bag of apples that rolled all over the crossing, and returned to the kerb.

'Watch out for the Yellow Peril,' bawled Crook, charging on, and simultaneously Old Mother Hubbard ran forward to rescue her apples. The Superb reared up on two wheels, nearly carried away a road lamp—and the old dear's eyebrows—and shot into the distance.

A truck that had been on Crook's tail pulled up, the driver got out and helped to salvage the apples.

'The things women do,' he observed severely. 'Eve lost Eden for the sake of an apple, and you nearly lost your life.'

'Do you know,' said the old lady wonderingly, 'I think he must have been in a hurry.'

'And they wouldn't call that suicide,' Crook was observing to his companion. 'There's British justice for you.'

'What price we get held up in the next town?' Oliver reflected aloud. 'Someone's bound to have taken our number.'

'That's why I've got you. If there's trouble, you take over. You know your way around well enough to double-cross a cop. Anyway it won't do us any harm to have the police on the trail. We don't know precisely what we're up against, but we do know there have been two deaths to be laid at the same door, and multiple murder carries the rope. And now there's this girl. I wonder how she got onto him.'

'Who?'

'Rhodes.'

'What, the porter chap?'

'That's right. I dunno how he persuaded her to go with him, we'll have to wait for his story. I dare say he could beat a best-selling lady novelist like Mrs Christie at her own game. Here '— as they approached a market town—'turn on the radio, full blast.'

The car had been fitted with a radio when Crook bought it. Hitherto he had never used it except to pick up the news. Now, turned full on, the blast nearly lifted him out of his seat.

'Put it down a bit?' offered Oliver.

'No,' bawled Crook, even louder than the radio.

'I ought to have brought two or three of my Hirewire stickers,' said Oliver regretfully. 'More publicity in an hour ...'

'If you'd put anything of the kind on my car you'd have been the next corpse,' Crook assured him, grimly. 'This ain't an advertising campaign, or a bit of fun and games on Workers' Playtime, this is life-and-death. Ever heard of a chap called G. K. Chesterton, or was he, like Kipling, before your time? Well, there was a story of his about a chap who wanted to attract the attention of the police—he was travelling with a thief and the thief didn't know he'd been caught—and this chap—Father Brown was his name—did a lot of fool things, changing sugar into salt, smashing windows, that sort of thing, so that people would remember. . . .'

'So when the police hear that a lunatic in a yellow car nearly ran down an old duck on a crossing—and they'll back the pedestrian every time, you bet—there's something about a motorist sends every Bobby in the force absolutely berserk—they'll get around and find out the same car deafened everyone in—what is the name of this place? Was, rather,' he added, as they came out the other side, the radio still blaring.

'And the same car that overturned a fruit stall and waltzed across a red light and down a No Entry street—here, for the lord's sake, switch that thing off. I can't hear myself think. I wonder what wised up the girl,' he repeated, apparently skating the Superb over a four-foot ditch and rushing it through a piece of waste ground—'something must have happened at that petrol station.'

'Why doesn't she just refuse to budge, tell 'em to call the police?' Oliver inquired.

'Anyone would know you weren't a married man,' Crook told him, pityingly. 'Women's minds don't work that way. Besides, this one is a Lady Knight Templar with a purpose. Daddy was a doctor and she had a nasty experience when she was a youngster, a drug case in the neighbourhood. She knows our little lot are in for drugs and she ain't going to fade out and let them carry on. Not if she can help to run 'em to earth.'

'You mean, she took a chance like that? She's nuts,' said C. Oliver.

'Oh, no,' said Crook simply. 'Just female. How goes the enemy?'

Oliver glanced at the watch on his wrist. 'Twelve-forty.'

'We've been a hour and ten minutes on the road. They had a long start, say eighty minutes, though they won't have made our pace. Still they could be at the coast by this time. One place I'll tell you they won't be, and that's The Manor House, Pursey.'

'Why Pursey?' asked Oliver. 'You didn't say.'

'That's where the fiancé's mum lives.'

'What's the fiancé doing?'

'Raking in the shekels in li'l ole Noo York, according to her.

144

Well, he'll be able to stand her a handsome funeral, silver coffin and all.' His hand jumped for a moment on the wheel.

'Here,' said Oliver as gently as a woman, 'like me to take over for a bit?'

'She's my old girl,' explained Crook. 'Thanks all the same. . . . What made you come at the drop of a hat?' he added.

'Try anything once,' said Oliver. 'Besides, I guessed it might be the girl. . . .'

'I always knew you were a fast worker. Now if someone was to propel *you* to the moon—hallo, could that be the garage? We're making better time than I thought.'

The Lion Garage, announced the sign, and Crook drew up with an empressement that would have done credit to royalty.

There was a big chauffeur-driven Bentley taking in sustenance, but Crook, like the Lord God, was no respecter of persons. He jumped out and caught the boy, Roy Bartlett, by the shoulder.

'You the chap that telephoned me this morning? Crook's the name.'

'That's right,' said Roy.

'Now think—did that fair chap give any idea where he was heading for?'

'The girl said Pursey, other side of Whitestone. I warned them there was a detour at The Shepherdess.'

'Stop long?'

'Fifteen minutes say. Could be longer. Had some sandwiches and a cup of tea.'

From within the Bentley an indignant voice cried, 'Take your turn in the queue, sir,' and Crook turned like a flash.

'Civil Service?' he exclaimed. 'Not Home Office, I take it? I was afraid not.' He caught Oliver by the arm. 'Meet Detective Inspector Oliver of the C.I.D. Chasing a stolen car—drugs. Now then . . .' he turned back to the boy.

'I should like to see your warrant,' said the large man stiffly.

'So should I,' said Oliver. 'No, I'm afraid I can't show you that, but can I interest you in a TV set? We're doing a model now for car use. Of course, it doesn't help the little man, the chap with the ten horsepower, but a car like this . . .' He was leaning through the window talking eagerly, and flipping a folder that he'd apparently taken out of his ear. 'A busy man like

145

you,' he went on, not giving the other chap a chance to get a word in edgewise, 'can't afford to lose time or lose touch. There are newspapers, yes, but—have you tried reading the *Times* in a fast car? Now a set like this, geared against any interference, can keep you right up to the minute with the news. Or say you need relaxation, as don't we all . . . O.K. Crook? Are you through? Fine. I was just running out of patter.'

'They stopped there and had tea,' said Crook.

'Women will, won't they?' Oliver agreed. 'Even the most sensible.'

'I don't think it was so much that Miss Carter wanted tea as that Rhodes was resolved she should have it. And the stuff he put in the cup. If she'd refused the tea I dare say he'd got other ideas.'

Oliver said something unprintable; Crook drove on like an avenging fury. There was a scurry of small birds from a hedge as he went by.

Quite soon they found the parking spot, with the car in it.

'Changed cars, possibly changed drivers,' said Crook. 'You know, Lochinvar, it wouldn't surprise me a bit if the driver of the rescue car wasn't someone you've seen before. Well, hell's bells, where do we go from here?'

SIXTEEN

'Keep your chin up,' said Oliver, undaunted. 'Perhaps little Miss Lonelyheart left another message here.'

He popped out and went over to the car. 'Come,' he called after a minute and Crook came to join him. 'What do you make of that on the window?'

They walked around the car so that they were approximately where Kay had crouched before entering the big white car.

'Someone writin' with red pencil?' suggested Crook.

'Lipstick I'd say. Got her wits about her, hasn't she? Pity about the sun melting it a bit. AX 1906 is what I make of it.'

'So do I,' agreed Crook, 'and two of us should be enough. Must have gone straight on, the road leads ahead like the path of the righteous moving on to the eternal day, and if he'd come back we would have run into him head on.'

'Ever noticed,' inquired Oliver conversationally, 'that if you want an auto club man or a chap in blue they never surface? We need the word put out for that car. It's not likely they'll change again. Thirty miles the boy said to Whitestone, and another sixteen to Pursey. We've done twenty, it only leaves twenty-six. Do it in about fifteen minutes, the way you're driving.'

'I dare say,' said Crook, dryly, forging ahead. 'Point is, are they going to Pursey?'

'Whitestone's a big centre, trains raying out in all directions. If they changed cars that looks as though Deadwood Dick's taking over. You must admit these boys think of everything. Your chap Rhodes has got to get back this evening and not too late or he'll have to answer some uncomfortable questions.'

'He'll do that in any case,' said Crook. 'Your idea is he'll drop off at Whitestone, and let X carry the torch from there.'

'Well, it seems reasonable. You know, if this was a film or something, I could begin to be sorry for D.D. I mean, he must be up against it. We're always told the criminal's real headache is getting shut of the corpse. Of course, we don't know for certain that Caroline Chisholm is a corpse. . . .'

'I do,' said Crook, 'didn't I mention it?' And he told Oliver where she was now. Oliver didn't turn a hair.

'Well, that's one. The second he left about for anyone to find. Now he's got to make a fresh plan. And where's it going to end? There's no security for him while you're walking the earth, and now you've pulled me in and the girl's pulled that lad at the garage in. . . .'

'And it's up to us to pull the girl out again,' said Crook heavily, slowing down behind some sheep that came straying through a defective hedge. 'Here, make those chaps get a move on. Our time isn't just money, it's life.'

Oliver obligingly hopped out of the car, caught two of the

sheep by their thick dirty fleeces—'and what sort of a farmer is he that he's not sheared 'em in this weather?' he demanded wrathfully—and pushed them toward the ditch. A head appeared over the hedge.

'What d'you think you're doing?'

'You should teach your animals the Highway Code,' Crook retorted.

'What is it, anyway?' the shepherd demanded. 'Motor Rally or summat? Two of you in twenty minutes, going hell-for-leather . . .'

'This other car?' said Crook like a flash. 'Notice what it was like?'

'I said so, didn't I? Big white job, thought it was on the M.I., I suppose.'

'Happen to notice who was in it?' wheedled Crook. 'Oh, come on, a clever chap like you . . .'

'Two fellows in front . . .'

'Passengers?'

'Could be.'

'But you didn't notice.'

'That's right.'

'Did you notice that there weren't any?'

'I said I didn't notice.'

The sheep, discouraged by Oliver's cavalier treatment of their fellows, had obligingly fallen back.

Crook trod on the accelerator and the yellow Rolls moved with the grace and silence of some great floating bird.

'She certainly has something my little bus has overlooked,' commented Oliver, generously. Not that he fancied a Rolls himself. You needed a something, a *je ne sais quoi*, to carry it off, if you didn't sport a chauffeur, and he admitted, surprisingly, that Crook had it.

'It don't matter if that chap saw anyone or not,' said Crook. 'The girl must have been in the car. There hasn't been a single place where they could have ditched her, not in broad daylight and with the chance of some innocent shepherd lad like the one we've just parted from, strolling down the road, straw in mouth and eyes on sticks.'

The road ran straight for a time, then branched.

'Which way?' Crook wondered.

'Railway,' said Oliver without any hesitation.

Crook shot him a glance. He sounded jaunty enough but there was some taut quality about the thin face, the long thin clever hands, that made the big man feel he'd just as soon not meet the chap in a dark alley if they weren't on good terms.

'You could be right,' he agreed. They flew along the road, where the surface befriended them, had to slow down a bit for a truck taking lambs home from market, got caught up with some cars and carts . . .

'But if this is market day in Whitestone the other car will have had to reduce pressure too,' Crook observed.

At The Shepherdess, as they had been warned, there was a detour where a water main had burst and men were repairing the road. Crook slowed down.

'Remember seeing a big white car go by not so long ago?' he asked.

One of the men said, 'Going to Whitestone. Two chaps in the front.'

'How long?' asked Oliver, putting his hands in his pockets and clenching them hard.

The man looked at his companion, they hesitated. 'Quarter of an hour,' he ventured.

'Good-oh! Well, we're gainin' on 'em all right,' Crook said. 'I dare say Rhodes didn't hurry—didn't see the need for it— and then they stopped at the filling station, and there may have been a bit of delay transferring from one car to the other. I don't suppose they'll be rushing to such an extent that they'd risk an accident. The last thing they want is anyone asking questions.'

'Your guess about their doping her must be right,' acknowledged Oliver, 'or a girl with her wits would have raised almighty cain as soon as they ran into some of these gigs and gocarts.'

'They wouldn't overlook a little thing like that, and if by chance she didn't fancy the tea, well, there are other ways— if there are two of you.'

By way of relieving his feelings Oliver leaned across and smote the horn a tremendous blow, at which the car in front nearly rose off its four wheels. The driver was so agitated that he swerved and like light Crook was past him and racing for the town whose church spire could just be discerned on the horizon.

The road wound quite unnecessarily, but Crook, refusing to be flustered, pointed out that it had rolled just as uneconomically for the car they were following.

In Whitestone the traffic was heavy again and they were caught by lights. The station was at the north end of the town, over a bridge. On the bridge various small boys sat with paper and pencils watching the trains.

'Taking numbers?' Oliver asked as they slowed to a crawl. 'Trains?'

'And cars,' said one of the boys.

'Large white car, two chaps in the front?' cried Oliver swiftly.

One of the boys turned up his notes; behind them a car hooted.

'We're buying info,' Oliver promised. They moved out of the stream of traffic and parked by the kerb. The boys raced after them.

'AX 1906', said one of the boys.

'That's ours,' Oliver pounced.

'You cops?' asked another boy.

'You could call us that. Look, you've got sense. Anyone in the back?'

'A lady,' chorused two of the boys.

'Lying like this,' amplified one, who was clearly a born mimic; he drooped his head and folded his hands. 'All curled up in the corner. Cor, she could be a deader, I said.'

'You don't miss a trick, do you?' suggested Oliver. 'Didn't notice what she was like, I suppose—apart from being possibly dead.'

The boys looked at one another; they'd thought this chap quite sensible up till now. A small boy bearing a ridiculous resemblance to a Fra Filippo Lippi angel, a fact for which life was doubtless going to pay him out for the next thirty or forty years, piped up sweetly, 'She was pretty.'

'Don't listen to 'im, mister. 'E's soppy.'

'So am I,' said Oliver, calmly. He put his hand in his pocket and brought out a lot of loose change that he jingled suggestively. 'Notice if the car stopped at the station?'

'That's right, stopped in the yard.'

'It's there still,' added Fra Filippo Lippi, Junior.

They turned unbelieving eyes to the station yard. There she stood, the long white car they'd been chasing. But now there was no one in her.

The two rogues, pursuing their plan, drew up at Whitestone Junction, and assisted their more or less comatose passenger to alight.

'Come along, my dear,' said the driver, and Kay stirred druggishly. She could move her own feet and with their assistance she passed through the ticket barrier and was conveyed to the little local train which passed through Overhampton, Longhampton, Sheepdale, Farley and ended up at a station called Thorpe.

At this time of day there were very few passengers and they had no difficulty in getting a compartment to themselves. It was an old-fashioned link of carriages with no communicating corridor, so that once the train started you could be sure no one would burst in. Rhodes was carrying the girl's case and this he had placed in the rack over her head. They had hung about until a moment or two before the train was due to start, and Rhodes stood squarely at the window presenting a stubborn back to any other passenger who might feel inclined to enter the carriage. But no one even tried. He didn't think there were more than fifteen or twenty people on board.

As soon as the train whistle blew, Rhodes leaped out, crossed the line by a bridge and set himself to wait for the London express that was due in another ten minutes. As for Brown, when his share of the work was done, he'd come back on a local to Whitestone, pick up the car and return it to the renting garage whence he had collected it earlier in the day. The plan wasn't foolproof, of course, but no crime ever is. The perfect murder, the perfect burglary, the perfect forgery—you can scheme and plot and protect yourself against every conceivable trap, but even Solomon, said to be the wisest of men, couldn't arm himself against the invisible witness, the man or woman who for no reason whatsoever crosses your path and later when questions are being asked—against all likelihood and fair play—remembers you and even what you were doing.

The local train moved out of the station, running for a while between fields burned honey-gold by the sun. Then it rounded a corner and the Whitestone Tunnel came into sight. This was the chosen site of the crime. It would be easy later for inquiries to deduce that a girl, feeling a bit dizzy perhaps, had got up to close the window against the foul air, and somehow pushed the door open and fallen to her death. There couldn't be much doubt that when the girl was eventually found (probably by chaps walking through the tunnel at the end of the day), she'd be past giving any kind of evidence. A sturdy bang on the head just before the door flew open would be explained away by the violence of the fall. Brown stood up and made his simple preparations, lifting the limp body from its place, holding it firmly with one hand while with the other he made ready to open the door and send the body flying into space.

And then he heard it, the long furious roar of a car horn. It screamed in the quiet countryside, bringing travellers to their windows to see the big yellow Rolls, with its two passengers, racing along the road parallel with the track. It was going hell-for-leather and it shot past the carriage where he was standing. Hastily he dropped the body onto the seat. At that pace it wasn't likely anyone would notice an individual traveller, and by the time they reached the tunnel—they had already begun to slow down—it would be out of sight.

'There she is,' yelled Oliver. 'My God, Crook . . .' Crook drew alongside the engine, the placid elderly driver turned his head. Silly young chaps, he thought, trying to race the train. It wasn't the first time, and, now he came to notice, one of them at least was old enough to know better. Then the younger stood up waving an immense red silk handkerchief in his direction and yelling words that the wind carried away. Red stands for danger everywhere, in the bull ring and on the railway. The driver slowed down, and the passenger in the fifth coach felt the sweat prickle through his skin. 'Get on, get on,' he muttered. But he knew it was all right really, because the tunnel would work for him. The driver saw the younger man leap from the car before it had properly slowed and come hurtling down the side of the bank, still shouting and waving the red handkerchief. Heads at the windows were staring at them. One or two joined in the general hullabaloo.

'What's to do?' demanded the driver, slowing to a crawl.

'Danger,' yelled Oliver. 'Stop the train.'

'The signals aren't against me,' said the driver, in mild tones.

'Not that kind of danger. You've got a murderer on board.'

The driver stiffened offendedly. 'That kind of lark,' he said.

'It isn't a lark,' bellowed Oliver. He came scrambling alongside the engine. 'Here, let me up.'

'You keep out of my cab,' said the driver, preparing to put on pace.

Oliver jumped for the step. 'Stand away,' bawled the man, but at that instant the ginger-headed one, who had also left the car, came charging down the bank like a buffalo crashing through to the water place. He caught his foot in a trail of bramble and finished the last few yards by rolling. But he was up again, bouncing like a ball and running between the rails.

'Get her, Oliver,' he shouted. 'They can't run a man down in cold blood—though if ever I saw hotter blood I must have been bottled.' He stood squarely in the path of the train. 'Look to your right,' he invited the driver, ' and see if one of your passengers ain't leaving the train against King's—Queen's regulations.'

The driver instinctively turned his head and, sure enough, a little dark chap had jumped down and was beginning to scramble up the opposite bank, catching at grasses and thorns, making his way on his hands and knees.

Someone else opened a carriage door. 'Let him go,' yelled Crook. 'Why should we do the police's work for them? That's what they're paid for, ain't it?'

Oliver had walked precariously along the footboard till he reached the carriage where a girl lay slumped against the upholstery; she was too dazed to realise what was happening. Oliver opened the door, hauled himself in and sat down beside her and put his arm around her shoulders.

'Tell the chap to drive on,' he bawled to Crook, shoving his head out of the window. '"I will see thee at Philippi".'

Crook courteously removed himself from the line. He recognised some of his limitations, though he hated to admit them, and he knew he had as much hope of scrambling on board as of winning a marathon. It was going to take him all he knew to get back to the Superb.

But he made it—if he'd been a fox-hunting man he'd have been in at every death, though it meant breaking every bone in his body. No wonder I called him young Lochinvar first time I set eyes on him, he reflected, driving like a zany, irrespective of the thorns in his big hands and the trickle of blood down one cheek where he'd scratched it when he fell. After this I'll make it a condition to all my clients to rent a set from Hirewire.

He and the train came to Pursey more or less at the same time. The road, that had been so friendly, branched away after the tunnel and he had to make a wide detour before he reached the wayside platform. There was no sign of the girl or Oliver, but the other passengers were milling about as inconsequently as the sheep Oliver had cleared out of their path during their crazy race with death.

SEVENTEEN

He found Kay in the house of the sole railway official, who combined the jobs of stationmaster, ticket collector and, when required, porter. Oliver was on the telephone to the local doctor, Mrs Stationmaster was brewing tea, while her husband, who had heard half a dozen times what had (or hadn't) happened, stolidly produced some beer. Crook thought better of the countryside and its denizens than he had in a dozen years. He asked if he could use the telephone and rang through to the Whitestone police. He told them about the little dark man and said to look out for a car with a (spurious) H.C.S. label on the windscreen, now in a parking spot about fifteen miles from East Portsea garage. He told them the number.

By the time he'd raised the alarm, the doctor, a rosy little man called Cripps, had arrived and was examining his patient, who was still in a dazed, not to say comatose, condition.

'What has the lady taken?' he asked severely, and Oliver snapped: 'That's what we're waiting for you to tell us. You do realise, I suppose, she didn't take the stuff herself. She's been doped, with murder in view.'

The little rosy man stiffened. 'I presume you realise you are bringing a serious accusation against some person or persons. This might develop into a police case, if what you suggest can be substantiated.'

'That bus has started already,' said Oliver in the same tone.

'Don't take any notice of young Lochinvar,' interposed Crook. 'He's had a shock and it's bad at his age. Good of you to come at such short notice,' he went on heartily, 'but it seemed to us the young lady wasn't in any shape to go visiting her prospective mother-in-law—that 'ud be Lady Julia Forbes—I dare say you know the name.'

We're a democracy nowadays, and Jack is as good as his master and frequently a good deal better, but there was no doubt about it, the rumour hadn't reached Pursey yet. The mere mention of Her Ladyship induced a hush of the kind associated with a judge's entrance into the court. Crook got the idea that if they hadn't all been standing already they'd have risen reverently to their feet at the mention of that august name.

'I think Lady Julia should be informed that her visitor has been delayed,' said the doctor in a voice as smooth as cream.

'Tom 'ull take a message,' said Tom's wife. 'Once the up train's gone through—it's due any minute—there'll be nothing doing for the next hour.'

'Won't they be sending a car for her, though?' demanded Oliver. 'She's expected.'

'I haven't heard anything of that,' said Tom.

'Well, I suppose she imagined Miss Carter would take a taxi on her own account.'

Tom and his wife shook their heads like a pair of mandarins. 'This beats London,' said Tom, and Crook thought, You're telling us. 'There's only two hire cars hereabouts, one from the Golden Goose and the other from Joe Bates, who has the shop.' He didn't say what sort of shop—it was obviously the only shop this side of Whitestone and sold everything from cough drops to cotton gloves. 'And this being market day both of them cars would be spoken for.'

Kay opened her eyes and looked unseeingly at Mrs Tom. 'Now you lay there,' said Mrs Tom soothingly, 'just as long as you please.'

The eyes, of a vivid Mediterranean blue, moved incuriously from face to face.

'Here, they haven't put her out, have they?' exclaimed Oliver.

'What, with you and me on the track? Be your age,' said Crook. He added that neither he nor the Rolls was proud and it 'ud be a pleasure to beetle along to the Manor himself. He saw the Toms exchange glances and knew they were thinking that if he knew his place he'd present himself at the back door.

'I'll sort Lady Clara,' he assured Oliver, cheerfully.

Mrs Tom said the name was Julia, adding, 'You should look out for your hands, all those thorns. Blood poisoning you could get.'

'I bet she thinks it'd be a lot too good for me,' Crook mouthed to Oliver, but he stayed patiently where he was while Mrs Tom, who was having a whale of a time, fetched an unsterilised needle and hacked at his hands till he began to think the thorns were preferable. Then she brought him hot water and a small clean rough towel. 'You'll want to wash before you go to The Manor,' she said. Oliver grinned and produced a packet of chewing gum that he passed over.

'Sweeten the breath,' he remarked. 'You don't want to go blowing beer fumes into that rarefied atmosphere. It might blow up or something.'

'When you get to the pearly gates,' Crook assured him, 'you won't need to be issued wings, you'll have them in your own rucksack.'

He took the gum though he felt pretty sure Lady Julia wouldn't let him come that near, and he'd be lucky if he wasn't left standing in the hall like a fancy hatstand.

'Is it far?' he thought to ask as he turned to go.

'Better part of three mile,' said Tom.

'Give him five minutes,' said Oliver, 'and the trusty steed 'ull be neighing at the door.'

Lady Julia was slightly more animated than a darning needle, but it was a near thing. When she saw Crook stamping up the drive she felt as Macbeth must have when he saw Birnam wood coming to Dunsinane, as if some fearsome and hitherto unrecognised prophecy were being fulfilled.

'It was like suddenly finding yourself in the zoo,' she told her son later, seven weeks later to be precise, when he got back from his trip.

'I fail to understand the situation, Mr Cook,' she said, when this extraordinary visitor had contrived to rush the hall. 'I am not expecting my prospective daughter-in-law.'

'Crook's the name,' her visitor pointed out sunnily. 'Well, that's funny, didn't your son . . .?'

'I received a telegram from Miss Carter informing me of her proposed arrival by the train arriving at 2.40 and shortly afterwards this was cancelled. No explanation or apology.'

'You'd hardly expect an apology from a corpse,' said Crook, respectfully. 'Not a bad title that. Apology from a corpse. Not that there's going to be one, not this time, and no thanks to Mr Bryan Forbes at that. Well, I called to say the young lady's up at the stationmaster's house with Dr Kipps . . .'

'Cripps.'

'. . . Cripps in attendance. He thinks when she's recovered from the shock . . .'

'Shock?'

'Well, it 'ud be a shock to most people,' protested Crook, and to his chagrin he realised he was beginning to sound apologetic, 'to be abducted and drugged and nearly pitched out of a train, in a tunnel, too . . .'

He was prepared to embroider, but the audience wasn't interested. 'It all sounds exceedingly melodramatic, Mr Cook, but hardly my concern.'

'Not your concern? Don't give it a thought,' Crook assured her. 'Your turn's coming. Why, this 'ull be all over the local press. Marchioness' daughter-in-law . . .'

'I am not a marchioness, Mr Cook, and Miss Carter is not my daughter-in-law.'

Crook relented suddenly. Awful, he thought, to be this frozen old cow, with no one in the world but a heartless tycoon of a son, who let other chaps go around rescuing his girl friend from a fate as bad as death.

'No, and she ain't going to be—not ever. We've got someone lined up who didn't come out of the small reptile house. . . .' Anger suddenly overwhelmed him again. 'Did you get what I said, Your Ladyship? *Miss Kay Carter is giving your son the push.*'

And on that reprehensible note he turned on his large well-worn heel and ostentatiously shook a lot of dust off his feet all over the polished cottage hall.

EIGHTEEN

The man now calling himself Frederick Brown was in a very awkward situation. He had jumped from the train at a point practically equidistant from Whitestone and Pursey and when he gained the narrow path on the farther side of the embankment the world seemed empty as a blank card, except for the train now snaking around the corner to enter the tunnel. He knew he had not much time, that in such a landscape at this hour of a blazing August day he would be as conspicuous as a pimple on a clear skin. His one hope was to get a lift back to Whitestone, return the big white car to the garage from which he had hired it that morning, and catch the next train to London. There wouldn't be another express for some hours, but it would be safer not to wait.

His first task was to recross the line and gain the road down which Crook had so unsportingly driven the old Superb. The path on which he was now travelling was unfit for any traffic heavier than a bicycle. Everything was so still even the minute creatures of the air, the bees and ladybirds, seemed to lie on solid gold beams. He passed, without noticing them, a beautiful clump of elms, their fluffy green trousers untouched by the wind, their branches cascading over in a green fountain. But then he had never taken much account of nature. When he felt sure he was not observed he scrambled down the bank again and recrossed the line.

Once on the road he slowed his step, waiting for the sound of a vehicle coming up from behind. A small black car presently flashed by, paying no heed to his lifted hand; the second to pass him had a man and his wife and a couple of children in it and, from the sound of it, half a dozen dogs as well. But he was more fortunate with the third, whose driver slowed of his own accord to offer a lift. He was a young man wearing a white drip-dry shirt and thin grey trousers.

'Hot for walking?' he suggested.

Brown nodded. 'I'm making for Whitestone. Missed the local at Pursey,' he said. 'There isn't another for some hours, and I couldn't get a car.'

'Market day,' his companion agreed.

'There don't appear to be any omnibuses in this part of the world.'

The young man grinned. 'Pursey's known as the place where the bus runs once a fortnight; this isn't one of the lucky days. Were you really going to walk the whole way in this weather?'

'I suppose I counted on getting a lift. Hallo, isn't that the train?'

From behind him he heard the steady sound of wheels rounding the bend of the track. Pulling out a packet of cigarettes he offered one to the driver, then stooped his head, cupping his hands around the flame of the match, so that his face would be quite obscured from view. Not that the driver of this train would be the one who had been taking him to Pursey, but a rumour might have got out. He was a man used to taking chances, but when things began to go wrong, not just one thing, but one after another, he began to lose his nerve. When he started this racket he had never intended to include murder in his programme, and his warped moral sense laid the blame for all that occurred at Caroline Chisholm's door.

The train went by, no one leaned out of window to yell, 'There he is,' or pointed an accusing finger, but he knew he'd feel a good deal happier when he had rid himself of the white car and was on his way back to London. He even toyed with the notion of leaving the car where it was, but that meant it would be the subject of inquiry and it would be easy to establish ownership. He wouldn't have chosen one so conspicuous but that there hadn't been much choice. He had had to show his driving licence to the garage proprietor, and though he didn't imagine he had taken much notice of the name, still there was the deposit to be collected. To ignore that would be to attract attention at once. It was very hot in the car; at some period the owner must have left it standing in the sun, for the leather scorched to the touch. He could feel himself sweating in his London clothes.

'Catching the London train?' asked the boy.

Brown started up. 'I didn't say . . .'

'You were looking at your watch, as though you had an appointment. You missed the train from Pursey and nobody would be going to the market at this hour. Perfectly simple, my dear Watson.' He laughed good-naturedly. 'Besides, you don't wear clothes like that in the country.'

Brown had an appalling suspicion that it was all a trap, that this young fellow was something to do with the police, had been sent out to pick him up, but he was quite wrong. Playing at amateur detectives is quite a usual game, and all the quizzes in the press and on the radio were sharpening people's wits.

'Well, do I drop you off at the station?' the young man asked, laughing, and he stretched his wide thin-lipped mouth into a sort of grin and said that would suit him. Brown wished he'd been picked up by a different kind of fellow, someone to whom he could have given a tip and who would forget him as soon as he'd turned the corner. This young spark, if he were questioned, would be able to give quite a useful description of him. All he could do was put the newly opened pack of cigarettes on the passenger seat saying gruffly, 'You might run short.'

Then he was out of the car and turning sharply left to walk

up the ramp to the outgoing platform. The car driver, who had stopped to light a cigarette, watched him curiously. If he was returning to London, as he claimed, he was going toward the wrong side of the station. Then he saw him stop by the big white car and put his hand in his pocket. A minute later a policeman walked up and asked him something and some tireless small boys joined them, like a kind of fringe. The man seemed put out, threatening, even apprehensive. The young man opened the car door and swung himself to the ground. If, as seemed likely, there was trouble brewing, he wanted to make his situation clear. Besides, he was curious. Who wouldn't be? He even had visions of his own picture in the paper. Johnny Blair, who gave the wanted man a lift . . .

'Your car, sir?' the policeman was saying, and Brown replied, 'No. No, that's not mine. I'm travelling by train.'

The policeman looked at him. 'Where are you going, sir?'

'London, if you must know. Though I can't see what concern it is of yours.'

'This is the wrong platform for London,' said the policeman.

'Is it? I didn't know. I don't know this part of the world. I'm a Londoner myself.'

'Came down by train this morning perhaps.'

'That's right.'

'Funny you shouldn't notice you alighted this side,' said the policeman. He wasn't one of the old country codgers beloved of playwrights, but a smart young fellow as keen for promotion as the next man.

'Well, I didn't. I'll have to be getting over on the other side or I shall miss my train.'

'Plenty of time,' said the policeman. 'If you're going to London it 'ud pay you to wait for the one after. Get you there sooner,' he added. 'And give you a bit more time,' he added.

'I've told you I don't know anything about this car,' said Brown sharply. 'I don't know why you're making inquiries or how it can conceivably concern me.'

'We received a message to look out for this car and its driver.'

'Well, you've got the car. All you want now is the driver.'

One of the small boys, lovingly licking an orange sucker, drew closer. 'That's 'im,' he said.

Brown turned in a flash. 'What are these kids doing here?'

'They're not doing any harm,' said the policeman mildly.

'That's the one, mister,' said the boy again. 'Car got held up by the lights the other side of the bridge. He was driving.'

'Nonsense,' said Brown. 'If you're going to listen to a boy— for one thing he couldn't recognise someone seen in a flash like that.'

'Dressed posh,' said the boy.

'Have you any identification with you, sir?' the policeman asked civilly.

He began to feel in his pockets. 'I don't think so. I didn't expect to be stopped by the police.'

The young car driver had drawn closer. 'Anything I can do to help?' he offered.

'If you can identify this gentleman . . .'

The young man shook his head. 'Only picked him up eight miles out of Pursey. Missed the up train.'

'You mean, you'd walked from Pursey?'

Now his heart began to knock, now danger drew very close. 'That's right.'

'Six miles?'

'I thought I'd get a lift before I did.'

The constable glanced instinctively at Brown's feet. After six miles of road walking the shoes should have been white with dust.

'Must have been walking about two hours,' the constable hazarded.

'It certainly seemed like it.'

'And you had another eight miles to go.'

'I told you, I expected to get a lift.'

'Wait a minute,' said the amateur Sherlock Holmes, 'There's something here that doesn't fit. When the train passed us he said, "That's the one I should be on". But if he'd been walking for two hours he must have missed the train before that. He could have caught that one at Pursey.'

'You said you were a Londoner,' said the policeman. 'Did you travel down today?'

162

'I told you so. . . .'

'Then no doubt you can explain your business at Pursey, produce someone to vouch for you.'

'What country is this?' Brown demanded. 'I've just come in from Pursey to catch the next London train. There's nothing criminal about that, I hope.'

'No, sir. But we've received instructions to look out for a man answering your description driving a white Ranger car. Number supplied. This is clearly the car in question.'

'I've told you I'm not the chap you want. I came down by train and took a connection into Pursey.'

'What time would this be, sir?'

'I don't recall the actual times. . . .'

'But you'd remember what train you caught from London.' The policeman leaned forward and touched Brown's coat.

'That's a nasty rent you got, sir. Looks new.'

'I caught it on a hedge,' muttered Brown.

'Would you tell me your name?' the policeman inquired.

'Brown.'

'The name of the man we're looking for is Brown.'

'There can't be more than about ten thousand of us,' Brown said. 'What's the trouble? If you're bothered about the car, well, there she is in perfectly good trim so far as I can see. Who's put forward a complaint? The man who hired her out?'

'Who said she was hired?' the policeman dropped like a hawk on a field mouse.

'You told me. . . .'

'I said we were told to look out for a man driving a white car, with this number, who left her here and went on to Pursey.'

'In that case you're still looking, aren't you?'

'I shall have to ask you to come down to the station, sir.' The policeman was inexorable. 'The car-rental manager can tell us if you're the one who hired the car. . . . You have to leave a deposit when you hire a drive-yourself car,' he added.

'Look, Officer,' said Brown desperately, 'this is a case of mistaken identity. I assure you. . . .'

'In that case the quickest thing would be to come to the station and if Mr Clutterbuck doesn't recognise you we'll get one of our chaps to drive you back in time to catch the London train. Of course if you could prove your name wasn't Brown . . .'

'It's a bit late in the day to think of changing it,' Brown said. 'In any case, if I were hiring a car I'd insist on something less conspicuous.'

'Chaps hang themselves,' Crook could have told him. 'They will open their mouths too wide.'

'Then you do drive a car, sir? In that case, you'll have a licence on you, and . . .'

'Of course he's got a licence,' said a new voice, and they turned to see an outsize ginger griffin come pounding toward them from a car as unforgettable as himself. ' I meant to offer you a lift in the Superb,' Crook went on, turning to Brown, ' but someone jumped my claim.'

It was obvious that all the small boys recognised Crook. 'That's the one,' they said, 'asked about the white car.'

'Who are you?' asked Brown. 'Plain-clothes police, perhaps.'

'You should ask them.'

'To the best of my belief I never set eyes on you before.'

'Your faith seems a bit shaky,' commented Crook. ' In another minute you'll be telling us you never set eyes on Miss Chisholm. Come on, let's go.'

'We'll ask the questions if you don't mind, sir,' remarked the policeman, frostily.

'Ah, but do you know the right questions to ask? What happened to the ticket?' he went on to Brown.

'Ticket?'

'Yes. You bought one, didn't you, Whitestone to Pursey, about forty minutes ago. You didn't give it up at Pursey because you never got there; and you won't have to give it up here because you didn't come in by train. *Ergo*, it's still in your possession.'

'What of it?'

'Questions are being asked about a chap answering your description who left the train just before it reached the White-stone Tunnel. Quite a lot of people saw him. If you've only got the return half of your ticket, well, then, we're barking up the wrong tree. But my guess is the officer here will find the complete ticket, punched this end and not punched for the return journey—and the number will show when it was issued. . . . Talk yourself out of that one, if you can.'

All criminals, they say, make one mistake which brings them low. Sometimes they can talk their way out of it, but Brown was not among that fortunate number. He had been so busy thinking of how to extricate himself from his present dilemma, he had forgotten that incriminating bit of pasteboard. Because Crook had guessed right. Naturally he had booked a return; he intended to alight at Pursey but not to give up his ticket. No, he would cross the line by the bridge and come back on the return train that linked up with the London connection. He would destroy the outgoing half, which had been clipped, and no one was likely to notice that the return half was untouched. In country stations they take life easy, you buy your ticket and wander where you please. He had had ample opportunity to throw the thing away if only he had remembered it.

Down at the police station, whither Crook insisted on accompanying them—' Well, if it wasn't for me where would you be?' he demanded of the police—Mr Clutterbuck identified Brown as the man who had hired the white car. He remembered him particularly because he had wanted something less spectacular but this was the only car immediately available. Clutterbuck had asked to see the licence and had noted the name and address; and of course that was the end of it. Because when they came to search their suspect they found the keys of the white Ranger in his pocket.

Crook, who had the ignorant man's idea that the point of waging a war is to win it and to hell with the Queensberry Rules, had the last word.

' By the time you're back in your home town,' he said, ' they'll just about have finished digging your wife out of the cellar.'

And then he stopped dead, as rigid as Lot's wife. ' Cor stone the crows,' he whispered, when he had recovered the power of speech, ' if I didn't forget to give Inspector Perrin the glad news. Let's hope Mrs S. will have tumbled, that's all.'

He didn't feel too worried. In his experience, these old girls always got there in the end.

NINETEEN

Sometimes, in her dreams, Mrs Sagan had seen herself as the kingpin of a situation both romantic and perilous. During the first war, when she had been a little girl, she had lived in week-long daydreams of running into one of the great leaders, Admiral Beatty, say, he was so handsome, and in some extraordinary fashion uncovering a German plot. During the second war she saw herself putting out fires single-handed or dashing into burning buildings or buildings that were tottering to their fall, to rescue some poor old creature who was trapped.

'Stand away there!' the Heavy Rescue chaps would cry, but she would pay no attention.

'My life's not important,' she would declare. 'And she's so—alone.' Breathless the crowds watched the intrepid woman vanish through clouds of dust. And presently she would reappear, sometimes at a window with an inert bundle in her arms urging the chaps below to put up a ladder and chance the whole place coming down. Sometimes she dragged her victim out single-handed. Now suddenly an actual opportunity to take the centre of the stage was offered her and she grasped it with both hands. She never even thought about the danger. The police had annoyed her, taking no notice of her as a person, and not remotely interested in any of her theories. Besides, one of them had bothered her about her astrological activities. She knew they thought she was a dotty old so-and-so and in the real Communist state toward which Britain's enemies worked tirelessly night and day she'd be shut up or put painlessly to sleep or something.

They're always declaring against the profit motive, she told herself fiercely, but if you don't show a profit for the community or them they're the first to want to put the kybosh on you.

After she had got Crook's call on that momentous morning

she sat down and gave herself over to mental arithmetic. 'Now why did he want to know . . . I must figure it out.' She was still figuring when Mrs Rollo came in for her weekly session.

'You *are* lucky,' she panted, being of the school that finds luck most unevenly distributed and never looking her way. 'You must have boiling water day and night.'

'We pay for it,' said Mrs Sagan, shortly. She didn't want to be interrupted just then.

'It's nice that you can afford it,' sniffed Mrs Rollo. 'We're supposed to have constant hot water where *I'm* living, but if *we* run out of fuel, well, we just have to make do with lukewarm till the new supply is due. *They* wouldn't dream of ordering any extra.'

'Rhodes is an excellent manager, he never lets us run out,' said Mrs Sagan severely.

'I know. That's what I mean, you're lucky, having such an easygoing landlord. Coal last week, coke this . . .'

'That's it,' shouted Mrs Sagan so loudly it seemed surprising the ceiling didn't cave in. 'That's what he meant. Now, Adela, you do remember the coal being delivered.'

'Of course I remember. I nearly fell through the coal hole. I might have broken my leg, I should certainly have sued your management if I had. And Prothero,' she added vehemently.

'Who's Prothero?'

'The coal merchant, of course. I have him for my wee fire.' For Mrs Rollo was one of those who believe in making life as difficult for themselves as possible, didn't approve of gas fires, they might blow out and poison you with carbon monoxide or whatever it was; wouldn't have electricity—never know when there might be a cut, and anyway it eats up all the air, so she retained her little grate and had her coal in a little bin on the landing.

'Prothero,' repeated Mrs Sagan. 'He'd remember delivering, wouldn't he?'

'Well.' Mrs Rollo frowned. 'If it wasn't for *me*, he mightn't. *I* know that man.'

'But we only use coke here,' Mrs Sagan insisted. 'Rhodes hates coal. He says it's all wrong for our kind of boiler, makes so much dirt.'

'Well, he was having coal all right that morning. Begging for it, in fact. I heard him. " You oblige me and you won't be sorry," he said to the coalie. Gave him a tip before he'd so much as unloaded a sack.'

Mrs Sagan snatched her friend's hand and nearly broke a bone. 'You'd swear to that—in court, if you had to?'

'There's no need to do me a deadly injury,' said Mrs Rollo, withdrawing her hand. 'If you mean am I sure of my facts, yes, I am.'

'Come on,' said Mrs Sagan. 'We're going down to the police station. Oh, yes, we are, and if you withdraw you can be taken for accessory after the fact. Did you never hear of Crippen?'

She dragged her friend into the street, saw and hailed a taxi, and was driven up to the handsome new police station at the top of the road.

Here she learned that Inspector Perrin was not available.

'Having one of his nonstop cups of tea, I suppose,' snorted Mrs Sagan. 'Why we don't all of us get murdered instead of only a few is no thanks to the police.'

'Who's talking of murder?' asked the station sergeant, wearily. He had these old battle-axes with a screw loose fourteen times a week and it wore the strongest man down.

'I am—if you'll deign to pay attention. No, not my murder, not yet, though it could well come to that.' The station officer thought he could believe her. 'No. Miss Chisholm's.'

'We don't know yet that Miss Chisholm is dead,' said the officer, in severe tones.

'You may not, but Mr Crook and I do, as well as a number of other people; but possibly at the moment only he and I—and the murderer, of course—could tell you where you'd find the body.'

And she told them.

'Have you,' asked the station officer, disappointingly stolid, 'any proof?'

'That's for you to find. All you want are some willing arms and a good supply of elbow grease.'

Then, when they still didn't seem enthusiastic, she cried, 'I wish I hadn't told you, I wish I'd found the corpse myself.

And then I suppose you'd have arrested me for trespass or something.'

'Deirdre,' broke in Mrs Rollo. 'Oh, do listen, dear. I've got the most wonderful notion. I'm practically certain any private individual has the right to bring a charge of murder against another citizen—I don't believe even the *Corps Diplomatique* is immune when it's *murder*—so if you charge—whoever it is you have in mind, with murder, the police must move.'

But Mrs Sagan hesitated. She hadn't any doubt Miss Chisholm was dead, she knew it wasn't a natural death, she was darn well tooting she could tell the world where the body was—but she couldn't swear to the murderer's identity.

'Accessory after the fact,' hissed Mrs Rollo. 'If you ask me the police are all in it, or they wouldn't be so afraid to act.'

It wasn't, of course, so easy for the police as it might appear on the surface. Mrs Sagan was the only tenant at no. 2 in immediate occupation, and the coal cellar didn't belong to her. 'Very well,' she told them, 'I shall go along to the agents. I'm certain Mr Allen will give you permission to search, it's his property.'

Finally they went around to see Mr Allen, the house agent who managed no. 2.

'Body in the coal cellar?' said Allen. 'Who says so?'

'I do,' stuttered Mrs Sagan. 'And Mr Crook.'

'Where's Mr Crook?'

'I don't know. Probably preventing another murder taking place somewhere.'

'Have you a grain of proof?' asked Mr Allen, flabbergasted.

'Only common sense. I did think you'd recognise that, even if the police don't. Look, Miss Chisholm disappeared, that's admitted. There have been pictures of her in all the papers but no one's come forward to say they saw her. Her letters are still coming to no. 2, her car was left behind and her pet was found murdered. Then the car's discovered but no Miss Chisholm. You're supposed to think she's under the sinking sands, but my bet is she's under the coal, the coal that should never have been ordered.'

'What is the arrangement about coal?' the police inquired.

'Hot water is one of the amenities included in the service charge,' replied Mr Allen, rather pontifically. 'An adequate supply of coke is delivered on the first of every month, unless that should be a public holiday, when it is delivered on the day previous. This arrangement has been in force for the eighteen months that these flats have been occupied under the new tenancies, and we have never run short of fuel.'

'You mean not till this month.'

'I'm not aware we ran short this month.'

'You mean'—Mrs Sagan couldn't contain herself—'you mean Rhodes never told you he took four hundredweight of *coal* last week?'

'Certainly not.'

The police took over again. 'Who would pay for the additional fuel, assuming that any was delivered?'

'The point has never arisen,' confessed Mr Allen, pulling at his long loose lower lip.

'Four hundredweight at present prices would be something like two pounds.'

'Summer prices still operate,' said Mr Allen, mechanically.

'Well, then, a few shillings under two pounds. Would the management pay for that?'

'It's a fine point,' said Mr Allen.

Mrs Sagan was dancing with impatience. 'In one minute,' she said, 'I'll get a shovel and start digging in the cellar myself.'

'The obvious course to pursue,' said Mr Allen, who had been so educated that he couldn't use a word of one syllable if a polysyllabic word would suffice, 'is to interrogate Rhodes.'

'If you know where he is,' countered Mrs Sagan neatly.

'At present,' continued Mr Allen, 'we have no corroboration of the statement that an unspecified quantity of coal—'

'Yes, we have,' interrupted Mrs Sagan rudely. 'My friend, Mrs Rollo here, she saw it being delivered.'

'Nearly broke my ankle,' agreed Mrs Rollo nippily. She had had no idea when she set out this morning that she was going to have such an exciting day.

'And surely the time to start looking for the body is *before* Rhodes comes back. Then you can present him with a fait accompli. That man's so clever he could probably spirit a body from under the coal if he knew you were going to look for it. . . . Ring up Mr Crook if you don't believe me,' she added.

The police recalled that there had been a message from Mr Crook to Inspector Perrin that morning, but the inspector had not yet returned. Crook's name carried a lot more weight than Mrs Sagan's, so they rang his flat but of course he wasn't at home.

'He's got a business address,' howled Mrs Sagan.

So they tried that and Bill Parsons told them that Crook wasn't there, he was out after victim number three, name of Carter, tenant of the second-floor flat, and a bit more to the same effect.

That did the trick. The inspector gave the order and his chaps got to work.

The cellar at no. 2 was under the front steps; coal was delivered through a chute; entry to the cellar came from a passage running from the front door of the garden flat, and only Rhodes had the key.

The Whitestone express took one hour and twenty minutes to reach London and about fifteen minutes after that Rhodes came strolling out of the Underground station and around the corner into Brandon Street. It struck him at once that there was an air of unusual activity about, and more people doing nothing than usual. Then he saw the reason for it. There was a police car in front of no. 2, and as he came to a dead stop, thought froze, feet even petrified. Something that looked like a visitor from outer space hurled itself down the steps and came clawing at him, shouting, 'There he is, there's the villain, there's the man you want.'

He had the sense not to turn and fly, not then. He simply stayed where he was and watched a policeman fend off the lunatic whom he now recognised as Mrs Sagan, and then asked, 'What's it all about?'

'As if you didn't know,' bawled Mrs Sagan.

Rhodes looked around. 'What is all this? What are those chaps doing in my cellar?'

Mr Allen who was hanging around, leaving his secretary to

cope with the office said uncomfortably, 'A suggestion has
been made . . .'

But the police intervened.

'Well,' said Rhodes mildly, 'your timing's let you down all
right this time. Why didn't you come yesterday? Coke came
this morning, the cellar's nearly full.'

'Not nearly so full as it was,' shouted Mrs Sagan, indicating
a great pile of coke already dislodged by the diggers.

'I don't get it,' said Rhodes simply. 'What are you expecting
to find anyway?'

So they told him.

'You're crazy,' Rhodes assured them. 'How could she be
there without me knowing?'

No one answered that one.

Mr Allen bustled forward. 'Is it a fact that you ordered an
additional supply of fuel last month?'

'No,' said Rhodes. 'We didn't need any.'

'It isn't true,' said Mrs Sagan. 'He bought it off a coal cart.'

'But we don't use coal,' Rhodes explained.

'That's why it's so odd you should have been begging a man
to let you have some.'

'Madam, I must insist . . .' the sergeant began, but he was
like King Canute ordering the waves to retreat.

'If I'd needed more fuel I'd have come to you, sir,' said
Rhodes in a straightforward kind of voice to Mr Allen. 'I
suppose if the police like to dig through the cellar there's no one
can stop them. I only hope they'll leave everything as tidy as
they find it. I take it there's no objection to me going into my
flat,' he added. 'I could do with a cup, and if these chaps
are going to move a ton of coke I should think they could,
too.'

He produced his key and walked in as cool as a cucumber.
The sergeant of police hung around the door.

'Come and take a seat, Sergeant,' Rhodes offered. 'You'll get
tired standing while they get through that little lot.'

He set out a tea tray handily, produced cakes and a bowl of
sugar. 'How many of you are there?' he inquired, taking cups
out of a cupboard.

The kettle whistled and he made the tea.

'How about you, Mr Allen? Sergeant? P'raps one of your chaps would fetch theirs.'

Mr Allen took the cup.

'Sugar, sir?'

Mr Allen took three lumps.

'Sugar, Sergeant?'

The policeman knocked and came in.

'Come for the tea?' inquired Rhodes cheerily. 'It's all ready.'

The man paid no attention. 'The chaps have got down to the coal, sir,' he said.

As the sergeant turned to Rhodes, the porter seized the cup of scalding tea and flung it full in his face. Before anyone could move he had bolted into his bedroom, slamming and locking the door behind him, and scrambled through the window into a little cul-de-sac that ran up behind the houses. He dashed down this toward the High Street, thinking, If they've put anyone on guard I'm done, but all the police were around at the front and he had gained the Underground station before any of them surfaced. He must have known he stood no chance; he had no passport, no luggage, very little money. But he was counting on Brown. Brown had got him into this, now let him get him out.

He shoved a sixpenny bit into an automatic ticket machine and fled through the barrier. A train going east was just leaving but he flung himself at it, heedless of the cry of the coloured platform attendant, and squeezed himself in. There were not many people travelling and he went to the farthest end of the car. At Holborn he got out and boarded a bus. A few minutes later he dropped off again without paying his fare—the conductress was busy inside talking to a passenger—and made for Francis Street. He had a key on his ring that admitted him to Brown's flat, and not until he was inside and had sunk onto a rather womanish-looking divan affair in the living room did he dare relax.

They won't find me here, he thought. Why should they? Brown would be back this evening, and they could puzzle something out. Brown was amply supplied with passports and he kept plenty of money on the premises. In fact, this seemed an opportunity to learn a little more about his evasive partner, so, having first locked the front door, Rhodes casually drew the curtains part way across the window and got to work.

They found the broken, disfigured body of Caroline Chisholm under the piles of coal. A doctor said she had died of a broken neck.

'It's very simple when you know how,' he assured his colleagues. 'One hand over the mouth, the other under the chin, a sharp jerk back with the victim held close so that she can't struggle, and it's all over. The spine snaps. If any death can be called merciful, this is it.'

Now all they had to do was trace Rhodes. It should be remembered that no one at the London end had heard of Brown at that stage.

Brown was playing it dumb. No one, bar Rhodes, could swear on the Book as to his identity with the chap they were after. Caroline and Smith were both dead, the chap who had called on the night of Caroline's death certainly hadn't got a sufficiently clear view of him to swear to him in court, and the same went for the police who had seen him at the wheel of the truck in Hebberden Mews. He doubted whether Kay could pick him out at an identity parade. She had been dizzy with dope when she staggered into the white car, though not quite so dizzy as he had anticipated, and he had never turned his face toward her. By the time they got into the train she was much too far gone to see anything straight. He hadn't met Crook face to face. It still seemed to him he might get the benefit of the doubt. In some countries you were regarded as guilty till you could prove your innocence. Here the onus of proof lay with the authorities. If Rhodes stood by him and said, 'No, I never saw him before,' Brown optimistically believed he still stood a chance.

The fact was he couldn't believe that after so much planning, so much risk taken and danger circumvented, he was going to fail now. When Rhodes had telephoned that morning that the girl was going to Pursey he had seen his chance. He knew now that she was the one who had exchanged the hats and that meant she was dangerous. Like most criminals he didn't look far ahead. Kay was the obstacle in his path and if obstacles won't get out they must be destroyed. Caroline had been in the way and she was gone; the same was true of Smith. Now it was Kay's turn. It so happened that he knew the Whitestone district and told Rhodes he would catch the express, hire a car at Whitestone and be waiting about ten miles out near a crossroads. It would be market day and people would be busy and unlikely to notice him. He hadn't bargained on getting such a striking car, but it so happened none other was available.

He had motored back by side roads and brought the car to a standstill in a lane where not much traffic came. He saw the little blue car go past and knew the parking spot was a bare half-mile distant. He waited a bit longer—Rhodes had to discover the car was unserviceable, and it might look suspicious if he turned up in the nick of time. On the other hand, he dared not wait too long; some Good Samaritan might pass and stop, and it was of the essence of the plot that there should be no third-party intervention. When he drove out of his quiet lane, where even the horses in the adjoining field paid no attention to him, he found the girl lying back in the car, and Rhodes waiting alongside. He played hard to get, you couldn't afford to overlook the smallest detail, then allowed himself to be persuaded.

Rhodes had given him the V-sign by that time, and he knew the girl had swallowed the dope and so should give a minimum of trouble. By the time she was found all the effects would have worn off, the coroner might add a rider about careless passengers or even hint that the authorities would do well to make certain all their carriage doors were in tiptop condition, but the verdict would be accidental death. Crook had had the wool pulled well and truly over his eyes, and whatever he might suspect he couldn't prove a thing. So Brown argued. But then Rhodes had pulled a boner that even an easygoing girl couldn't overlook. Murder isn't a hit-and-miss affair, whatever amateurs might think. It's a matter of check and double-check all along the line. He'd trusted Rhodes and Rhodes had proved he was an amateur and sunk them both.

With Crook prodding them from one side and Mrs Sagan from the other, the police got a prize wiggle on. Whitestone had sent them Brown's address, on the assumption that sooner or later Rhodes would go around there. It was just a matter of time, the sergeant told Crook.

'Time!' retorted Mrs Sagan scornfully. 'Yes, but how long? Don't forget the man who escaped from a north-country prison last year, and wasn't caught *for eight months*.'

Brown hadn't expected his confederate to look for him at his home address.

'Go to The Two Pigeons,' he had said, 'and wait for me there. If I don't turn up by, say, six o'clock, go on home to Brandon Street and wait for me to telephone.'

He didn't know that for quite a while Rhodes had had a key to the flat in Francis Street, or he might have put everything into a safe. He didn't realise that there's no such thing in the jungle as honour among thieves, and that the law there is every man (or beast) for himself. By the time he came back to London his partner had sold him right down the river.

TWENTY

To Rhodes in Francis Street time moved like a cripple. The room faced due west and as the afternoon wore on the heat became stifling. He was afraid to raise another window lest he be seen from the street, but he did at length carefully ease one curtain across the blazing pane. There was no way of warning his partner what had happened; Brown would presumably go the The Two Pigeons and wait for him there. Rhodes wished he had the courage to keep the appointment, but he knew the hue and cry would be out for him, and every publican would have been warned. His chief fear was not that he would be tracked to Francis Street but that Brown, grown tired of waiting, would oil around to Brandon Street in search of news—and run his close-cropped bullet head into a wasps' nest. His unease growing with every maddening tick of the clock, Rhodes presently moved softly across to the highly polished and sophisticated cocktail cabinet in one corner of the room and poured himself three fingers of Scotch. This seemed to calm his nerves, so he repeated the dose. He had intended to add a little water, but, with his hand outstretched to the tap, he decided to take his medicine neat; and really it tasted better that way.

There was a morning paper on a chair, and he read it from end to end. When he'd read the news, including the radio programmes, he turned to the advertisements. 'Love Laughs at Locks,' he read. 'Affectionate Poodle Offers Three Adorable Labradoodles to Good Homes.'

Somebody had swum the Channel and somebody had crashed a plane with twelve people on board, no survivors, and somebody had taken an overdose. Patersfamilias objected to the American rocket bases in England and someone else was beefing about the undue profits made by one of the television services. The mixture as before, and nothing to hold your attention. He looked at the crossword but that kind of thing had never interested him. As the clock moved around to news time he could resist the temptation no longer. Stealthily he turned a knob and a voice in a whisper like a grasshopper's whirr said, 'Police today found the body of a woman believed to be Miss Caroline Chisholm, the West End milliner who has been missing for a week, in a cellar under her flat in Earl's Court. The death is reported of Sir Bertram Peacock, the landscape artist. Sir Bertram . . .' He flicked the switch off again, and had the second half of the whisky. It was going to be all right, of course—Brown wasn't the kind of fool that puts a foot wrong—but because he had to pass the time somehow he began to work out a statement, if the police caught up with him.

It would be useless for him to pretend he hadn't known Caroline was there, hadn't, in short, put her there himself, since no one else had the cellar key, and anyway the boiler had to be stoked daily. Accessory after the fact—he couldn't deny that, but it wasn't a hanging matter, he assured himself. As for the girl, Smith, he knew nothing of her, hadn't in fact even set eyes on her, and on the evening she died he had been hanging around the house on Brandon Street waiting for a chance to break into

Kay's flat and look for the hat. As for today's activities, he had been in the London express when Brown put his plan into practice. Apart from Kay Carter's evidence there was nothing against him. And unless Brown had come a cropper, her evidence wouldn't be available. If we hang together, he thought with unconscious irony, they can't shake us. With only average luck Brown would get away with a manslaughter charge on Caroline Chisholm's account—didn't you have to prove malice aforethought for murder?—and Brown swore he hadn't intended to do the woman any harm when he walked into her flat.

He faced the obvious truth, that he would get a long stretch if the police found out anything about their drug-peddling activities, but why should they unless his confederate let him down? And he'd not do that, because he'd want to save his own skin. The Hebberden Mews premises had been vacated—all incriminating evidence removed. Brown ought to be back by now, he fretted, looking at the watch on his wrist, and at that moment he heard a key being carefully pushed into the lock.

He jumped up and came into the hall as the door opened. Caution made him refrain from putting on a light.

'Well, Fred, you've taken your time,' he exclaimed, and then someone pressed a switch and two men came in, neither of them remotely resembling the missing Brown. Before he could even think about a break this time, they were either side of him, had him by the arms, one was saying, 'Herbert Benjamin Rhodes, I arrest you for . . .'

'I didn't kill her,' said Rhodes quickly.

'Less you say at the moment the better,' the officer warned him. 'You're being held for complicity, the rest we can sort out at the station. Come on.'

He didn't ask what had happened to Brown. He knew. The fellow had bungled it, otherwise the police wouldn't have come here. Could they hang you for complicity in two murders? (They couldn't touch him where Smith was concerned.) A few people were standing about as they emerged, a press camera flashed; he tried to wrench an arm free to cover his eyes but they held him too firmly, he could only duck his head and seek the welcome obscurity of the police car, where he sat at the back between two men in blue and started desperately to plan his defence.

Rhodes told his story in considerable detail to the lawyer assigned to him after his arrest.

'I first met Brown when I was a porter at Litchfield Mansions about two years ago. He had a flat there at the time, and he asked me if I wanted to make a bit of money on the side. All I had to do was deliver parcels to addresses he would supply, and sometimes bring parcels back that would be handed to me. He never said what was in them. I thought most likely he was trying to dodge the purchase tax. By the time I realised he was involved in drug-peddling it was too late for me to back out. He had known Miss Chisholm for several years; I think at one time they had either been married or had passed as man and wife.

'About eighteen months ago Brown changed his address and suggested that I might apply for the tenancy of the garden flat at no. 2 where I would have more leisure, as it was only a part-time job. The flat went with the work, and Brown said he would make it all right about the wages I would be forfeiting. I am a carpenter and decorator by profession, and during the past few years have worked as a one-man business, on a part-time basis. I never had any trouble getting work.

'Brown told me that Miss Chisholm had a flat at no. 2, and would probably want me to co-operate with her. I did messenger work and carried on with my decorating etc., which proved a very good entrée to various houses where Brown wanted me to go.

'On the last Tuesday in August I received a telephone call from her flat soon after 7.30 p.m. It was Brown's voice, which surprised me, as I had not known he was coming. He said I should come up at once, we were in trouble. When he let me in I saw Miss Chisholm's body on the settee in the living-room, and Brown said she was dead. He explained that he had come to see her, because he had discovered that she was holding out on him. Brown himself was not in charge of operations, only a kind of agent for someone he called the guv'nor. I never saw this man and do not know his name. Miss Chisholm, like me,

179

was supposed to take her orders from Mr Brown. I never knew the details, but I know the hat shop played some part in the scheme. You might say Miss Chisholm was like a sub-contractor, who had been accepting other contracts unknown to the boss.

'There had been a scene, and Miss Chisholm had told him he could do nothing, because he could not bring a case. Brown had said, " I could tell the boss," and she had laughed and asked, " What would you tell him? That you let yourself be bamboozled?" He was furious at being cheated and more furious still at being laughed at. The little bird was flying round the room all this time, calling out its five words, and flapping near Brown's face. He said he had a kind of horror of birds, sometimes had nightmares about them, and he told Miss Chisholm to put it back in its cage. According to Brown she said, " I can't imagine what the guv'nor would think if he knew you were nervous of a budgerigar." Then Henry—that is the bird's name—settled on the back of Brown's chair and he caught it and twisted its neck and threw it back into its cage. Miss Chisholm started to scream and he put his hand over her mouth; she was a good deal stronger than she looked and she struggled hard. Brown told me he must have suffocated her without meaning to do so. Suddenly she stopped fighting, but he said it had been an accident.'

At this point his lawyer, Mr Morcam, intervened. ' According to the medical evidence Miss Chisholm's neck was broken. That is not in accord with your version of what took place.'

' I don't know what took place,' asserted Rhodes, sullenly. ' I'm only telling you what Brown told me. He said that if the police were called in, my name couldn't be kept out of it, and that would mean a long prison sentence for my share in the drug-running, even if they didn't accuse me of being an accessory in Miss Chisholm's death. I said, " I wasn't even here when she died," and he said, " There's only your word, isn't there?" I suppose I panicked. I didn't know at that time it was Brown who opened the door to Oliver. He said Miss Chisholm had sent the young fellow away, and nobody but myself knew that he, Brown, had called that night. Brown said it would be easy to close down the workshop for redecoration and give out that

Miss Chisholm had gone abroad a bit unexpectedly that day. She generally did go abroad about that time of year. There was only the one girl at the workshop, and she would swallow whatever she was told. She could be sent on holiday at once, and later on we could come to some agreement as to the story to be told to account for Miss Chisholm's not returning. He had thought everything out, was as cool as you please.

' He suggested we could remove some of her personal belongings from her dressing-table and bathroom and wrap them in newspaper and put them in her little dust bin. She always wrapped everything in newspaper so no one would notice anything unusual. I would then collect as usual the next day. I was to take her car round to the garage and leave it to be decarbonised! I had often done this before; later I could call for it and we could either get rid of it or change it so that it would not be recognised. I would have taken it round that night but the garage would have been closed. The main trouble was to conceal the body. Obviously if it was left in the flat it must be found sooner or later, and Oliver could give evidence that she had been at home that night.

' Brown said he had formed a plan. The cellar of no. 2 is a big old-fashioned affair with a flagged floor; nothing was done to this when the rest of the house was modernised. To reach the cellar from inside you go down a flight of stairs at the far end of the hall. This door leads to the garden flat, and if you go through that you come into the passage leading to the cellar; it can also be approached from outside, but once the body was through the hall door there was no danger of anyone seeing it. Brown said I should take the body down without delay, as we did not want rigor mortis to have time to set in. He said it would be quite safe, he had sent the young man I now know to be Mr Oliver up to the top flat, and we could hear the sound of television programmes through the ceiling. I knew Miss Carter was out, which only left Mrs Sagan, and Brown said he would keep her occupied on the telephone while I went down the stairs with Miss Chisholm. This was a good idea, as Mrs Sagan is a very sudden lady and liable to pop out at you without warning.

' I did not like the idea, but I could not suggest anything

181

better. I did think, if Mr Brown could get the body into Miss Chisholm's car and then drive it away, it would be safer for me, but he said it was too dangerous, the cellar would be best. I knew the supply of coke was running low, which meant it was a good time to try taking up the floor, so at last I agreed. I also took her handbag that I later passed to Brown; I forgot about her glasses. Probably Mr Brown did not know she wore glasses, she only put them on for work and did not like talking about them.

' Miss Chisholm was a little thing, but she seemed very heavy to carry when she was dead, and awkward, too. Her hair brushed against my cheek and I almost dropped her, and one of her hands kept jogging against my shoulder. I think carrying her downstairs was almost the worst part of the affair, but at that time though I knew she was dead and I had her body in my arms, I could scarcely believe it. I put her in the cellar, at the far end, and scooped a little coke over her. I did not like to put on the light as it can be seen from outside, the cellar being under the front steps, and having glass risers—I suppose, for the sake of light. Then I went back to my flat and destroyed everything I could from her bag; the creams, etc., I scooped out and later threw away the jars. That same evening I found to my horror that it would be quite impossible to put her under the flags. One or two were loose, but most of them were heavily cemented in, they could only be shifted with a pick, and that would bring everyone running.

' I went back to my flat and rang up Brown. He said, " Wait till the morning when the others will be out, and if anyone should hear you they will think you are breaking coal." I said, " No, they won't, because they all know we only use coke, which doesn't require breaking,' but he had given me an idea. Next day I heard a coalie selling in the street, so I asked him if he could oblige me with four hundredweight. I said I had unexpectedly run out, and there would be trouble if there was no hot water. I told him the flat went with the job, and he saw how important it was and made no trouble; I had told him I would make it worth his while. I saw to it that Miss Chisholm's body would be completely concealed by the coal; the coke was due in a few days and after that I thought we should be safe.

I still think the plan might have succeeded if Miss Carter had not become suspicious about Miss Chisholm's absence. She spoke to me before I had time to move the car, and after that it was too dangerous. I did not dare say I knew Miss Chisholm had gone away, because of the things in the box that the milkman had left.

'Then Mr Crook came into it and things got worse than ever. But Brown told me to drive the car round to his garage with Miss Chisholm's things in it, and this I did. That evening I changed the licence plates and Brown drove the car away. I know nothing of any visit to Sheepford or how the girl, Smith, came by her death. I had never set eyes on her. Of course Brown thought the sands would swallow up everything left on the seat of the car, and with a different number it might not be associated with Miss Chisholm; it was a piece of shocking bad luck the mirror getting caught in a crevice.'

Rhodes made this long statement in an injured and outraged voice, suggesting what in fact he felt, that men who had taken so much trouble and so many risks deserved to be successful.

His lawyer was quite unsympathetic. 'The least you can look for—apart from any charge in connection with drug-running —is a verdict of accessory after the crime. You'd probably have been wiser not to get that coal.'

'I had to get the coal,' asserted Rhodes fiercely. 'Suppose I'd had an accident, got knocked down on a crossing or even twisted an ankle, first thing Mr Allen would do would be to send in a temporary to keep the boiler stoked, and no one could have missed her, I tell you, no one. . . .'

'It will be interesting,' Mr Morcam observed, 'to know how far your story tallies with Brown's.'

'Mine's the truth,' said Rhodes at once. 'And you don't frighten me with any suggestion they could take me for murder. Miss Chisholm was dead before I got into the flat, I don't know anything about the girl, Smith, and as for Miss Carter, she was alive all right when I left her.'

'If Brown chooses to say he came to the flat and discovered you there with Miss Chisholm . . .'

'He didn't. He opened the door to Oliver, and Oliver can swear to it I was downstairs on my own premises.'

'Lucky for you,' said Morcam. 'You shouldn't have removed the silver though, because that constitutes theft, whether you meant to keep the stuff or not, and homicide plus theft constitutes a capital charge. Still, no doubt you'll be able to duck that, and the taxpayers will have the pleasure of investing eight hundred a year on your behalf—that's what it costs to keep a chap in prison—for an indefinite period.'

'Here, you're supposed to be acting for me,' shouted Rhodes.

'Which involves making the best I can of the story you tell, and that I shall do. But don't go to bed dreaming of being acquitted without a stain on your character.'

He wished he hadn't been picked for the job; he was hard-hearted as well as hard-headed, and he'd like to have seen the pair of them written off. Caroline had asked for what was coming to her, but poor little Smith had been squashed as ruthlessly as if she were a bluebottle, and it was no thanks to his client that Kay Carter was still in the land of the living.

TWENTY-ONE

'Who says fairy stories have gone out of fashion?' asked Crook, when he heard all that. 'Of course Brown knew what he was doing when he put out Caroline Chisholm's light. If you lose your head you strangle or suffocate; you don't daintily break a lady's neck. And it was the same with the Smith girl. He knew what he was doing and he did darn well. All that guff about the little bird fretting his nerves—he killed it because he was a natural killer. He hadn't a pang of compunction at the idea of shoving you off the line, and it wouldn't have kept him awake at night if the plan had come off.'

He was talking to Kay Carter and the man he had christened young Lochinvar in his flat on Brandon Street.

'Why did he do it?' Oliver wanted to know.

'Rhodes said she was double-crossing him and that was probably true, I don't see any other explanation for the hatbox with the stuff in it going to her private address. She may have had other registered parcels there, no one would notice and Rhodes would take them in. In addition, she was very likely blackmailing him and he couldn't or wouldn't take it. He was in the racket in quite a big way. The police have discovered they were passing marihuana—among other things. Henry, the budgie, was all part of a blind, Indian hemp seed mixed with his diet—they were up to all the tricks. Rhodes had a perfect disguise for passing the stuff, no one was going to question an odd-job man coming to paint a cupboard or mend your electric bell. They've been cleaning up for quite a while. Some of the names that are going to be involved in this before they put our little gentleman in quicklime are going to stagger you. . . . What put you wise to him?' he added to Kay.

She leaned back, her hands linked behind her head. 'It was such a little thing. It was just before we came to the petrol station. I'd accepted everything up till then. I thought it was being a bit—well, fuddy-duddy—sending Rhodes with a car when I'd meant to go by Underground, but I suppose people have got pushed off platforms just as the train's coming in. I was a bit surprised, too, to see the label in the front of the car, but I decided that was all part of the Arthur Crook service. Even when he told me he was driving me the whole way because you'd been thinking it over and you didn't like the idea of my changing trains and perhaps having to go by a subway—well, it was a lovely day for a drive. And then I happened to say Lady Julia might be sending a car to meet the train and he dropped his brick so hard it nearly crushed my foot. He said you'd rung her up and explained I'd be coming by road. But you couldn't have told him that because *Lady Julia hasn't got a telephone.*'

'You can hardly blame Rhodes for pulling that boner,' suggested Crook. 'Anyone out of the nuthouse living in the country has a line.'

'But, look, Cinderella,' urged Oliver, 'why didn't you put down your little glass slipper right away? You were in a strong position, I should have thought. The car was stationary, you had a witness at the petrol station, you only had to say, " I'm not moving from here. . . ." '

' I had to make up my mind so quickly,' Kay explained. ' It seemed to me the essential thing was to get *you* on the scene.' She turned a glance on Crook that nearly melted his barnacle heart. ' The garage attendant was a boy of—what?—eighteen, I was travelling in a Hospital Car Service vehicle, Rhodes was in charge, he only had to explain he was a doctor, that I'd had a breakdown, had a persecution complex—after all, if I wasn't sick, what was I doing in a car with a Hospital Car Service sticker on it? A boy of that age wouldn't have dared try to stop him, and anyone would have supported Rhodes, even if he had. But I worked it out that if I could leave a message in some way, then most likely he would ring up. I made a point of mentioning your name and said where we were going. I didn't dare do more, because once Rhodes got the idea that I'd—rumbled him, is that what you say?—I was certain we wouldn't get to Whitestone, let alone Pursey. As a matter of fact, he was much cleverer than I was. He came back with the tea and what he said were aspirins, and I wouldn't have them because I said I was allergic to aspirin. I didn't think that's what they were, of course. I was convinced they were some sort of sedative. What a clever girl I am, I thought, seeing through that.'

' Did he try and urge you?' inquired Oliver.

' Of course not. Why should he?' The stuff was already in the tea. I dare say those two were genuine aspirin. But it foxed me all right.'

' It was taking a whale of a risk going on with him in any case,' Oliver growled.

' But, don't you see, I knew once Mr Crook understood, he'd bring me out like Mr Standfast on the other side. It was just a question whether I could get the message through.'

Oliver shook his head. ' How do you do it, Crook? Win their hearts and yet always sidestep the hoop?'

' I did have a bit of a shock when I saw we were going to change cars. I didn't know how I was going to leave a message there, but don't they say when you're desperate your brain functions at double rate? I pretended I was going to be sick and of course even Rhodes didn't like to offer to hold my head, and as I leaned against the far side of the car I scrawled the number with a lipstick. It was as much as I dared do.'

' It was enough,' said Crook, simply.

' What will happen to them now?' Kay inquired.

' Well, Rhodes has indicted Brown for the murder of Miss Chisholm. He might have played it tricky and said it was all yarn on Rhodes' part to get out of an accusation himself but you'—he pointed one of his pudgy fingers at Oliver—' could testify there was a chap answering to Brown's description in the flat that night.'

' Would they have taken my evidence at an identity parade?' Oliver sounded scandalised.

' Well, they'd know it wasn't Rhodes you saw, and once they'd got onto Brown they went round to his place and found the card index and files he'd removed from Hebberden Mews. He was so sure of himself he hadn't even destroyed them. Anyway, he hadn't had much time, what with murdering that poor girl . . .'

' Will they get him for that?' Oliver asked.

' He can't say he never heard of her because her insurance card, stamped by Miss Chisholm, was in his flat. She was nearly run down by a Martin Tourer the same night as a similar car was wrecked off Benton Cove; that young couple at Sheepford can testify to a dark chap at the wheel; we know a chap answering to a similar description was in the Mews the night the premises were raided—" some circumstantial evidence is very strong, as when you find a trout in the milk." And there was the little effort against you—I'm not a bettin' man, not in the ordinary meanin' of the word—but if I were I wouldn't risk a postwar tanner on his chances.'

' And Rhodes?' persisted Oliver.

' Well, he knew Brown had murdered Chisholm, but he'll soft-pedal it, say he believed it was an accident and he lost his head. You can't hang a man for that. It's probably true he didn't know anything about the Smith girl, but there can't be any question that he'd known Brown's plans for you.'

' It's awfully silly, though,' Kay suggested. ' So long as your head bobbed above water, they hadn't got a hope. Why didn't they start with you?'

'They might have got hurt,' said Crook, simply, and Oliver leaned forward and slapped him on the knee.

'Come clean, Crook. You know quite well that if they'd turned their guns on you, little Cinderella here would have come swimming to the rescue, if necessary in a homemade submarine. Besides, your evidence was mostly hearsay once she was silenced. . . .'

'I dips me lid,' acknowledged Crook, simply. 'If ever you get tired of selling radios you might do worse than join my racket. . . . All the same, it don't pay to try too long odds,' he added warningly to the girl. 'I know a lot about feminine intuition being better than proof, but what you don't know is that to a chap like Brown the individual simply doesn't count. If he's a nationalist he's called a fanatic and they string him up just the same, but sooner or later someone goes and hangs a martyr's crown on his picture in the town hall. Brown was a fanatic all right, he'd swat you as easy as a fly, same way as he swatted Miss Chisholm and that miserable girl. And Rhodes was his A.D.C., same like Bill Parsons is mine.'

'Why was Brown so sure that Kay was dangerous?' Oliver wanted to know. 'Because of the hat? Could he be sure it was she who'd swapped it?'

'Well, it wasn't little Miss Smith and I'd say Rhodes knew the box had been opened at no. 2.'

'How did he know? Or do you think he found the hat?'

'If he didn't it wasn't for want of searching. He'd given my place the once-over—well, he told me himself that he could open any of those flats, given a little bit of celluloid. Only the hat wasn't there.'

'I hadn't got it either,' Kay pointed out.

'Remember what you did with the original bit of string that was round the box?' Crook inquired, artlessly.

'I put it in the rubbish. It was just a piece of string. . . .'

'With marks of the wax on it. And who empties the rubbish? Oh, you handed him that on a dish. When he came upon it that virtually signed your death warrant, and if they had pulled it off,' he added savagely, 'the law would have been justified in taking me as accessory before the fact. Yes, they would. That chap was giving me the red light from the start, and I was colour-blind. That registered parcel you took in—how come Brown knew you had it? Obviously because Rhodes told him.'

'I don't think I mentioned it to Rhodes,' said Kay, wrinkling her brows.

'You didn't have to, sugar. You left a little note under the door, Miss C.'s door, telling her you'd taken in a registered packet. Rhodes saw it there and so did I and I didn't connect. Then there was the coal—Mrs Sagan mentioned that to me, and I let that one go by, too. Rhodes took the car when the house was empty and no one would notice, and I'd guess he was the one that changed the licence plates. Chaps in his and Brown's position have to be ready for all emergencies. But he played it smarter than Brown, because when it came to the actual blow bein' struck he melted away. You know, if you hadn't been nosy and found the butter and what not in the fridge, and noticed the car in the street, they might have got away with it. The police have every reason to thank you, and if they knew the meaning of gratitude they'd give you the handsomest wedding present on record—a stuffed policeman for a hatstand, say.'

'That reminds me,' observed Kay, calmly. 'Did you really tell Lady Julia I was jilting her son?'

'Oh, teach the orphan girl to sew,' exclaimed Crook. 'Someone's got to do your thinking for you. How could you marry a chap like that? Any time he heard someone had struck oil he'd be off like a vulture, probably wouldn't even take time to attend your funeral. I'd feel like accessory before the fact if I let that go through.'

'Don't give it another thought,' Oliver soothed him. 'If he withdraws gracefully it'll save me the trouble of breaking his blasted neck. You know,' he went on, turning to the girl and drawing her hands down to hold them as if he'd never let them go, 'I'll tell you a most astonishing thing.' He said it as solemnly as if he'd just discovered the eighth wonder of the world and he probably thought he had. 'That first night I saw—well, hardly saw you, come to that—but the mischief was done. You know, I've been congratulating myself for years on missing the ball and chain, nice quiet evenings planning a new campaign to bring a Hirewire Telly into every home, but that night—no, I found myself with pencil and paper working out things like rent and credit buying and dress allowances and two living as cheap as one. My sales resistance was definitely lowered for a day, heart not in it, see. Naturally I shall make up for lost time because—well, you have to have something besides yourself to offer.'

'Don't you do it, honey,' said Crook sturdily. 'You'll find you're married to an animated television set, like having a spy in the home.'

'Come off it,' said Oliver softly. 'You know you love it.' He leaned forward and turned a knob.

'What's the most wonderful thing you can think of?' said a voice, and they waited entranced till the picture faded in.

'Is that Sally Hawksbee or only her twin sister?' demanded Crook. 'If it's the girl herself she must have as many passports as our Mr Brown.'

Sally Hawksbee (or her identical twin) treated them to a smile that would have made an alligator envious and coyly produced a huge box of chocolates with First Love in great gold letters across the front.

'Make an appointment with First Love tonight,' she cooed. 'There's nothing like First Love.'

'Blow me down,' said Oliver. 'Fancy me agreeing with a television ad.'

Sally disappeared and the now familiar frill of faces took her place.

'Take it cold, take it hot,' they began.

'This,' said Mr Crook, 'is where we came in, and here,' he added a moment later, 'is where I go out. If there should be any messages,' he added blandly, 'you'll find me at The Two Chairmen, where I'll be setting up a tankard apiece.'

But when he reached the bar he only ordered his usual pint. He knew he wouldn't be having any guests this evening.

Mobile Library
Isle of Man

Withdrawn
From Stock